THE PRINCE
BUYS THE MANOR

THE PRINCE
BUYS THE MANOR

An Extravaganza

By

ELSPETH HUXLEY

1982
CHATTO & WINDUS
LONDON

Published by
Chatto & Windus Ltd
40 William IV Street
London WC2N 4DF

★

Clarke, Irwin & Co Ltd
Toronto

British Library Cataloguing in Publication Data

Huxley, Elspeth
The prince buys the manor.
I. Title
823',912[F]

ISBN 0-7011-6251-5

For Norah,
silken spur,
incisive counsellor, and
warm-hearted friend

Chapter One

IT WAS not to be expected that the intention of a royal personage to buy a country estate on the outskirts of an English market town should pass unremarked by the local inhabitants.

For several weeks, rumours had been twittering round Shipton Wick, a pleasant little town lying under the lea of the Cotswolds, and within easy reach of the M4. Princes had been there before and at least one king – Ethelbald the Elder, who'd founded the place by building a monastery around St Ninian's hermit cell. Historically speaking, a prince wouldn't be anything new. Like an oak tree, Shipton Wick had grown slowly and without fuss through two thousand years or so, adapting to change rather than resisting it. So the citizens were not going to work themselves into a lather about the prospect of a prince in their midst.

But this Prince's arrival, if it came to pass, would be, undoubtedly, a topic of interest, whether in the bar of The Red Lion or The Goat and Compasses, or in any other of the seventeen pubs in the town and its immediate environs. Or whether at Squibb and Squirrels, the only surviving grocers; or in the Town Hall, where the magistrates sat every other Wednesday; or in the canteen at Buggins' Brushes, Shipton Wick's largest employer of labour; or in the council houses on the Dudgrove Turville road; or of anywhere else where two or three might be gathered to enjoy an exchange of news.

Cantilevre Manor had been on the market for about six months. There had been plenty of viewers. At least one Emir from the Gulf; a pop singer from Sunderland with magenta hair and a sliver of ivory piercing the septum of his nose; a Dutch businessman believed to be involved in a scheme to extract iridium from the Quantocks (in the course of which those hills were to be levelled); a former Minister for Urban Development seeking investment for generous sums derived from property deals in various boroughs; a consortium of animal-lovers hoping to establish a wildlife sanctuary and deny access to the local hunt; and several other potential purchasers.

The offices of Doolittle and Dalley, Chartered Surveyors, Valuers, Auctioneers and Estate Agents, were in a state of pleasurable activity. Tony Borrowdale himself, the senior partner, conducted those considered to be serious viewers round the estate, laying stress on its drawbacks rather than its virtues. It was his belief that clients were more apt to be won by frankness than by panegyrics. Anyway, they'd find out the defects for themselves when it came to the survey. The Emir of Hufuf got as far as paying a deposit, but the complications involved in creating a separate flat for each of his wives, plus quarters for concubines, proved too formidable, and the prospects of getting planning permission for a change of use of the stables looked sticky. The deal fell through.

Then came the first rumours of a personage who, quite without ceremony, had been seen to turn into the tree-lined drive in a Rover 2600 with a lady beside him, and a neat-and-tidy, fit-looking, short-back-and-sides individual in the back. Mrs Sproggs, cycling from her morning's work at Hartley's Farm, would have noticed nothing special had not the driver turned his head, just as he passed her, to present his profile, bestowing on his companion, as he did so, a smile which acted on Mrs Sproggs like a sharp but not paralysing electrical impulse.

"It was him," she said later to her husband, and later still to her daughter Astrid when both were back from work. "Couldn't mistake him could I? Not with that smile, those curls up the neck. Going to buy the place, that's what he's up to. You mark my words."

Harry Sproggs stirred his tea. He worked on one of the farms that went with the Manor and was in two minds as to how to take this news, if news it really proved to be. So adept was his wife at starting and purveying rumours that Lady Evers, who'd lived in foreign parts, had called her the bush telegraph.

"There's plenty been to see the place." he commented. "Doesn't follow he'll buy, if it's him."

Astrid, bringing a jar of cherry jam from the kitchen unit asked: "What was *she* like, mum? Seen her in the papers?" Astrid worked as a stylist in the Marie-Louise hairdressing salon.

"Wasn't time. Swept by they did. Detective in the back, stood out a mile."

"Security," Harry Sproggs said gloomily. "Coppers all over the bleeding place. That is, if it's right."

"Course it's right," Mrs Sproggs said huffily, cutting more slices. "What did I tell you – an auspicious month for business deals and welcome strangers bringing good news in latter half. What's clearer than that?"

"Mud."

"Oh, come off it, mum. You and your stars. . ."

All the same, as she dug in the jar for more cherries, Astrid's mind took one of those sudden leaps to which it was prone. She saw a girl with peachy skin, long curved eyelashes, a *retroussé* nose and shapely head in the chair by the window. One of the salon's rose-coloured nylon robes harmonised with her slacks and polo-necked sweater, dark blue but not quite navy. Her hair was blonde, not ashy, more of a ripe corn shade. Rinsed and set, she was waiting to be escorted to the dryer. "Of course" – a low-pitched voice and slight drawl – "there'll be a party for the hunt ball. All the toffs" – perhaps she wouldn't say toffs? – "and the Queen sure to be there. Tiaras of course. I like the way you've fixed those side curls – " Her father's voice interrupted.

"Creepy crawlies, too."

"Creepy crawlies?"

"Coming out of holes to get themselves taken notice of, like at the horse trials – crowding round, as if it was a murder or something."

"Go on with you, they don't do you no harm," said his wife. Harry Sproggs partially relented.

"Well, might have been Arabs I suppose." He turned to a more interesting topic. "There's badgers back in Lammas wood."

"Their faces look like bullseyes," his daughter remarked.

"Ever seen one?"

"Only on telly."

Now that Harry controlled his high-speed, power-steered, air-conditioned tractor from the cushioned seat of a heated cab, peering ahead through a perspex panel, lulled by the wireless and in constant touch with the manager's office, the countryside around him was, in the main, invisible. Sometimes he missed the green hedges, circling seagulls, an occasional rabbit. So he had formed the habit of alighting at lunchtime from his cosy tower, unzipping his protective clothing and eating his sandwiches beside the wood, or in some other convenient spot. The day before he'd spotted a freshly dug badgers' sett.

"I'll show it to you sometime," he promised his daughter – she was the one who kept the bird table replenished and fed the cat.

Astrid's first customer next morning turned out to be Lady Evers, come for an early shampoo-and-set before a bit of shopping and then a coffee morning in aid of the Church Restoration Fund. Lady Evers hated coffee mornings, especially ones with a tombola thrown in – they reminded her too much of all those dreary functions she'd had to preside over during Hubert's last term as Governor-General of the Laxative Islands. But duty was duty, and the habits of a lifetime couldn't be lightly set aside. She could see at once that Astrid was heavily pregnant with news.

"Good morning, Astrid. Not so cold today."

"Bit of ground frost first thing, Dad said."

"Soon be time to take up the dahlias, I suppose. The usual, please."

Lady Evers is putting on weight a bit, Astrid thought, settling in her client for the shampoo. A handsome face, strong features, nice soft grey hair, complexion weather-beaten, you could say. If Lady Evers was putting on weight, it wasn't for lack of exercise. Astrid had often seen her striding across the fields, calling at intervals to a spaniel who paid no attention.

"Heard from your brother lately?" Lady Evers enquired, probing gently for the news, rather as people thrust skewers into the turf at a church fête to hit upon the hidden treasure.

"Not one for writing, Roger isn't. Will you be wanting a rinse today?" Astrid deftly tied the strings of the rose-coloured nylon overall. No longer able to keep the matter bottled up, she added: "They say there's a new viewer been seeing round the Manor. Very distinguished."

"Really?" Lady Evers said, non-committedly. "Another Saudi, I suppose."

"Not this time, Lady Evers. Someone nearer home."

Lady Evers raised her eyebrows, then shut her eyes as she leaned back over the basin. She'd heard a faint rumour too. Good news or bad – if true? She and Hubert would of course have to sign the book. But would there be a book, leather-bound and open at a half-blank page, with a chained pen, awaiting signatures on a table under the portico? Was there, come to that, a portico? Probably no book, if this was to be a quiet country retreat. Still, book or not, she and Hubert were sure to be invited. Clothes. . . with prices as they were, she'd just about given up trying. At least informality was everywhere these days. No doubt there'd be girls in jeans. Perhaps Charlotte. . . She sighed, and gave herself over to the pleasures of the shampoo.

Lady Evers disapproved of gossip. Long service overseas as helpmeet to a husband who had climbed steadily up the ladder, had taught her to keep off gossip as if it were a deadly poison. Perhaps it was. Such abstinence had virtually restricted conversation to the weather, not so easy in climates which stayed exactly the same for six months on end (or more; in one of their postings, it hadn't rained for seven years, and in another rain had fallen every day for two); to fund-raising events in aid of good causes, family news from home, and – luckily this didn't count as gossip – postings of colleagues to various dependencies, protectorates, condominions and islands. How dull it had made the conversation! But now. . .

This particular coffee morning struck her as especially drear. There was, as usual, a tombola. Mavis Pellett, proprietor of the newly opened Health Food Shop was going on about the vices of caffeine and the virtues of comfrey tea. The rector's wife, ferrying around cups of weak instant coffee, was passing on a tip about crab apple jelly. Mrs Rufford, flushed with her husband's triumph as newly elected president of the Lions, was commending a petition being circulated in the town about dogs fouling pavements. Lady Evers, thinking of her spaniel Cherub, eyed Mrs Rufford warily.

Then, as she afterwards put it to herself, something snapped. The rebel in her, so long suppressed, the bandit, gunman, hijacker, planter of bombs in public places – suddenly she felt an alarming spiritual kinship with those upsetters of society's equilibrium. She approached Mrs Rufford, whose finger rested firmly on the pulse of Shipton Wick.

"Your husband will be busier than ever, now we shall be making the headlines," she remarked.

"Headlines?" Mrs Rufford looked startled. A bye-law forbidding dogs to foul pavements was undoubtedly important, but headlines? Lady Evers must mean the weekly *Star and Echo*. And she'd better watch out for that spaniel of hers with a silly name, Cherub.

"You haven't heard about Cantilevre Manor?"

"Cantilevre Manor? Oh yes, of course. Plenty of nibbles, Mr Borrowdale was saying, but no fish landed yet."

Lady Evers gave a short laugh which sounded, Mrs Rufford thought, rather like Cherub's bark. "Bordering on *lèse majesté*, surely? Calling the Prince a fish. Still, salmon are sometimes called royal fish, I believe. Hubert once caught a thirty-pounder in the Usk." She turned her attention to Mrs Paxton, circulating in her wheel chair. Mrs Rufford's hand trembled slightly and a little of her coffee spilled into the saucer as she put down the cup. Cantilevre Manor. . . the Prince . . . she left before doing her duty by the tombola. Robert didn't encourage her to phone him at his office, but on this occasion she didn't think he'd mind.

In the offices of Doolittle and Dalley, the secret was being properly guarded. Tony Borrowdale had reminded his staff: "You know our work is always confidential, but in this case especially. . . When the time comes, there'll be an announcement from the Palace. Until then, not a word, not a whisper. No moles." Here he glanced at Daryll Pringle and smiled engagingly. "Not even you, Daryll, knowing your fondness for the little furry creatures of our woods and fields. I know I can rely on you all. If there's a leak, at any rate *our* water works won't be to blame." Everyone laughed, uncertain whether Tony Borrowdale had made a slip of the tongue or intended a joke.

Daryll extracted a little plastic mug from its burrow in the vending machine and carried it back to his desk. Try as he would, some of the contents always spilled. So the Prince was getting Cantilevre. A cool three-quarters of a million of taxpayers' money. Then he remembered that the cash wouldn't come from taxpayers but from land, investments, property, all the rest of it, handed to him on a plate by accident of birth, without his lifting a finger. What could be done with three-quarters of a million by dedicated ecologists! Badgers immunised against tuberculosis, underpasses made for hedgehogs desirous of crossing motorways, nature reserves established for rare butter-flies, protection for nesting sites of the Dartford warbler, wetlands set aside for the Natterjack toad: and then, beyond that, a great drive for the liberation of battery hens, hibernation centres built for tortoises, even perhaps a step towards achieve-ment of the highest aim of all, the greatest of all causes – the salvation of the whale. Daryll's heart beat faster and seemed to be expanding in his chest, a gentle glow suffused his body. If that goal could be won? That squalid, brutal chapter in the gory history of mankind be ended! Beside such an achievement, the triumphs of vainglorious persons strutting their little hour upon the stage, of generals and tycoons and dictators and liberators and so-called statesmen, would pale into insignificance.

Why couldn't the Prince donate his three-quarters of a million to the cause and live like any other young man in a comfortable flat, or even in a detached architect-designed compact country residence, centrally heated with easily maintained garden and double garage? That should be enough for anyone. Daryll sighed, and drew towards him a file on a poky little terraced house with dry rot in a back street of Shipton Wick, to be offered as an ideal retreat in a picturesque market town, equipped with old timbers and stone-flagged floors, convenient for shops, with main services, vacant possession on completion. Pity the Prince didn't buy *that*.

Obedient to his employer's instructions, Daryll considered his lips to be sealed when he turned up, a few days later, at the Annual General Meeting of the Shipton Wick and District Ecology Group, of which he was Hon. Secretary. Not an easy job, with so many conflicting points of view. Ecologists, as he often reminded himself, were individualists, and you couldn't expect them to agree about everything. But if they agreed about nothing, as he had more than once pointed out, nothing would be achieved.

This was going to be a difficult meeting. The time had come when the Group really must define its policy on the issue so forcibly presented by its fellow movement, Stop the Hunt. On the face of it, there was no problem. Fox-hunting was cruel, barbaric and socially divisive, and should be stopped. But some ecologists thought this view too simplistic. Foxes (they said) are natural predators, predation is part of nature and you can't change nature, however cruel. Men, too, are predators, and while of course it's silly to chase foxes in fancy dress with all those yippings and halloaings, humans have always liked fancy dress and you can't stop that either.

Daryll wasn't sure where he stood. Emotionally, he took the side of foxes. On the other hand he didn't care at all for the Stop the Hunters, especially Judy Mustard, a toothy loud-voiced, bosomy lady, over-fond, he considered, of bossing other people around. To foxhound meets she took a kind of giant flour sifter containing a powder so distracting to the hounds that they ran round in circles, raised their heads and howled. Cruel to dogs, surely? Colonel Martingale, the Master of the Hunt, brandishing a long-lashed whip, had threatened to give Judy Mustard a thrashing and, Daryll had felt at the time, this proposal had a lot to recommend it.

"Well, here we go, Daryll," said the retiring chairman of the Group. "Elderberry, parsnip or sloe mix?" The hall wasn't licensed, but several members had brought along home-made wines which were being dispensed from a trestle table, together with squares of goatsmilk cheese and tasty little cookies made of stone-ground, compost-grown, unsprayed wholemeal flour.

"Sloe mix." Daryll was sorry that the chairman was resigning. It meant upheaval. Barry's wife wanted to move nearer to a sister in Bedfordshire, and Barry had acquired an interest in a health food shop in Milton Keynes. "Great future, Daryll," he assured his colleague. "Open University. Courses in fungi, medieval herbs, tissanes. A very active group in Milton Keynes."

"All very well," Daryll said gloomily. "But what about Shipton Wick? Who's going to take over? We need strong leadership or else. . ." The words remained unspoken, but the name Judy Mustard hung in the air.

Barry drained his glass of elderberry and put a hand on Daryll's skinny shoulder. "Don't you worry. There's a new candidate in the field, a real humdinger, way up at the top of the food chain. He'll dump Judy right in the disposal unit, chewed down to molecules. Ever heard of Angus MacBean?"

Daryll shook his head.

"New on the market. Really high-powered. Moved here from Aberdeen, perhaps it was Dundee, where he was Regional Experimental Supervisor of Ecological Studies at the College of Further Education. Not been here long, but he contacted me and he's coming along, should be here any time. He's my nomination for our new Chairman."

"But – " Daryll started to protest; he'd never even heard the name. His protests went unheard. In at the door came a bulky figure clad in a kilt with all its trappings, with a kind of knobkerry in his hand. A mixture of envy and repulsion struggled for ascendancy in Daryll's mind at the sight of that bushy red beard. Daryll's own beard was trim and modest, a neat edging to the chin; but undeniably wispy. Daryll knew he couldn't ever grow a beard like that red monstrosity; but then, he wouldn't want to. The personality it expressed was domineering, brash and, in Daryll's opinion, frankly vulgar. A bad day for the Group should it fall into the coarse-boned hands of Angus MacBean.

Two hours later, after a show and then recount of hands, Angus MacBean was elected Chairman by a single vote. Judy Mustard was the runner-up.

"Seeds of discord planted." Daryll believed that he was thinking, not talking, but evidently he'd muttered the sentiments aloud. He found himself standing next to a new member, pretty if a bit gormless-looking, who worked at the hairdresser's with a fancy name, the salon Marie-Louise.

"What was that you were saying?" she enquired.

"Nothing much. Rather a surprise result." A closer look caused Daryll to revoke the word gormless. Not gormless, more – he searched for a word. Guileless? The sort of girl men used to feel they wanted to protect. Not, of course, any longer. The opposite of Judy Mustard, now licking her wounds by enlisting recruits for a monster Stop the Hunt rally to be held at the Opening Meet.

"She'll have to stop that nonsense if the sale goes through," Astrid surprisingly said. A touch of asperity in her voice dispelled any lingering thought of gormlessness.

"The sale?"

"Don't pretend you don't know all about it. He's been seen here, you know."

"He?"

"I suppose you're under an oath of secrecy but it's all round the town. I only hope he won't find out about the badgers or, if he does, keep it to himself."

"Badgers?" Daryll realised that as a conversationalist he wasn't doing very well.

"I should have thought you'd have known. There's a sett in Lammas Wood and we've got to keep it secret, so the Ministry won't come and gas them all to death. That's why I decided to come along and join the Group actually. To help save the badgers. Dad found the sett."

Daryll was about to say that, as Hon. Sec., he would guarantee that the whole weight of the Group would be thrown behind the preservation of the badgers, when the new Chairman, sporran swinging, was upon them, eyeing Astrid with what Daryll felt to be a positively lecherous look.

"I'm greatly encouraged," he pronounced, ostentatiously rolling his r's, "to see so many young people here in the Group. With youth on our side, we can't fail. The future is ours!"

Astrid was gazing as if hypnotised at the spreading beard. No doubt about it, the man exuded some kind of animal magnetism, a sort of primeval force. Daryll fingered his own callow appendage and felt as if, like Alice down the rabbit hole, he had shrunk.

"But not without a struggle!" Angus continued, rolling his r's more than ever. "Daryll and I must map out our strategy. How fortunate we are to have so devoted a Secretary, eh Daryll? One who'll rise to the occasion. Opportunity. A great opportunity beckons. The spotlight of the media is about to be turned on Shipton Wick. We shall be in the eye of the world. How can we turn this to our advantage? That's the question. Ecologists of Shipton Wick and District, unite! We are about to become internationally famous!"

"Scarcely the way to keep secret the whereabouts of the badgers." Daryll hadn't meant to sound sour, but he did. He was encouraged by what he could have sworn was a slight wink of Astrid's skilfully pencilled right eye.

"Turn it to our advantage, that's what we must set our sights on. And how? I'll tell you how!" Angus couldn't lay hands on a button as Daryll was wearing a sweater, but his bushy beard loomed close to Daryll's wispy one.

"This royal personage who's soon to live amongst us, isn't he famous for support of conservation? A wildlife enthusiast? Enemy of pollution? Countryman at heart? Tailor-made to be our President! Yes, President of the Shipton Wick and District Ecology Group! Entering into local affairs – photographed stalking a rare butterfly – nature trails across his land – crouching in a hide to badger-watch. . ."

"More likely to be photographed galloping after a hunted fox," Daryll interrupted, his ego boosted by that near-wink. "We shan't get anywhere with him if the Stop the Hunt crowd go gallivanting all over the countryside giving nervous breakdowns to the hounds and apoplexy to the Master."

"Now, then, my dear chap, we needn't leap to hasty conclusions. We all endorse the aims of Stop the Hunt but there are ways and ways of reaching them. In my father's house are many mansions. I'm sure we'll find that loyalty to the Crown. . ."

Judy Mustard was bearing down on them, hand outstretched.

"No hard feelings, Angus, a fair fight and a fair win. Narrow, you'll admit – one pip. Now we must work together for a Better Britain, an end to badger-bashing, a fair deal for our fair country and Stop the Hunt!"

Angus was clasping her hand. "Judy, this is a great day! The proudest moment of my life! I'll strive to be worthy of this great honour, I can promise you that. Shoulder to shoulder, we'll march together and achieve our aims!"

"Well said, Angus. And the first task is to plan our strategy for our demo at the Opening Meet. The press will be there in force. For a start – "

Daryll slipped away. That, he thought, will give the new Chairman something to bite on. Show him that all's not a bed of roses when it comes to holding office in the Shipton Wick and District Ecology Group. At the door he paused and found Astrid standing beside him.

"Can I see you home?"

She smiled. "Thanks awfully, Daryll, but I came on my bike."

Daryll swallowed hard and felt his heart thump: sensation not to be blamed entirely on the sloe mix plus the tension generated by so momentous a meeting.

"I hope we'll meet again – soon."

"I'm sure we shall. I daresay you'd like to see the badgers."

"Oh, yes, very much."

"I'll talk to Dad about it. The best time is when it's full moon."

"That would be marvellous."

An understatement, Daryll felt. A full moon – badgers – perhaps a Death's head Hawk-moth or even a Rosy Footman attracted by the torch's beam – the hoot of a barn owl – the smell of damp leaves. And Astrid. Perfection. Daryll walked home light-footedly. Let Judy Mustard do her worst. Only one fly – hornet, rather – threatened the purity of the ointment. A fly, or hornet, with a red beard.

A week later, contracts were exchanged for the sale of Cantilevre Manor and the secret was out.

Chapter Two

WHILE the objective was in doubt, the means of achieving it divided the Shipton Wick Town Council into almost as many factions as there were councillors. The Mayor, Councillor Mrs Hussey, proposed the immediate presentation of a Loyal Address, inscribed on vellum in Old English lettering with the town's emblem at the head and the councillors' signatures at the foot.

"What is the town's emblem?" Peter Paxton enquired. As a newcomer to the Council, his ignorance might perhaps be excused.

"A kind of bird," the Mayor informed him. "A wyvern, I think."

"Looks like a topheavy pelican with very short legs," Councillor Rufford added.

"That sounds more like a roc," Sir Hubert Evers put in. "Extinct, of course." He was an authority on birds, as well as on the physiology of the gastropods, with special reference to their reproductive systems.

"I don't think a topheavy, extinct bird with short legs is very suitable for a Loyal Address," Councillor Paxton observed. The Mayor looked displeased. Councillor Paxton, as the newest member, was too much inclined to throw his weight about. The fact that he had bought not only Hartley's Farm, right next door to Cantilevre, but Buggins' Brushes, Shipton Wick's largest industry, as well, didn't entitle him to dictate to the Council and criticise its traditions.

"The emblem has come down to us from Saxon times," she said reprovingly. "Something to do with Ethelbald the Elder. Are there any other suggestions?"

There were. A Medieval Fayre, with tumblers, jesters and possibly a tournament enacted by members of the Pony Club; a triumphal arch over the entrance to Cantilevre Manor through which the Prince's car would be drawn by stalwart citizens dressed as verderers; a reception by the Beauty Queen and her Maids of Honour in the Civic Centre decorated by the Floral Art Club; a lawnmower race combined with a rally and a massed ascent of balloons. By contrast, Councillor Paxton made, the Mayor was ready to concede, a sensible suggestion.

"I think we should invite him to a banquet."

"Costly," objected Councillor Rufford.

"On the contrary, we'd make a profit. People would be treading each other underfoot for tickets and prepared to pay the earth."

"Especially those with daughters," Councillor Snape said in a snarky kind of voice, "of marriageable age." Councillor Snape was well known for his snarkiness, exacerbated, in the opinion of many, by repeated failures to win the County Challenge cup for six varieties of vegetable, combined with his wife's blatant carryings on with the attendant at the swimming pool.

How Councillor Snape, certainly no Humphrey Bogart, had come to espouse so winsome a lady as Ermyntrude was a matter for conjecture among his acquaintances. The more charitable discounted the theory that he had taken her over in settlement of arrears of interest on a mortgage he had assigned to her father on a property in the town. Be that as it may, by one means or another Councillor Snape had managed to acquire a good many houses, shops, yards, plots and other freeholds, leaseholds, appurtenances and curtilages in Shipton Wick. Planning permissions seemed to fall into his lap, even when it came to converting the old slaughter-house in Crumble Street into a supermarket. A sharp man, it was generally agreed, the tip of whose sharp nose, like a terrier's, could be observed to give a slight twitch when the whiff of a bargain came to his nostrils.

"Of marriageable age," he repeated. His fellow councillors got the point. Peter Paxton's daughter Jo was of a marriageable age, although whether of a marriageable inclination was another matter. Clad in patched jeans, a sweat shirt and a lumberman's jacket, her long hair golden but matted, she was living in a commune over towards Charlton Mansell, barefoot and eating berries and, it was said, taking part in heathen orgies presided over by some kind of oriental monk.

"A banquet," Sir Hubert Evers said reflectively. "That seems, if I may say so, an appropriate way in which to express our gratification at the honour the Prince is conferring on our community." Sir Hubert also had a daughter of marriageable age, and possibly of a more marriageable nature. In the past there had been ups and downs but now she had come to roost, temporarily at least, under the parental roof, and taken to horses and eventing, cricket in summer and cooking the rural equivalent of directors' lunches (dinner parties, buffets, weddings and the like) all the year round. A competent girl.

"Yes, I can see a profit there." Councillor Rufford had given the notion of a banquet close attention. "Souvenirs, too. We could have souvenirs. Plates? Mugs? Plaques bearing the Prince's profile? Glasses with our emblem on them, hand engraved?"

"*Not* a top-heavy extinct pelican with short legs, I hope," said Councillor Paxton. "I suggest we appoint a sub-committee to frame our strategy, and report back at our next meeting." This was agreed.

So far, so good, thought Peter Paxton as he drove to Hartley's in his Volvo. For once, the sun shone. The combines' work was almost over; long, even swaths of straw gave the fields a neatly combed look. That Royalty had smiled on Shipton Wick couldn't but be beneficial to the town and all concerned. Good for trade, good for tourism, excellent for property values – the fact that Hartley's land marched with Cantilevre's would double its value, treble it very likely, overnight.

And then, Buggins' Brushes. Could there be a tie-up there? Royal Approval, By Appointment? Change the brand-name to Prince's? Peter had bought the factory only two years ago. It had been started in 1886 by an enterprising farmer seeking to find a use for the bristles of his pigs. Brushes, and especially toothbrushes, had proved to be a lucrative answer. Now a new name was needed to match the New Technology that Peter was about to introduce. Prince's – too pinched a word somehow, not sufficiently robust. Majesty? Highness? Emperor? Sovereign? Or something oriental perhaps – Caliph? Sultan? Satrap? Vizier?

Difficult. With reluctance, he directed his thoughts to a less congenial topic as he approached his home.

Jo. A problem, as no doubt most daughters were. Opting out on a derelict airfield used as a rubbish tip with someone she called a Munshi and various unsavoury looking creatures of indeterminate sex. Living on bran and cannabis, eked out by baked beans pinched from the supermarket. He'd heard that her commune was suspected of making bombs. Well, maybe Sybil had got something worked out. Sybil wasn't often defeated.

Peter felt a glow of satisfaction every time he drove up to Hartley's. Forty years ago, it had been a tumbledown old farm-house with a cheese-press in the cellar, apples in the attic, a perpendicular staircase, worm-eaten beams and buildings of an obscure but rustic nature all around. After the war, a London couple had done it up from top to toe and turned various sheds and yards into stables where disdainful hunters had been kept. Since then it had changed hands twice. Each new purchaser had added on, subtracted, rearranged and generally improved the house. The stone remained mellow, the stone-tiled roof was still beautiful but no longer leaking, in place of the perpendicular staircase was a graceful stairway in Regency style. Turkish rugs, cabinets displaying porcelain, Adam chimneypieces, had appeared.

Peter had installed concealed lighting and turned the stable yard into a swimming pool. The stables stood empty, but one of the barns had become a studio-cum-music room to which the Paxton's son had brought pop groups from time to time. Now that he'd gone to the Gulf to make pots of money, they came no more. Sybil, who from her wheelchair had caused shrubs to be installed wherever shrubs would grow, and an assortment of interesting trees to be planted behind the stables, was proposing to make a vineyard on a gentle southern slope beyond.

Peter found his wife inspecting the orchard, accompanied by old Donkin, who was breathless from trotting after her electric chair propelled in top gear round about flowerbeds, up and down banks, in between apple trees. He sometimes wished his wife would take things a little easier. Old Donkin would drop dead one of these days.

"Frau van der Schnorkel is strangling poor Lord Lambourne," she announced. "Donkin must use his saw on her. A pity, she's a peach."

Peter felt confused. Who, or what, was Frau van der Schnorkel? Lord Lambourne, he seemed to recollect, was a kind of apple. Or could it have been a peach?

"A man has been to see the attics," his wife informed him as she charged a bank at full speed and sped towards the lily pond. Pounding after her, Peter was too breathless to enquire why. The attics were empty except when friends of Jo's turned up, mostly with rucksacks and wearing moccasins, wanting to doss down in the stables, only to be orderd upstairs by Sybil. Even Jo's friends seldom disregarded Sybil's instructions. She wasn't, Sybil had said, going to have girls sleeping about all over the floor like pigs. Anyway, there weren't any stables.

The attic windows offered a wide view over the surrounding countryside and included part of the roof of Cantilevre Manor, nestling behind some fine oaks and lime trees. Could this be something to do with security? A word, he feared, that they would hear only too often in days to come.

"I suppose we shall have to get used to this sort of thing," he said gloomily. "I hope they won't have alsatians."

"Certainly not. Heloise and Abelard would never tolerate alsatians."

"Heloise and Abelard may not be consulted." They were yappy little Yorkshire terriers, taken out for exercise by Miss Cheer, who looked after Sybil, organised the household, typed letters, cooked, froze the vegetables, chauffered, and did virtually everything that needed doing at Hartley's. "A gem," Sybil had conceded, "but unfortunately she does not sparkle." In fact, most of the time she gloomed.

"There will be no alsatians," Sybil confirmed. "I shall ring up the Palace." Sybil was a great believer in going straight to the top.

Back by then in the sitting room, Peter told her of Shipton Wick's plans to welcome the Prince into their midst. Sybil emitted a sound formerly expressed in romantic novels by the word "Pah!", though it did not sound like that, more like a cross between a sniff and a throat-clearing. "A dreary municipal function like that. Mrs Hussey dressed up like a birthday cake and that Judy Mustard cracking whips all over the place. Poor young man! We must do better than that."

"We?" Peter saw rocks, not to mention rapids, ahead.

"Jo must be recalled. Not a ball, of course, out of keeping. Informal dinner? Cocktail party? Buffet lunch? Fashion show? Rock concert?" What Peter called her egg-laying look had settled on Sybil's powerful countenance. A high forehead, a thin, almost beaky nose, a wide mouth and fine eyes. A face born to command. Now she was giving birth to ideas. Brooding came later. As with many birds, the male was expected to take his turn at brooding.

"One can't just ask the Prince to dinner," Peter pointed out.

"No one spoke of just asking. First I must find out who's coming with him. In charge, I mean."

"Ah, yes. The equerries."

"Jeremy Baxendale. He married a niece of Phyllis Barbeton-Miles who came from Rutland, her mother was a Garrard, they had interests in Canada, something to do with asbestos, I think. His brother-in-law married a Masterton-Spencer and was killed by a poisonous spider in northern Australia. *His* first cousin was a Beasley-Adams, he was drowned off New Guinea in a trimaran, and *his* brother was Keeper of the Privy Purse. My book, please, Peter."

Peter handed her a fat and much-thumbed address book oozing telephone numbers and left her pressing buttons on the instrument. What a wonderful breeder of prize cattle or champion race-horses she would have made! No computer could have stored pedigrees in its memory-bank more accurately. Within the half-hour, she'd have the answer to this immediate problem.

So it proved. "Captain Longshott is to be Comptroller. His wife was a Pardoe-Mustang, they're divorced now, but she's a cousin of Amelia's former husband's niece. Of course she knew Amelia well. Captain Longshott is coming to drinks on Sunday. He'll be staying at the Gwents. A small party, I think, just close neighbours, quite informal. The Prince wishes to integrate."

She reached again for the telephone. It was lucky, Peter reflected, that he could afford the bill. Still, it was cheaper than owning race-horses or yachts, foreign travel, keeping up with fashion or whatever Sybil would have taken to if she hadn't, poor dear Sybil, been run into by a drunken driver and broken her spine.

So – staying at the Gwents. The Gwents had been something of a disappointment to Sybil. The Marquess was amiable enough, in no way standoffish, but inhabited a different world from that of Shipton Wick and its environs. Perhaps all those generations that lay behind him of crusaders, valiant warriors and border chieftains had exhausted the red blood corpuscles, or directed the genes into different channels. Perhaps, too, it was his Welsh heritage – he claimed descent, if somewhat obscurely, from Owain Glyndwr – that had led him to become an authority of dragons. His book *The Anatomy of the Dragon* was recognised as the standard work. His skill as a needleman was no less remarkable. He had for some years been engaged on an ambitious set of kneelers for the Cathedral of Sodor and Man, soon (it was hoped) to be erected in the Orkneys.

The disposition of the Marchioness was more practical. She sat on committees, sold cakes on the Womens' Institute stall in Shipton Wick on Fridays, did Meals on Wheels on Wednesdays, had a small herd of pedigree Jerseys and endeavoured to keep track of the activities of her offspring, numbering seven. Some were still at school but Lady Pandora, the eldest daughter, was sometimes to be seen in Shipton Wick, parking her red sports car on the yellow lines and looking in at The Red Lion for a Bloody Mary.

Sybil had hoped that she and Jo would make friends. What an old-fashioned ring, Peter reflected, there was to those words! Making friends with others of their own sex was something girls didn't seem to go in for these days. Lady Pandora had round blue eyes, long lashes, full lips and practically no buttocks. Beside her their own Jo, Peter feared, munching her muesli, brewing mead and smoking pot in her commune, couldn't hold a candle, or only a flickering one at best.

Sybil was never one to admit defeat. "Jo must be summoned",

she repeated.

"Summoned, I daresay. But will she come?"

"Then you must fetch her."

"I can't *abduct* the girl. Besides, I'm very busy. Important meetings. New developments."

Peter seldom discussed business affairs with his wife. She wasn't really interested, and such matters were highly confidential. Big things were indeed afoot at the factory. Buggins' Brushes were well known in the trade. An old-established product, reliable, hygienic – never a hint of thrush or anthrax in their long history – contemporary in design, reasonably priced and with a satisfactory export market in face of stiff competition. Now there was to be a dramatic development. Buggins' Brushes were about to make history. Shipton Wick would be right on the map of progress in the field of industry, modernisation, British inventiveness, New Technology and everything the country needed, regardless of the town's coming fame as the Prince's shopping centre. The world's first microchip automated toothbrush was about to be launched.

"Jo must be fetched." Sybil repeated. "She must be here by six o'clock tomorrow. I will inform Miss Cheer."

The fires of Miss Cheer's natural gloom were stoked – or, more appropriately, the marshes of her natural gloom were flooded – by her employer's instructions, passed on next morning to Mrs Sproggs.

"Not much good making up the bed." Mrs Sproggs opined. "Last time Jo came, she slept in the potting shed – said she liked the smell of compost. Wasn't compost she was after, I'll be bound."

"She'll suffer for it," Miss Cheer prophesied. Not, Mrs Sproggs reflected, in the way she would have suffered when she was a girl. She wondered sometimes about the pill but never asked. So far as she was aware, Astrid was a good girl and didn't need it. But you never knew.

"Got the builders in at the Manor," she remarked. "Pulling the place about they say. Been measuring for carpets too. Sure to be changes. The nursery wing. . ."

"Now then, we don't want gossip do we? Enough troubles

of our own.''

''Permits for everything now Harry says, coppers all over the place. Plain clothes. Those badger people Astrid's taken up with, they've got to get a permit for Lammas wood.''

''Nasty creatures,'' Miss Cheer pronounced. ''Smelly, but I don't see why they need a permit.''

''It's the people need a permit, not the badgers. To go to Lammas wood, did you ever? People have been going to Lammas wood for centuries. Primroses in the spring. There's a foreigner called Mac something or other wants them to go and watch the badgers when it's full moon.''

''There's other names for *that* than watching badgers.''

Mrs Sproggs all but took offence, since Astrid was involved, but thought better of it and finished making up the bed.

''Why that girl doesn't settle in sensibly in a nice room like this and help her mother, goodness knows,'' Miss Cheer observed. ''Potting sheds! Compost! Dirty feet! Hideous clothes with fringes!''

''Boyfriends I suppose. There's someone there they call a Banshee I'm told. Think the world of him they do. Well, it takes all sorts I suppose.''

She smoothed down the bedspread while Miss Cheer put a vase of flowers on the dressing table, remarking as she did so: ''Wasted on her. If Mrs Paxton thinks Jo's going to catch the Prince's eye, she's barking up the wrong tree. Now, if it was Lady Pandora. . .''

Mrs Sproggs made no comment. She didn't think much of Lady Pandora. Astrid said she'd heard Lady Pandora say one day in the salon that she'd papered the walls in her flat in London with parking tickets. What a way to go on. Thank goodness Astrid didn't carry on like that. In spite of all the airs and graces of the Lady Pandoras and Jo's of this world – though airs and graces didn't exactly fit Jo – Astrid was worth a dozen of them any day. If it came to catching the eye of royalty, that eye would do a lot better if it were to be cast in the direction of girls like Astrid. A fleeting vision passed through Mrs Sproggs' mind of Astrid in a billowing lacey gown, peach or perhaps shell pink, her blonde hair garlanded with rosebuds, floating through a ballroom hung with chandeliers to the muted throb of music in the arms of a smiling Prince.

"I'll do the bathroom now," she said. The tinkle of a handbell reached the upstairs quarters. "Drat the woman, what is it now," Miss Cheer complained. "Always something." Mrs Sproggs fetched the Vim and rags from the airing cupboard and got on with the job.

The behaviour of daughters was also concerning Lady Evers at the Old Coach House behind The Red Lion, a tastefully restored grade II listed building with a small garden at the back overlooking the river, and fields beyond where Cherub took his exercise. Lady Evers knew that she was lucky with Charlotte, despite a worrying period with that Italian owner of a chain of fish-and-chip shops who was supporting at least two families, and ample ones at that, already. It proved to be fortunate, in the long run, that one of his consorts threw a pan of boiling fat at his head, thus as it were, cooling his ardour. But the incident had got into the papers with Charlotte's name dragged in just at the time when Hubert was retiring with his well deserved knighthood. If it hadn't been for that, and the publicity, Hubert was sure that the order would have been a "G" and not merely a "K".

Privately, Lady Evers doubted this. There had been that bother in the Laxative Islands when Queen Chotonopohaggis' seventh husband had disappeared in mysterious circumstances and the Queen, incensed by police harassment – they'd even searched the kitchen middens of her palace for bones – had appealed to the Russian fleet to rescue her from British oppression. Hubert had handled this tricky situation with admirable calm and diplomacy, but there had been a lot of fuss in Parliament when Queen Chotonopohaggis, removed for safe keeping to Government House, had complained to the Commission on Human Rights that her traditional diet of giant crabs had been denied her. It was not Hubert's fault that a Japanese fishing fleet had so depleted the surrounding seas of crabs, giant or otherwise, as to render them unobtainable. Nevertheless the Commission on Human Rights had delivered a reprimand and poor Hubert had scored an undeserved black mark. This was the more likely reason for Hubert's disappointment than Charlotte's entanglement with the Italian vendor of fish-and-chips.

"Seven Up has a swollen pastern," Charlotte observed, throwing her riding cap on to the sofa as she came in from evening exercise. She helped herself to a gin and tonic. "God knows if I can get him right before the Novice Hunter Trials."

"How annoying." Marjorie Evers was all too conscious of her inability to find the right words about horses. To her, they were a closed book and seemed always to be going wrong.

"And that bloody helicopter came so low it positively hovered over Coca Cola when I had him out this afternoon and naturally he panicked. Nearly threw me. I thought there was a law about low flying."

"It's Cantilevre, I suppose," Lady Evers said. "An aerial view for the newspapers."

Charlotte gave a sort of snort and finished off her gin and tonic. "Cantilevre, Prince, chitter-chatter. The place will be crawling with reporters, lurking behind every bush. So boring."

Lady Evers felt discouraged. Why was it so difficult to talk to one's daughter? But she must have a try.

"I daresay there'll be lots of parties when the Prince moves in. Dinners, lunches, drinks and so on. Domestic staff will need their times off. There may be occasions when outside caterers. . ." She left the sentence in the air while she helped herself to a dry sherry before going to turn on the oven for the casserole.

"Oh ho." Charlotte got the point. "Want to get me in there do you, running up canapés and mousses so I'll meet Interesting People and Pa will get invited to a do?"

"Really, Charlotte." As if Hubert was going to beg for royal favours – Hubert, who had served his Queen and country with devotion and fidelity since before the Prince was born! "It's you I was thinking of. A chance to meet and mingle with, let's face it, people of a less parochial background than we've got in Shipton Wick. A wider world, cultivated folk, cheerful parties. . ." She successfully avoided the word gay. Nothing irritated her more than the hijacking of this useful, attractive little word by a bunch of pansies, as they used to be called –

much too flattering, why not plain buggers? – and their female
equivalents who were about as far from being gay as you could
get.

"There'll be plenty of people wanting to meet and mingle.
You can count me out."

All the same, Charlottte reflected as she heated up some
oatmeal for a poultice, there just might be something in the idea.
The dinners-for-directors ploy had worked out well. No doubt a
staff of cooks and other servants would be installed at the
Manor, if such folk still existed in the world of royalty, but
occasional outside help might be sought. And be well paid. If she
built up a little business, a royal connection could be a help.
How did one go about it? Ring up and ask? Send round a
sample of one's wares? Get to know someone on the staff, she
supposed. Meanwhile, Seven Up's swollen pastern needed
attention. If it didn't improve, she'd call in that new young vet
Sebastian, who seemed a reasonably competent young man.

The light was on in Sir Hubert's study. He was working late,
as he often did, on his monograph on the reproductive methods
of the higher gastropods, a subject of endless fascination.
Especially remarkable were those of the Opsisthobranchs, her-
maphrodite in structure. "The penis," he had just written, "has
a wide and extraordinary variety of shapes, and may be decorated
with all kinds of accessories – teeth, scales, spines and hooks."
How fortunate that the human species had not adopted the
forms favoured by the Opsisthobranchs! Although no doubt
these would have contributed towards a higher standard of
sexual morality, and possibly towards a lower birthrate, so much
to be desired. Several theories had been advanced about the
purpose of those teeth, scales, spines and hooks, but no
satisfactory theory to account for their evolution had as yet been
established. That he might be the one to settle a controversy
which had rocked the world of molluscologists for many years
was Sir Hubert's dearest ambition.

Sir Hubert sighed, and put down his pen. He missed, at times,
the prosbranchs, aplacophorans, polyplacophorans and other
creatures, so colourful and mysterious, to be found on the
beaches of the Laxative Islands and other tropical dependencies

wherein he had served. Gastropods did not argue, write stupid minutes in official files, forget appointments or demand lavish hospitality with no notice just when the monsoon had delayed the monthly steamer bearing supplies.

All that, of course, was in the past. In the present, the affairs of the Shipton Wick Town Council did not quite replace the interest to be found in the fauna and flora of the 976 scattered atolls of the Laxative Islands, now fully independent under the rule of Queen Chotonopohaggis, and a member (if not a fully paid-up one) of the United Nations. A nice little town, Shipton Wick, but no bustling metropolis. He heard his wife's footstep approaching, followed by her gentle knock – she never entered his study without knocking.

"Time for dinner, dear. I hope the monograph is going well."

"Slowly. But then, since the opsisthobranchs have taken several hundred million years to evolve their present forms, one should not be impatient."

"I suppose not. I can't help worrying about Charlotte. I do wish she'd settle down."

"We must be thankful she didn't settle down with the purveyor of fish-and-chips."

Marjorie Evers agreed. "She has so much talent, I feel it's wasted here. I've been wondering. . ."

Sir Humphrey inserted his biro into its holder, arranged his papers neatly and looked over his glasses at his wife. When Marjorie wondered, she generally had a plan on foot.

"This event could make a difference. New acquaintances, opportunities, wider horizons. If only Charlotte would co-operate."

"Event?"

"The sale of Cantilevre Manor."

"I don't see how that can affect Charlotte. We can hardly expect her to enjoy the favours of royalty. As it were," he added, conscious that his wording might lend itself to miscon-struction.

"I wasn't thinking of that, so much as of Charlotte's

catering."

'You mean, find her way in through the back door as a cook? Hardly a suitable procedure for our daughter to follow, I should have thought.''

"I hadn't quite meant that either," Marjorie Evers said, uncertain as to exactly what she had meant. Charlotte was a handsome girl, if only she'd take trouble with her appearance; she could talk intelligently if only she'd bother. The eyes of princes, like those of lesser men, had been known to rove. Besides, there'd be an entourage. Equerries, secretaries, comptrollers and the like. A wider world.

"I've no doubt," her husband added, "we shall get an invitation sooner or later." If it hadn't been for that undeserved disaster about the "G", he was sure it would have been sooner.

"I don't think there'll be official entertaining down here. Cantilevre is to be a country retreat." A door slammed downstairs. "There's Charlotte in from poulticing. The casserole is ready."

A casserole again. The truth was, Sir Hubert reflected, that Charlotte's cooking had undermined Marjorie's nerve. With a professional in the house, adept at such matters as choux pastry, fillet *en croute* and stuffed boned capons, his wife didn't dare embark on culinary experiments. You couldn't go far wrong with a casserole. Daughters might be blessings, but they were sometimes heavily disguised.

Chapter Three

SERGEANT Bullstrode had been so long in charge of Shipton Wick's police station that everyone regarded him as a fixture, including his superiors in the Constabulary. Other officers were moved about, got promoted or were sent on courses to widen their experience. Sergeant Bullstrode's experience was evidently considered to be wide enough already. There was not much that went on in Shipton Wick he didn't know about. An understanding of the intricacies of the international drug trade, the organisation of terrorist gangs, the operation of the world's art market and other similar matters was not considered necessary for keeping the peace in Shipton Wick.

But times were changing. The unmasking of a drug ring centred in the skittles alley of The Goat and Compasses; an armed hold-up at Lloyds' bank foiled by the manager who recognised the gangster's gun as the twin of one he had just bought in W. H. Smith's for his son's birthday; cannabis growing in the Garden of Remembrance by the church; drunken orgies in the barn at Eastcombe Farm where those harvest festivals Sergeant Bullstrode well remembered had been held; and so on. One had to move with the times, in whatever direction the times seemed to be moving. A young policewoman was the latest sign of progress to come to Shipton Wick. Nine O levels, and in the Sergeant's opinion a good deal too pleased with herself.

Change, within limits, could be tolerated; now it looked like getting out of hand. With Royalty imminent, things couldn't be expected to go on just as they were. But the authorities seemed to have gone overboard about Security. The words were on everyone's lips. In his more fanciful moments, which visited the Sergeant now and then, Security seemed to him like some strange animal, large and furry, that hid in bushes and growled. You couldn't tell what it would do next.

Experts from Scotland Yard came and went unobtrusively and

immersed themselves in conferences which seemed to go on indefinitely. An operations centre had been set up in an empty back room of The Red Lion, pending the building of a new police station which was being rushed through as a matter of urgency with top priority at such a rate that it might well be completed within two years, or three at most. Officers from County headquarters were being very tactful. Their duties, they explained, would relate solely to Security. So far as local matters were concerned, Sergeant Bullstrode was assured, all would be as before. Including, he thought a little wearily, all those driving without due cares, the shoplifting of two cans of beans and a packet of Daz from the supermarket, vandalism in the childrens' playground in the Jubilee Park, the theft from the church of several kneelers, and farmer Stubbins' failure to keep his cows off the highway.

The empty room at the back of The Red Lion had been transformed. Desks positively jostled each other, and on them stood telephones with direct lines to several highly important places. Large-scale maps of Shipton Wick and its environs covered the walls, and various sophisticated pieces of equipment, electronic no doubt, of whose purposes Sergeant Bullstrode was ignorant, had been installed. In his own modest office a direct line linked him to this operations centre, by means of which he could communicate with Mr Whackers, or with one of the gentleman's minions, at any time, night or day.

Mr Whackers, the Chief Security Officer, must certainly, the Sergeant opined, possess some other official title, Chief Superintendent perhaps, or possibly a military rank. He bore the unmistakeable stamp of a uniformed service, but uniforms and ranks were being sternly suppressed. A low profile, informality, were the orders of the day. "Reggie Whackers," that gentleman had said, introducing himself by shaking the Sergeant's hand instead of expecting it to be at the salute. He wore a tweed jacket, a maroon sweater, grey flannel trousers and a pair of rather cracked brown shoes. "Glad to meet you, Sergeant. We're relying on you for local intelligence. Personalities, records, who does what. Absolutely vital. For instance, footpaths."

"Footpaths, sir?"

Mr Whackers moved over to one of the maps. On it could be seen Cantilevre Manor, sheltered from the main road by a belt of trees. The farm buildings were less than half a mile away, with the bailiff's house nearby and two cottages, one occupied by Harry Sproggs and his family, and the other by the herdsman, and his. Various other sheds and barns and buildings were indicated, and another cottage on its own down towards Lammas Wood. A wiggly dotted line snaked across the fields, skirted the farm buildings and orchard, and came out on the road less than a hundred yards from the entrance of the drive leading to the Manor.

"We've got to get that footpath moved," Mr Whackers said. "Can't have the public wandering right up to the Manor."

"There'll be opposition," the Sergeant observed. He well remembered the commotion several years back when old Stubbins, who farmed the land adjoining Cantilevre, wired the gap where the stile had been – the stile had crumbled – and turned a bull loose in the field to deter ramblers who, he said, left gates open and let their dogs chase his sheep. There had been letters to the *Star and Echo,* protests in all directions, and a 'walk-in' up and down the path led by Judy Mustard brandishing a stock-whip to keep off the bull, which was a Hereford and quiet as a lamb. The ramblers had taken the matter through the Parish Council, the District Council and the County Council right up to the Department of the Environment, and it had appeared that an Act of Parliament would be needed to interfere with a right of way established, if he correctly remembered, by King Ethelred, or it might have been King Athelstan. He hoped that wouldn't all start up again.

"The ramblers, I suppose," said Mr Whackers. "Pressure will have to be applied." The ramblers, Sergeant Bullstrode reflected, were exceedingly resistant to pressure, and those Ecologists who'd recently shown up would make matters worse.

"Who lives in that cottage?" Reggie Whackers indicated the cottage down near Lammas Wood.

"Fellow called MacBean, sir. Newcomer. Foreigner," he added.

Reggie Whacker frowned. "What sort of foreigner?"

"Aberdeen, sir, I think. Or may be Dundee. Wears a kilt."

"Newcomer, eh? What's his line?"

"Runs an outfit calling themselves Eggologists, sir. Eat bran and nettles, so they say. Fond of badgers. Harmless, we regard them as."

"Mmm. We'll check on Mr MacBean."

"Any other foreigners? Irish accents, oriental appearance, things like that?"

"There's Ah Wong, Takeaway Meals in the High Street, sir."

"Been here long?"

"No, sir. Somewhere about ten years if I remember right."

"Well, we can easily check on Ah Wong. Anyone else?"

Sergeant Bullstrode knitted his brows in thought. It was not easy to recall exactly who came when, and what sort of accents they had, when it was sprung on you like that. There was the brush man who came round every couple of months or so and looked Italian. A couple of Pakis who took a room in The Red Lion every so often to display cheap carpets, or what passed for cheap, but they came from Birmingham or somewhere like that. Then of course there were the Irish labourers laying pipes and cables for Stimsons' the contractors, who showed up now and then at The Goat and Compasses, rough types they were. The Gwents at Cockscombe Castle had employed a German girl groom, and Lady Pandora had at one time kept company with a brown-skinned boyfriend with fuzzy hair said to come from Syria or some such place. Then there was a female who held classes once a fortnight to do with Indians, contortionists he called them. He wouldn't be surprised if there was something funny going on there. Worth mentioning to Mr Whackers.

"Then there's a lady, sir, teaches yoghurt at the Christadelphian hall."

"Yoghurt?"

"That's what they say. Sort of oriental PT. Both sexes. Not much on below the waist I've heard."

"Ah, yes. We'll look into that too."

Then there was the commune over towards Charlton Mansell that the Paxton girl had got herself mixed up with, all living in each others' pockets, or more correctly beds, with some kind of foreign teacher supposed to be in charge. Nut cases. Sex, sandals and pot. But Mr Whackers would know about that, the County drug squad having had it under observation for some time. And alien as the commune and its customs were to the life of Shipton Wick, he really couldn't see it as a nest of bombers from the IRA, PLO or Red Brigades.

Mr Whackers had gone back to the wall map which seemed to fascinate him. Now he was concerned with Hartley's, separated from Cantilevre Manor by the road but not more than a quarter of a mile away. He pursued his enquiries.

"Newcomers, sir. Not been here above two years."

There seemed to be a lot of newcomers in and around Shipton Wick, Reggie Whackers reflected, if you counted ten years as yesterday. He already had a dossier on the Paxtons, and had sent a man to look at their attics. The roof of the Manor was clearly visible from there.

Further away, almost off the large-scale map, was Cockscombe Castle. The name was misleading. There was no castle, or only a few green mounds and hollows in the garden to suggest the grey walls, towers, keeps and courts that had stood there centuries ago. The castle had left as its heir a shapely Georgian edifice that had replaced the mansion built mainly from the Castle's stone in early Jacobean times. The Georgian edifice was able to accommodate the Gwents' ample family and leave half a wing over, which had been placed at the disposal of Captain Longshott, the Prince's Comptroller, and others of his entourage whose presence might be deemed necessary during the moving-in process, complicated as this was likely to be.

Even princes were not immune from planning permission, especially as Cantilevre was a listed building. The royal status of its new owner might have been expected to hasten and smooth over the necessary processes, but one of the planning staff had raised a query as to whether the change in ownership did not amount to a Change of Use, arguing that as a royal residence it would fall into the category of a Palace. In that case, a whole new set of procedures would have to be invoked and a minimum of six months allowed for the raising of objections.

Even without the Change of Use complication, plans to knock a window in what had formerly been the butler's pantry to light a downstairs lavatory were causing a lot of concern in the Planning Department. Opinion had grouped itself round two opposing viewpoints. One held that loyalty to the Crown called for the smoothing of minor procedural objections from the royal path, and expedition of the due processes of law. The opposing viewpoint was that, on the contrary, democracy demanded that royalty should not only be treated the same as everyone else, but more so.

Argument raged hotly in County Hall, and in the meantime decisions were in obeyance. It looked as if Captain Longshott would spend some time in the spare wing of Cockscombe Castle. It was even rumoured that the Prince himself might take advantage of the Gwents' hospitality from time to time. This rumour was causing Mr Whackers some anxiety. The Gwent family seemed to be if not a nest of vipers, a cluster of question marks.

Lord Eustace, for instance, had recently brought from Eton a pop group believed to include at least one Arab to ply their art and doss down in the old coach house. Lady Annabel, a pupil at Westonbirt school, had formed a Magic Circle and her expertise in escaping from a sack tied up in a cocoon of ropes, chains, padlocks and fetters had recalled shades of Houdini. Clearly no training could fit an individual better for coping in later life with high security prisons. Lady Griselda was studying art in Florence and in touch, perhaps – who could tell? – with members of the Red Brigades. Lord Nigel was a pillar of the Socialist Syndicalist Sodality group at Cambridge University, a body so far to the left that it had almost got round in a circle to the right. Lord Roland was with a TV unit somewhere in the Middle East engaged, allegedly, on making a film about the sex life of camels. Lady Veronica was an activist in the Tintagel Resurrence movement dedicated to a free and independent Cornish nation. So the scene was something of a headache for a conscientious Chief Security Officer.

"There's one thing I should mention, sir," said Sergeant Bullstrode, laying a finger on a spot on the map. "Lammas Wood."

"Yes sergeant?" The Wood, he could see, lay just inside the Cantilevre property, near its northern boundary.

"There's badgers in there now, sir."

Mr Whackers stared at the sergeant. Surely to goodness he hadn't got to deal, on top of everything else, with a bunch of seditious, revolutionary, regicidal badgers, manufacturing bombs down in their holes and secreting Soviet-made automatic weapons?

"There's a lot of interest, sir, in them badgers. There's a group, call themselves Eggologists, go down there nights to watch what they get up to. Harmless, sir, but I thought you'd better know. Might see flashlights in the dark, that sort of thing."

"Not on your life we might. A bunch of nut-cases roaming round the place at night with flashlights! We'll put an end to that."

The Sergeant scratched his head and looked puzzled. "Yes, sir, but – ".

"But what?"

"Well, sir, they're a very active group. Got powerful friends. That right of way goes through Lammas Wood. If they was to be stopped, they'd create."

"Well, let them. Of course we don't want to tread on toes but security comes first, you know that."

"Yes, sir." Mr Whackers had his job to do but Security didn't come first, not with the Eggologists. Beside, there was another aspect. The badgers had now become royal property. "The Prince, sir. He's a sort of patron, you might say, of the Eggologists."

"He's a patron of a lot of things. Doesn't entitle members of whatever he's patron of to roam about his property at night flashing lights."

"It's been said, sir, they've had a favourable reply to a request to join them next full moon."

Mr Whackers put his hands to his head and was rendered speechless.

The Sergeant's information, although seldom very wide of the mark, was not always a hundred per cent accurate. On this occasion the score could be reckoned at around eighty per cent. Urged on by the dynamic new Chairman, Daryll had despatched a letter proffering to the Prince a loyal welcome from the Shipton Wick and District Ecology Group, referring to his well-known support for all forms of conservation and wildlife (Daryll wondered how fox-hunting fitted into that), hoping that the Prince would honour the Group by his patronage, extend protection to the badgers now resident on his property, and join the members in a badger-watch on the occasion of the next full moon.

A friendly reply from the Principal Personal Private Secretary had not committed the Prince to a badger-watch, but had expressed interest in, and approval of, the Group's aims. While it had not exactly promised full protection for badgers – they dwelt, alas, in an area where the Ministry's vets were under orders to destroy them – the letter had expressed the hope that badgers would continue to enrich the wildlife resources of the countryside, and had affirmed the further hope that HRH would in due course have an opportunity to meet members of the Group.

"Tread warily here," Captain Longshott had said to the Principal Personal Private Secretary, Martin Knox-Knox-Knox. "We don't want to get him mixed up with a bunch of nature nuts."

"Quite so. But the ground is delicate. There's an activist, I understand, in the Stop Hunt gang who's also active in the Ecologists. Might well cause trouble. Best not to give offence if we can avoid it."

"If HRH would lay off hunting and stick to polo it would make our job a lot easier."

"Not here for easy options, old man." Martin Knox-Knox-Knox was a slender, tidy individual who had been diverted, through connections of his wife, into the royal secretariat from an academic career.

"Then there's a drinks party we've been invited to by this Mrs Paxton," he added "I've accepted for us both."

"Why?" asked Arthur Longshott.

"Paxtons a local big-shot, owns a factory, on the Town Council, that sort of thing."

"Sounds an irresistible party."

"Well, there's a daughter of sorts."

"What do you mean, of sorts?"

"Moony, I'm told. Meditation and bedbugs and long golden hair. Just your cup of tea." Arthur, whose marriage had disintegrated, enjoyed bachelor status, whereas Martin was safely anchored, or at any rate anchored, to a stylish wife and elegantly decorated flat in Ennismore Gardens. Meanwhile he was dossing down, in a manner of speaking, in the spare half-wing of Cockscombe Castle. He and Arthur shared a spacious office overlooking a terrace set with flower beds, urns and statuary. Beyond, a lawn sloped down to a small lake. An agreeable billet, both were ready to admit.

The private line to the Palace flashed a light and Arthur picked up the receiver.

"Arriving tomorrow? Oh, I see. Coming down here? What for?" More conversation followed and he hung up. "The new equerry's coming tomorrow. As HRH is away, they're sending him here for a few days. "Accustom him to English country life," they say. "Ease him in gently." I suppose Lady Gwent won't mind."

"Isn't he accustomed to English country life already?"

"He's from the New Commonwealth. Gesture of solidarity and all that. Independent Republic of Hapana, if I remember aright. Captain Kidogo is the name."

"How shall we accustom him to English country life? Crocquet on the lawn? Rain spreading from the west? Coffee mornings? Hunter trials? Darts at the pub?"

"He was at Sandhurst I believe. Won the Sword of Honour. Splendid chap. Sure to fit in."

"We'd better kick off the fitting-in process at the party you've let us in for. Get him accustomed to moony girls with long golden hair for a start."

Sybil Paxton raised no objections to this addition to her party. A Captain from the New Commonwealth would make a change. Besides, he might become a Head of State at any time.

"Sandhurst you say?" she enquired of Arthur Longshott. "Sword of Honour? Which year?" Arthur chose a year at random. "Ah, yes, that would be in General Saddleback's time. His wife's nephew married one of the Ramsay girls whose previous husband was on the staff of Dickie Mountbatten. I'll get a dossier."

Despite rapid telephoning to the Royal Military College, the Ministry of Defence, General Saddleback's home and the Embassy of the Independent Republic of Hapana, the dossier proved elusive. In fact, Sybil was baulked, a condition to which she was not accustomed. However, there was no time to take the matter any further; the Captain would just have to be taken on trust, resting, as it were, on his Sword of Honour.

Plans for the party were nearing fruition. After wrestling with doubts, Sybil had invited Charlotte Evers to do the eats. She was by no means enthusiastic about Charlotte Evers. She made, in Sybil's opinion, too much parade of her so-called efficiency. Horse's ailments, cocktail canapés, cleaning plugs, typing letters – all calculated methods to worm her way in. Sybil had very little doubt that Charlotte had mapped out a cold-blooded campaign of worming-in. The Prince would be regularly seen on the hunting field; so would Charlotte. There would be parties at Cantilevre Manor; eats would be needed and Charlotte would provide them. Sybil had no intention of aiding and abetting the worming-in process, but there was no doubt that Charlotte was good at eats, and those supplied by her local rival in the business, Shipton Wick's leading bakery, were distinctly unimaginative. So, with reluctance, Charlotte had been taken on, but Sybil meant to keep her too busy to do much worming. A minor problem, really; over Jo hovered the real question mark.

Peter, with reluctance, had driven over to the commune wondering what on earth to say to his daughter. The teachings of the swami, or guru, or whatever he was, were not sympathetic, to put it mildly, to Princes and to those whom he would no doubt describe as their hangers-on; to drinks parties, capitalists, equerries and indeed to anyone likely to be encountered at Sybil's little social gathering. A matriarchal summons was likely to prove as attractive to Jo as a burst of gunfire to a covey of pheasants. Members of the commune were out to regenerate the world, and a drinks party designed to bring together the rank and fashion of Shipton Wick with members of the Prince's entourage would not, in Jo's opinion, be likely to promote this cause.

The commune had taken over a derelict RAF site whose abandoned buildings had been slowly and hideously disintegrating into component parts. A central building, once the mess and offices, had to some extent been made habitable. In it, meals of a sort were communally consumed and seminars, meetings and meditations were held.

There had been, of course, problems. For instance, bats. These animals had established a commune of their own in the roof. Should they be dislodged? Clearly not; the commune believed in the Right to Life of every living creature, bats included. Co-existence lay at the root of their philosophy. But leaks in the roof were almost as numerous as the bats, and repairs could not be carried out without dislodging them. It was on the question of co-existence with a leaking roof that opinion was divided. Some held that a state of dampness, being part of nature, was to be tolerated, even welcomed. The rival view was that while people might tolerate, even welcome, dampness, timbers did not; all of them were rotting and floors and roof had become unsafe. The argument was still unresolved and yellow plastic waterproofs had crept into the wardrobe of the weaker brethren. The bats were still in residence.

The door to the central building was open – probably it wouldn't shut – and Peter discovered within more evidence of past activities than of present ones. In one room, pots of various shapes and sizes, bits of pots and lumps of clay were strewn around; the remains of a meal, probably several meals, adorned another; a hand printing press, with tiers of type, stood in a third. Peter headed for a passage where he had caught a glimpse of something white. Rounding a corner, he found himself face to face with a goat. The goat nodded its head, scattered some droppings on the floor, turned and walked off with the supercilious air affected by all goats.

At last, entering a bare room larger than the rest, he came

upon human life. A figure with its back to him stood halfway up a ladder sloshing paint on to a damp and peeling wall with wide sweeps of the arm. Taking shape was a mural, whose scheme, design, or theme was not apparent to Peter's eye.

"Hello," Peter said. The figure did not respond. "Can you tell me where I'd find Jo?"

A sort of whistling sound, such as that often made by people grooming horses, was the only reply. A wide swath of purple was laid across a hatch of mustard-coloured stripes superimposed on a magenta background. The Apocalypse? Coming round after an accident? A trip on LSD? Peter tried a different approach.

"I like your mural. Powerful, expressive. Angry. But I'm afraid, on that damp wall, it won't last."

The approach worked. The figure turned its head, enabling Peter to sex it – a beard.

"Last? Endure?" the painter demanded. "Who wants art to last? Don't you understand its whole essence is to be ephemeral? Respond to changes in the ethos, reflect contemporary motivations? Constantly be born anew? One of the morticians, that's what you are. Want art laid out, embalmed, stiff on a slab. Then you can trade in it – buy and sell the corpses, invest your stinking money in the cadaver industry. Brounk!" A kind of snort, snuffle or choke ended the address. Peter felt crushed.

"Could you, I wonder, very kindly tell me where I can find Jo?"

Seeing it was to be a non-discussion, the painter turned back to his task, muttering. "Seminar I expect. Temple of the Sun."

How to find the Temple of the Sun? No further information was vouchsafed by the young man on the ladder. Temple suggested a large edifice, Sun was clearly metaphorical in this climate. There was a wet west wind, an overcast sky, a half-hearted but persistent drizzle. Peter headed for an ex-hangar he had observed among the complex of buildings.

Here indeed, something was going on. Inside the bare and draughty hangar was what appeared to be a large plastic bubble. Inside the bubble were rows of low wooden benches grouped around a central dias which had something like a lectern on it. There, no doubt, the high priest, the Munshi Jo called him, presided over the deliberations and readings from sacred books of different faiths. The commune wasn't merely ecumenical but pantheistic, if that was the word. The teachings of many prophets, sages and philosophers were studied and a kind of theological mix was the aim. Indigestible, Peter feared.

He approached the plastic bubble nervously, wondering whether he ought to remove his shoes. There was a discussion, going on. He had little difficulty in identifying the Munshi, a tubby little man dressed in sackcloth with a bushy black beard and very little hair on top, whether a sort of tonsure or natural baldness who could say. And there was Jo, conspicuous with her long hair flowing over her shoulders. She wore a kind of sari, hand-woven no doubt, perhaps from the fleece of some odd looking sheep he had noticed as he drove up – very small, dark brown, with four horns instead of two. He didn't think she looked very well.

"I still experience difficulty in accepting without reserve the principle of respect for blowflies," one of the Seekers, as Peter believed they were called, was saying. "Look what they do to the bottoms of sheep."

"There can be no exceptions," the Munshi pronounced. He had a fruity voice with a slight singsong accent that denoted the East, unless possibly parts of Wales. "The Web of Life embraces all creation."

"Then should we let blowflies rip? Lay their eggs all over the place and turn everything maggoty?"

"In the Web of Life, maggots have a place no less than men. Maggots deserve our respect."

Old Donkin would have something to say to that, Peter thought, when caterpillars ate his cabbages. Jo was looking in his direction and he waved a hand. Rather to his surprise, she left her place on one of the benches, emerged from the plastic bubble and greeted her father with if not warmth, with rather less hostility than usual. Evidently she was finding the subject of blowflies less than rivetting.

"Hello," she said.

"Hello." For hours he had been wondering what to say next without any bright ideas popping into his head. "Your mother wants you" hardly seemed a telling phrase. He glanced at her with more attention. "You look as if you could do with a square meal."

"Red meat of course. Corpses of animals. Slaughtered creatures."

"How about a creamy mushroom omelette, nicely browned on the outside? A lasagne perhaps, or a tasty pasta?"

"Is this bribery?"

"I suppose in a way it is."

"Mmm." Jo gave a little swallow. Had Peter actually made her gastric juices flow? The poor girl was obviously starved.

"No red meat of course. Squib and Squirrel have got an excellent counter of continental cheeses. Miss Cheer can make a very creditable spinach quiche, and then a cheese soufflé. . ."

"Well, we'll see." Better than blowflies, Peter felt inclined to add, but didn't. And the roof of Hartleys' doesn't leak.

"I think she'll come,"he reported to Sybil. It was rather like tempting a shy animal into a trap, or getting a sparrow to eat out of one's hand.

"The next thing," Sybil mused, "will be to get her into some decent clothes."

"Perhaps at least we'll get her to wash her sari, or whatever it's called, and comb her hair. But I'd keep off the subject of the Prince and his equerries. She's easily scared."

The trap had been baited: would the quarry enter it? The question was answered by the sound of a car's engine, switched off by the door, soon after dark. Despite a conviction that the only decent way to move about was on the back of a donkey, the Mini that Peter had given Jo for her birthday was evidently still in use, consuming fossil fuel and so further depleting the dwindling resources of a plundered planet. Peter believed she kept it at a nearby farm well out of sight of the Munshi, whose communal shopping was done by ox-cart. This vehicle caused considerable chaos in the narrow winding village street and there was a strong feeling among the locals that the commune should be summoned for obstructing the highway.

"Vegetable soup," Sybil instructed Miss Cheer. "Made with water, not stock. Croutons fried in vegetable oil. Then, I think, a cheese soufflé, she can't find fault with that."

Miss Cheer grunted. "Pandering, I call it. What Jo needs is bread and water and a good talking-to, spanking it would have been in my day." She grunted off to put on the vegetables.

What Jo needed was a good rest. A nasty prickly sensation at the back of her nose gave warning of unpleasant things to come. With all the vitamins, trace elements, roughage and stone-ground flour which sustained members of the commune, colds should have been unknown, but somehow bugs seemed to break in. The Munshi taught that this was due to Errors of Thought, which weakened the defences of the body. If you caught a cold it was your own fault and called forth blame rather than sympathy. Miss Cheer had the same approach. "All those draughts and damp mattresses and mooning about in barns, what can you expect?"

Errors of Thought. All very well to talk about errors, Jo reflected, but how does one avoid them if the object of one's thoughts is behaving like a right bastard? Stringing one along with a line of talk and all the time behind one's back stringing someone else along and pretending not to? Of course one believed in absolute freedom, no possessive shackles, no reactionary middle-class conventional stuff. Cosmic sharing, as the Munshi said. Freedom. Simon was free to shop around and if he wanted to ditch her, fair enough.

At least Jo supposed that it was fair though, considering all she'd done to help Simon, doubts, like the bugs, somehow got in. What wasn't fair was sneaking off with the half-witted little bitch always on about the two-bit parts she'd once had in some ghastly outfit called The Charnel House, and now working off her frustrations by making revolting bits of pottery whose shapes could only have originated, in Jo's opinion, in a diseased mind. Now Roseanne, for such was her absurd name, was putting on an act about a campaign for the Liberation of Laboratory Animals. Simon, heaven help him, had lapped it all up and even praised Roseanne's monstrosities. They'd had a row which had ended with Simon hurling a can of acrylic paint at her and then daubing an enormous depravity across a wall of the refectory. In this the teeth of a crocodile, the claws of a dragon, the belly of a pregnant spider and the vagina of a parturient cow could, with some imaginative aid, be discerned. The word "Jo" sprawled across the masterpiece in foot-high letters was less ambiguous. At times, Jo felt that she would welcome the release of laboratory rats in tens of thousands, all with pink eyes and pointed fangs and all half-starved, to converge upon the cornered person of Roseanne.

Late October sunlight was yellowing the bedroom when Jo surfaced to hear the rattle of a teacup and scrape of a chair as Mrs Sproggs put down a tray by her bedside. A sensation of guilt mingled with the prickling of her nose. To be waited on hand and foot by a woman of her mother's age, toiling upstairs carrying a tray! Contemptible. She started to get out of bed – a comfortable, warm bed, contemptible too, with all those destitute people sleeping rough in shelters. A sneeze disrupted her thoughts. Hot tea: contemptible too, but comforting.

"Nasty cold that," Mrs Sproggs remarked. "Going about it is, Astrid's had a shocker. Harry's sickening now. Wouldn't do for it to spread to Cantilevre, would it? Moving in, he is, they say, week or so from now, though how they'll get the carpets down in time the Lord only knows. Baynes and Buckle were hoping for the order but there's been a London firm come down. Cream and gold they say's the colours for the lounge. Very suitable."

Here we go, thought Jo, enough to turn the stomach of a hippopotamus. Toads, the lot of them, even Mrs Sproggs. An idiot she'd been, scuttling out from under when things weren't going her way. She'd have the tea and clear off back to the commune, in time for the weekly meditation on Transcendental Purity.

"There's a note for you on the tray," Mrs Sproggs said, drawing back the curtains. "Walked all round the place, he did. Harry was in Sproutings, drilling winter wheat. Round he comes in a Land Rover with a couple of fellows, bodyguards I suppose, Harry stops the tractor and they chats away free and easy as close as you are now, he asks Harry how long he's worked at Cantilevre and where before that and so on, ever so friendly. He even said he'd heard there was badgers in Lammas Wood. Harry found them badgers. The thing is whether they'll be gassed.''

Jo blew her nose and took up the note. It was from her mother. "You have a hair appointment at Marie-Louise's at 11 a.m. Kindly keep it. Lunch at 1. Your sari is in the machine.''

Marie-Louise's was a hive of activity, everyone at full stretch. Jo despised herself for entering its portals, but had to admit that facilities for hair-washing at the commune were minimal. In fact she couldn't remember when she'd last given herself a shampoo. Tresses that had once been golden seemed to have turned a dull bronze.

Female toads came and went in the salon. Lady Evers, having a blue rinse. Councillor Mrs Hussey swathed in curlers. Even Lady Pandora, who seldom patronised Marie-Louise's. She was having a tangle-toss, a bold cut advertised in *The New Stylist* as imparting the fresh, youthful fragrance of windswept moors, reminiscent of heather, billberries and peaty burns. This was taxing for Astrid, who wielded her scissors with a puckered forehead and a look of concentration on her heart-shaped face.

It was true that she was concentrating, but not only on Lady Pandora's tangle-toss. There was the question of Daryll. He was displaying a side to his character she hadn't suspected, a positively awkward side. He'd seemed so kind and gentle, so easy-going in a way, and now there'd been words that you could only call harsh and uncalled-for. She wondered whether she'd done right to join the Ecologists. Their last meeting, with the new chairman in command, had been stormy. The main bone of contention had been the hunt. Judy Mustard had proposed a massive demo at the opening meet. She was negotiating with some firm or firms to procure a huge inflatable rubber whale which, with appropriate slogans, was to be floated over the assembly. She had already organised aerosol sprays guaranteed to cause frenzy, disorientation and general mayhem among the hounds.

Daryll it was who had counselled moderation. The Prince's presence at the meet would certainly attract publicity, he had agreed, but wouldn't that publicity cast a shadow on the name of

Shipton Wick in the eyes of the nation? Was it in accordance with loyalty to the Crown and respect for others' rights to throw all this at the Prince at the very outset of his arrival amongst them? Of course, it was wrong that royal support should be lent to cruel sports, but Daryll suggested holding back until the Prince had, as it were, got into the saddle.

This had provoked an uproar. Judy Mustard had been incensed, thumping the table and shouting which came first, sycophancy or survival of whales, cow-towing or the struggle against revolting cruelty? While they argued, whales were dying in agony to satisfy the greed of man, foxes being torn to shreds for his amusement. She was ashamed of all of them. She'd threatened to resign from the Group and expose their servile boot-licking to the media. Their names would be dragged in the mud. Of course, the Group had given away, with Angus MacBean taking Judy Mustard's side and Daryll defeated.

"No hard feelings, old chap," Angus had said to Daryll over the refreshments. This time he wasn't wearing his kilt, but trousers with a strong check and a Norwegian sweater, very rugged, and much too hot for an October day. "Tell you what," he'd added, "why don't you all come down to my place, you know I've got that little cottage by the wood, and we'll work out a strategy for the demo? If we lay it on, and that's been decided, it's got to be done properly, we'll agree on that. I can foresee problems with the inflatable whale. Next Tuesday, seven p.m., how about that?"

Daryll had declined. Daryll belonged to the Shipton Wick Singers, and they had a practice on the Tuesday. Astrid hadn't seen any harm in accepting and had done so, and Daryll had taken offence. "You can do what you like of course," he'd said huffily. "No business of mine. But I should have thought you'd have the sense to steer clear of that hairy humbug. I don't trust him as far as I can see the nose on my face." These were strong words for Daryll. Well, after all, there was nothing between them except mutual interests and, you might say, a friendship in its early stages. A shoot that might grow or wither. At the moment, it looked as if withering would be its fate.

"There we are," Astrid said brightly, coming back with a

jerk to the business in hand and holding up the mirror. "Very becoming, Lady Pandora, if I may say so. Just right for this evening's party."

Lady Pandora examined her image carefully, nodded, and enquired "What party?"

"Well, *the* party at the Paxtons. For the Prince's entourage."

"I hardly need to go to Sybil Paxton's to meet Arthur Longshott and Martin KKK, if that's who you mean, seeing that they're staying at the Castle."

"Yes, of course, I forgot." Astrid, feeling crushed, undid the rose-pink apron.

"There's a new equerry coming," Lady Pandora added, relenting somewhat. "So I'm told. From the New Commonwealth, wherever that is."

Unexpectedly, a fellow feeling for Lady Pandora came to birth in Astrid's mind. She was glad that others, so much better educated than she, shared an uncertainty about the whereabouts of the New Commonwealth, not to mention the Third World. They must have a geographical location somewhere, but she'd never heard it defined or seen it on an atlas. The inhabitants, she knew, were brown or black, very numerous and mostly hungry, which gave her an uncomfortable feeling of guilt combined with an inability to do anything about it, like a mild attack of indigestion. And where were the First and Second Worlds? No one had ever explained.

"That'll be a nice change," she said vaguely, pocketing Lady Pandora's 25p. Difficult, the question of tips. Some people didn't tip at all, others fumbled in obvious uncertainty as to how much to fish out of their bags, others put the money into a box for Dr Barnardo's Homes. Daryll thought tipping demeaning, but Astrid didn't – she thought it a nice little personal touch, to show you weren't a machine but human.

Her mind turned to Angus, who appeared to live alone at Lammas cottage, which had been unoccupied for some time before he came because it was in a bad state of repair. He worked, he'd said, on and off, in the building industry, and did for himself. She wondered whether there was a wife or girlfriend up in Scotland. No mistake about it, he had pressed her hand when the meeting had ended and said: "See you Tuesday, then. Cakes and ale and a log fire, and we'll make the world safe for whales and badgers."

Chapter Four

A MESSAGE had come through to say that Captain Kidogo was due at the Castle sometime between five and six p.m. He was arriving in a military aircraft belonging to the Hapanan Air Force and a car from the Embassy would deliver him into Captain Longshott's care.

"Poor chap, bit of a plunge in at the deep end," Arthur remarked.

"Republic of Hapana," Martin said. "I looked it up. The president's someone called Mbogo. More or less Western-aligned, the F.O. think, which is why we're getting Captain Kidogo. A state visit's being laid on. Important reserves of molybdenum and castor oil. The president heads an ivory-smuggling consortium and is an honorary vice-president of the World Wildlife Fund. Kidogo's his nephew or something I think. We're to ease him in gently, the F.O. say, and keep him sweet. And here he is."

A large Mercedes drew up under the portico, the driver sprang out to open the passengers' door and out of it emerged a very large, broad and bulky gentleman in a sky-blue uniform with three rows of shiny medals, a revolver in its holster at his hip. Two more hefty figures followed, both in army battle dress with automatic weapons slung over their shoulders, caps at a jaunty angle, and straggly beards. There were three broad grins.

"Captain Kidogo? Surely. . ."

Arthur for once was at a loss. The resplendent visitor advanced with outstretched hand. Arthur had never had his hand gripped by a vice but had no doubt that this was what it felt like.

"Captain Kidogo you say?" There was a shout of derision. "Captain Kidogo!" If a spitting cobra had the power of speech, the resultant sound would have closely resembled that emitted by the splendid figure now confronting Arthur and Martin.

"You will hear no more of that viper, that dung-beetle, that hyena! Now that our great deliverer, our Good Shepherd, has freed our great country from the grip of that vile, corrupt, foul and stinking locust who called himself our president, the *late* president Mbogo, you will hear no more of that baboon, the former self-styled Captain Kidogo!"

"I see," Arthur said. "Well, that's a little awkward. It was Captain Kidogo we were expecting. Credentials. . . May I ask whom I am addressing?"

"Me? I? Who? I am General Mkubwa of our ever-victorious army. I have come to greet your Prince from our glorious president Dudu (since Saturday night) and Good Shepherd. I come to tell him, the people of our country stand beside your people in the struggle for peace, justice, freedom, the extermination of South Africa and the restoration of the stolen wealth of the Hapanan people by the late hyena Mbogo from the numbered account in Switzerland where it is buried like a dog's bone."

"Yes, I see. Well, I am sure the Prince will appreciate the message. But at the moment. . ." The bearded companions were showing restive signs. A statue of a naked Niobe mourning her daughters had attracted their attention. A running commentary, doubtless directed at her physique, had started up between them, while one of them swung his weapon lightly in his hand.

"Now lead me to your Prince," the General ordered, in tones suggesting that instant obedience was normally accorded to his commands.

"Actually the Prince, I'm afraid, isn't actually here."

"The Prince not here? What is this I am hearing?"

"No, I'm afraid. . ."

The look of puzzlement on General Mkubwa's face gave way to one of enlightenment. "Ah, I understand. A *coup*! There has been a *coup*! I am the man to deal with a *coup*, you will see. We are accustomed to *coups* in my country. Your Prince shall be rescued and restored. That is, if it is not too late. If so, I will have the traitors dragged through the streets attached to Land Rovers and driven over by tanks."

"Thank you, that won't be necessary." Arthur was beginning to regain his equilibrium. "The Prince is quite well, I'm glad to say. Merely on a visit to a friendly country. Back on Friday. Meanwhile. . . I'd be obliged if you'd tell your men not to indulge in target practice on Lord Gwent's statuary. It is quite valuable."

At a bark from the General, the bodyguard lowered their weapons, grinned broadly and, at a further bark, put the guns into the boot of the Mercedes. "I suggest your driver takes your men back to your Embassy, or wherever they came from," Arthur said. "You won't need a bodyguard here."

"Me? Without a bodyguard? What nonsense is this? At night, they sleep by my door. When my food is offered, they take first portion. Does the Prince not have a bodyguard?"

"Of a sort, certainly," Arthur admitted. "They keep a low profile. I'm afraid soldiers in battledress with automatic weapons. . ."

"This is talk I do not understand."

"Well, tell you what" Arthur rather desperately rallied his forces. "We're all invited to a party and we ought to go now. Right away. Our hostess is a lady who's a great friend of the Prince's. No, no, I don't mean that." The General's eyes had widened and another grin appeared on his face. "More like a mother you might say. You'll be as safe there as in your own home." Ill-chosen words, Arthur feared, as soon as they were spoken; the General's home might well be a nest of vipers hatching the next *coup*. "Mrs Paxton, that's our hostess, won't allow bodyguards in. Rule of the house. I'm sure – "

Martin interrupted. "Several young, attractive, unattached girls will be there – nervous, you understand, they'd be terrified if they even caught sight of a gun. Swoon right away, very likely. The Prince would be *most* displeased. Come with us, General, we'll look after you."

The General appeared undecided. "Very pretty girls," Arthur added. "Your bodyguards can rejoin you later. Please tell them to lock their guns into the boot."

"Before we go, I'll show you your room," Martin added. "I expect you need a wash."

Another mistake; the General stiffened and began to glower. "I mean, a pee. One should avoid euphemisms." Seizing the guest's bag, he led the way into the house and was thankful to hear the General's footsteps following. By the time Martin had deposited the bag in the last of the spare bedrooms, shown the General the bathroom and returned, with the General still in tow, the Mercedes with its bodyguards had departed. Fleetingly, Arthur wondered where they would fetch up. Well, sufficient for the day.

The rank and fashion of Shipton Wick assembled at Hartley's were expectantly awaiting the Prince's Comptroller, his Assistant Personal Private Secretary and the equerry from the New Commonwealth. Their hostess was keeping things moving in a literal sense. Her guests were obliged constantly on *qui vive* to dodge her wheelchair as it circulated briskly round the room, weaving about among the company with the agility of an experienced polo pony.

"Earth waves," she was saying to Sir Hubert Evers. "Neglect of earth waves is bringing us down. Have you had your bed aligned?"

"Not that I'm aware of," Sir Hubert cautiously replied.

"Then you must. If you lie across the earth waves you resist the current and the result will be disastrous – compacted muscles, inflammation of the bowel, ulcers, tumours. The current must flow *through*."

"I think perhaps it does. So far, I haven't got compacted muscles, inflammation of the bowel, tumours or ulcers. Touch wood."

"The contract for the light fittings had gone to a London firm," Councillor Snape was saying to Councillor Rufford. "Scandalous I call it. The Prince should patronise local firms. Baynes and Buckle have an excellent range of lamps and lampshades, couldn't be bettered."

"I don't suppose the Prince himself places the orders," Bob Rufford observed, stepping smartly to one side as the wheelchair sped by.

"Anyway, everything at the banquet will be local."

"I hope we shan't be confined to sausages and mash."

"A very varied menu. We start with jellied eels."

"The toads are late." Jo's high, clear voice pierced the hum of conversation, bringing looks of disapproval from several guests. But Sybil, with perfect timing, had positioned her wheelchair beside the door at the moment when Arthur led in his little party, bowed slightly over her hand to suggest a hint of royalty, and said: "May I present HRH's new equerry, General – ah – Kukuku?"

"General Mkubwa" announced that individual, seeming as he spoke to swell and fill the doorway, medals jingling. "I come to help your Prince to burn his enemies into ashes. The Prince is not here. But you are like his mother."

"Well, not exactly." Sybil was for once at a loss. "I wouldn't quite say that. But welcome, General, to our little gathering. It's a pleasure to have you here."

The General surveyed the scene with a look of puzzlement mingled with disdain.

"These people, they are the Prince's friends? These are some of his women?"

"Peter, bring the General a drink," Sybil said hastily. "Martini, sherry, whisky, gin. You have a preference?"

"That one over there, I think." The General pointed a commanding finger and strode purposefully across the room, brushing aside those in his path and making for Jo. "All of them are thin," he said over his shoulder to Arthur, following nervously in his wake, "Why do their fathers starve them? But when all the fat lambs have been slaughtered, the eagle must eat rats. That is a saying in my country. Aha there is food I see. I will drink whisky." He grinned down at Jo, gave her a pat on the bottom and added: "Milk will make you fat. Much milk. And tails of sheep and humps of camels. Then you will be beautiful and please your husband. You have a husband?"

"No, nor should I enjoy the tails of sheep and humps of camels."

"Best of all are monkeys. Monkeys are food for chiefs, very tender. When your Prince comes to my country, he will feed on monkeys."

Peter Paxton arrived with the General's whisky and a plate of canapés. The General drained the whisky, handed back the empty glass and exchanged it for the plate of Canapés. In a few capacious mouthfuls, he cleared the plate and handed it to his hostess, who at the moment reached his side.

"You must meet a fellow General, General," she said. "This is General Sir Alciabiades Mortimer-Fell. He has won great distinction in several evacuations. He is an expert on evacuations but I'm sure he hasn't as many medals as you."

Sir Alciabiades was small, wiry and brisk. In order to avoid being described as dapper, an adjective he disliked, he was clad in a pair of baggy trousers, a well-worn pullover and no tie, and in order that his voice should not sound clipped, spoke with a somewhat unconvincing drawl.

"I'd no idea your country had been engaged in so many military campaigns," he observed to his fellow-guest. "Twenty-seven, if I've counted the campaign medals aright. Yours must be a very warlike nation."

General Mkubwa's belly-laugh set all the medals dancing. "My nation is devoted to the cause of peace. We do not give our medals for fighting in battles. We give our medals to our commanders, and then if one of them fights a battle, our President takes a medal away. One at a time for each battle."

"So if you, General, were to take part in twenty-seven battles, your chest would be bare?"

"Impossible. I am loyal to our Good Shepherd, our great president Dudu. I fight only for him."

"You mean if you fight *for* your president, you don't lose any medals? Only if you fight *against* him?"

"That is more or less true."

"An ingenious system."

General Mkubwa's interest was still focused on Jo, who was looking up at him with an expression Sybil couldn't remember seeing since her daughter's childhood. Interest, certainly; could it be deference? Esteem? Even admiration?

"I think it's horrid to eat monkeys," she remarked, "Like eating children."

"Then you shall have no monkeys when you come to my

country. I bring an invitation to the Prince to pay a state visit. You shall come too.''

"Thank you, but I'm not going to turn into a toad.''

"A toad?'' A puzzled frown creased the General's wide brow. "You mean there is *mganga* here with such powers? You are in danger, I will protect you. Anyone who is under the protection of General Mkubwa is safe, quite safe.''

"And his enemies?''

The General waved a hand. "They wither like dried grass. They burn to ashes like bushes. The Prince – ''

"Don't let's talk about the Prince. Talk about yourself. Have you many wives?''

"Only one at present. Also concubines. You call them girlfriends I think.''

"Is your wife fat?''

"Fatter than she was. She is trying.''

"I wonder why people want to be fat in Africa and thin in Europe. The climate, perhaps.''

"Come to my country and you will see. It is a beautiful country. I will make you welcome. Fat sheep, honey, roast dog, porcupines, sweet potatoes. Everything you wish for, you shall have.''

Sybil arrived at the General's side in time to receive another empty plate from his hands. "I mustn't let my daughter monopolise your attention. You must talk to some of the others. Lady Pandora, over there, is longing to meet you. A daughter of the Marquess of Gwent.''

For a moment the General looked rebellious and glowered. He was not accustomed to taking orders from women. Women in general were of small account in matters of authority, but particular women – a chieftainess, a medicine-woman, a queen mother – could be possessed of spiritual powers which were not to be ignored. Clearly the Prince's mother was one such. This woman in the wheelchair was like a mother to the Prince. What could that mean but that she, too, was invested with such other worldly powers? Obediently he made his way across the room towards another of those thin, scrawny, underfed maidens the English seemed to prefer. Halfway there, he changed his mind.

If he had to make do with a thin scrawny maiden, he preferred the one with long pale hair.

What was this about a fellow General? Could that little man, scarcely larger than an uncircumcised boy, be a commander of warriors? He addressed himself to Sir Alciabiades.

"You are a commander of warriors? You have won battles?"

"Yes, indeed. Mainly on manoeuvres. Practices, you understand."

"Practices?" General Mkubwa looked puzzled. He had not done much practising for battles. "And when you fight the enemy?"

"There is a saying, you know, *réculer pur mieux sauter*. Sometimes it is more important to withdraw than to give battle. So as to attack with greater punch another time."

"So you have done this? Go back – " he swept an arm and narrowly missed decapitating Counsellor Mrs Hussey – "not advance?"

"I was considered quite an expert on evacuations. There is an art, you know. The logistics of evacuating are very complex."

"This I do not understand. In my country, we do not evacuate. We crush."

Sir Alciabiades looked sad. "I don't suppose you have a Minister of Defence constantly nagged by Parliament to cut the budget. Tell me about your last campaign."

The General needed no further encouragement. It had happened only the week before. The former president, it seemed, had been seized at the cinema while watching *Star Wars,* his bodyguard eliminated, the barracks taken by supporters of the General, and supporters of the president put to flight.

"Those vile dogs supporting that stinking hyena, the so-called president, that dung-beetle, fled like dust blown by gales before our brave soldiers. They took shelter in a field of tapioca and our warriors drove them out by fire. Canoes they had ready, hidden in the rushes, many canoes. Into the canoes they jumped and down the river they fled. Oho, you say, they escaped, they are not crushed flat like insects, they run like the cheetah and get away."

"And did they?"

"In your country, you have an army of maidens?"

"A womens' section of the army? Yes, indeed."

"I, too, have an army of maidens. Now I bring them into action. I place them on an island in the midst of the river. On that island is a meeting place for maidens who are newly circumcised. It is a dancing place. So, the maidens, they smear themselves with chalk and the fat of sheeps's tails, they bedeck themselves with beads, the drums are sounding, there is beer for the drummers and the maidens dance. They dance, they leap, they stamp their feet, their breasts leap up and down. They are not skinny like your maidens here." He glanced at Jo in a derogatory way. "They have good shapes. They dance."

"Ah, yes, I see," Sir Alciabiades gave a sage nod. "The men in the canoes reach the island. They hear the drums, they see the girls, perhaps they smell the beer. And then – "

"You are right!" With a shout of pleasure General Mkubwa clapped his fellow general on the shoulder. Sir Alciabiades gave at the knees, to be rescued just in time by Peter. "The fleeing traitors come, they see girls, they think we are tired, there is no one following, night is coming, Mkubwa's soldiers they have camped to feast, we will rest here a little and put aside our weapons and leave with these sprightly maidens something they will remember us for. So they leap from the canoes, the maidens welcome them, they dance, presently they enjoy the maidens in the bushes and then sleep, sleep – sweet dreams!"

"And then your men come up and tow away or sink the canoes."

"So you understand my tactics, you salute my skill. Battles are won here, you agree." He tapped his forehead.

"They must have felt like proper charlies when they woke up."

"Woke up?" The General's laugh again rang through the room. "You think they woke up? You think my maidens are fools?" With an eloquent gesture he drew his hand across his throat. "You have a maidens' army too. I will tell the Prince how he should train his maidens. I have drawn up a manual of instructions for the maidens' army. He shall have a copy." With a reminiscent smile, he briefly recalled other victories before finishing his drink and remembering his mission. A frown replaced the smile. "Where *is* the Prince?"

"Back on Friday," Arthur reminded him. "He's looking forward to your taking up your duties immediately."

The fuse of memory, once lit, burned briskly. "My duties, yes. Where are my bodyguards? Why are they not at my side?"

Silence fell upon the company. The same question had been troubling Arthur and Martin. With any luck, the bodyguards had gone back to London in the Embassy car. With a bit less luck, the automatic weapons had gone back to London locked in the boot, leaving the bodyguards behind, with who knew what result. With no luck at all the bodyguards with their weapons were roaming the streets of Shipton Wick creating who knew what havoc. Some comfort might be drawn from the fact that no SOS had, as yet, come through from Sergeant Bullstrode or any other branch of the law.

The bodyguards had not returned to London in the Embassy car. Loyalty to their General clearly demanded that they should stay if not actually at his side, at least in his vicinity, available instantly to resume their posts when the command came. Besides, they were thirsty. The driver, a fellow Hapanan more versed than they in the English ways, after checking that opening time had passed, deposited them at The Goat & Compasses and drove back to London.

While glad to welcome to his premises New Commonwealth citizens, still something of a novelty in Shipton Wick, the landlord, Mr Sweetapple, observed with apprehension the automatic weapons slung over their shoulders. Apprehension turned to dismay when the two gentlemen, evidently mistaking the darts board for a military target, appeared to be about to demonstrate their markmanship. While he tried to keep them engaged in conversation – a difficult feat, since they had no English – his wife slipped out at the back to telephone the police. Sergeant Bullstrode was off duty. W.P.C. Helen Wiggett answered the phone.

"Brandishing wicked looking guns they are," she concluded. "Come quick for God's sake they'll have us all laid out flat as kippers and the place knee-deep in blood."

Armed bandits loose in Shipton Wick! W.P.C. Wiggett knew the drill: buzz headquarters, send out a call to the patrol cars, set in motion the emergency machinery. Instead, she reached for her cap and walkie-talkie set and made for the door. For six months now she'd sat at that desk answering dull or silly calls, pounded the beat with nothing to look at but shops and shoppers, brewed tea, and entered a lot of nonsense in her notebook that no one would read. At least, she hoped they wouldn't. "Pair of bullfinches in the Memorial Garden" and "Barn owl nesting in oak tree back of childrens' playground" testified more to her interest in natural history, the subject of one of her O levels, than to the breadth of her experience in the police.

And now, had her chance come at last? Opportunity knocked? Was her skill, devotion and initiative about to be put to the test? Mounting her bike, she sped towards The Goat & Compasses turning over in her mind the best strategy to pursue. "New Commonwealth", Mrs Sweetapple had said. That gave her a clue. Among her varied studies – and she had been a studious girl – the subject of linguistics, and oriental languages in particular, had captured her interest. There were, it was true, a great many oriental languages and she had a smattering, the merest smattering at that, of only a few. But she could recite several verses from the Koran and, if the bandits were Muslims, these might ring a bell. On the other hand if they were animists, an incantation in use among the river people of the upper Volta, designed to repel crocodiles, might open a dialogue. Anyway it was worth a try.

The bodyguards had postponed their target practice and were drinking beer. W.P.C. Wiggett's first two tries made no impression but a few words in the third brought them to their feet with wide grins of delight. Weapons abandoned, they seized her hands and pumped them vigorously, uttering joyful cries. W.P.C. Wiggett was touched. All she had said was "the fleas of the goat are biting the baby," example number one in the first exercise in *Bantu Semantics,* but it had certainly struck a chord, and she went on to example number two, "the drunken European has killed the cook", which brought her to the end of her vocabulary. Taking advantage of the bodyguards' rapture,

Sweetapple removed the weapons and his wife hid them in an out-house behind some bags of pellets kept for the childrens' rabbits. W.P.C. Wiggett was able to say a few words into her walkie-talkie which resulted in a police car drawing up outside The Goat & Compasses. The bodyguards were coaxed inside and the crisis was over, the situation defused.

W.P.C. Wiggett felt a heel. They'd trusted her, they'd believed they were being taken to rejoin their General, that was why they'd gone not exactly quietly, roisterously in fact, but in the best of humour. They'd been betrayed. Still, all in all, perhaps it was just as well.

If W.P.C. Wiggett had hoped for praise, as indeed she had, she was disappointed. Next morning, Sergeant Bullstrode was grumpy and no mistake. Chit of a girl, you could almost hear him saying to himself, gabbling away in heathen tongues, he'd always known no good would come of all those O levels. He looked at her with disfavour.

"Complaint's come in, mud on road, farmer Stubbins' tractor suspected. Offence under section D, sub-section 29a, Highways Act 1910. Go and investigate."

Throwing him a dirty look, Helen Wiggett left the room and got out her bike. Initiative, resource, courage, coolness and devotion to duty, all went by the board. Unacknowledged, unrewarded. Still, it was a fine morning and the allegedly muddy road ran past Lammas Wood. Badgers there, she'd heard. Mustelidae (*Meles meles*), crepuscular and nocturnal, compulsive burrowers, omnivorous, practise delayed implantation. One evening, she must join the badger watch she'd heard was being organised. Or mustn't she? When you could see it all on TV a thousand times better, why bother to get cold and wet and not see anything, or maybe a dim shape half suggested in the dark?

Chapter Five

"ONE MAN in his time plays many parts." The words, Angus often thought, might have been written for him. To dress for each part, he believed, was expedient. The chairman of the Shipton Wick and District Ecology Group was, in appearance, a different person altogether from the individual who made his way to the seventh floor of the Adonis Hotel in South Kensington, London. The red beard had been trimmed, combed and disciplined. Hairy tweeds and rugged sweaters had given way to a tidy dark grey suit, polished shoes and an elegant tie, and he carried a briefcase and umbrella. Casual observers might have put him down as a director of a substantial company on his way to a board meeting.

On the way to a meeting he indeed was, but of a nature unconnected with the world of commerce. In room 707 was assembled a group of seven individuals who hailed from as many parts of the world. In appearance, hue, background and belief they were as different from each other as rockets from rosebuds, but they shared a common all-embracing aim. This was to overthrow the existing order wherever it might be (except in the empire of the USSR), eliminating in the process as many people, communities or nations as possible who disagreed with their views, and destroying as many capitalist installations such as powerstations, pipelines, airfields, banks, railways and bridges as could be bombed, blown up, cut or set on fire.

Funds were needed to advance these aims and the kidnapping of eminent, or merely rich, personages had a high priority. A gathering of the World Revolutionary Council was in session and Angus had been summoned to attend.

"You're late." The man who so abruptly addressed Angus was short and swarthy with a lot of frizzy hair and onyx-black eyes. He wore a scowl. Angus knew him as Hakkab, an activist in the Alliance representing the Levantine Liberation League.

"Traffic jams. Burst water-mains. Road works. Closed carriage ways."

"You should have taken a train."

"On strike."

Hakkab's scowl deepened. The room, thickly carpeted and furnished with expensive armchairs, was full of tobacco smoke. Pads and pencils lay about on tables. On one corner was a cocktail cabinet. Angus noted with regret that the only bottles in it contained lemonade, lime juice and soda water. Much as he respected his masters, he deplored their habits of austerity in this respect at least. No doubt Hakkab and his friends could seek their stimulus in other directions but he had, alas, no harem to go back to when the day's work was done.

"To business," Hakkab said. "you have the money, you have the means, you've had the time. Action now we demand. Action – when?"

Angus took a seat, frowned slightly at a glass of lemonade handed to him by one of the members and fingered his beard.

"Soon. When everything is ready. Sewn up, every detail right, mishaps ruled out. So far as they ever can be," he added.

"All mishaps must be ruled out. Now, give details of the plan."

"The plan is hatching. The chick is pecking at the shell of the egg. When will it step forth from the shell? At the moment when it becomes fully fledged. That moment. . ."

The truth was, Angus didn't fully trust his colleagues and masters. There were too many of them for one thing. For another, no one colleague trusted another. The plan was his. A fine plan, a bold plan, a plan that would startle, confound and amaze the world. A plan that would alter the balance of nations, go down in history as a *coup* to end *coups*. To reveal the plan in full and in advance to members of the World Revolutionary Council would be to ask for trouble. As a good Scot, Angus did not forget the warning delivered by his national poet about the schemes of mice and men. If all went well, the full scope and beauty of the plan would be revealed and they would have their reward. If, by some trick of fate, it went ill, he would still have kept open his lines of retreat.

"That moment," he continued, "is close at hand. Meanwhile, I need money."

Hakkab's scowl became positively ominous, his black eyes glared. "You have had money. Much money. A house, a helicopter, guns, and some extraordinary expenses, out-of-pocket you call them. Something called a kilt. Now what is it that you want?"

"An island."

Hakkab and his colleagues were momentarily taken aback. "Explain."

"A holding ground. The plan is hatched, we have our victim – or should I call him prize? – and all the forces of the kingdom are after us, army, police, air force, everyone. Where do we conceal him?"

Giuseppe of the Scarlet Brotherhood, who had been following the conversation with some puzzlement, intervened. "We want no island. An apartment, an empty house, a garage, that is all we need. With guns, bombs, explosives, ropes, adhesive tape. Then the phone call, the newspapers, the call-box, the announcement of terms. If there is holding back we send an ear, a finger, a toe." Giuseppe spoke from experience. He had played a prominent part in several successful kidnappings and a few unsuccessful ones, when the victim, or prize, had ended up full of bullet-holes in the boot of a car.

"No physical violence. We must respect the person of the Heir." The speaker was the Reverend Amigale Pyle, a lean, stooping individual with a pince-nez who hailed from Kicking Horse, Alberta, and represented the World Congress of Churches. How he had got on the Alliance council he was not quite sure.

"How does one kidnap someone without using physical violence?" Angus' question remained unanswered. A newcomer to the council intervened.

"What will be our terms for the release?" Dr Daniel Bongola spoke for the Freedom Fighters' Front, whose track record was unsurpassed in the way of blowing up aircraft and hotels, absconding with school children, slaughtering teachers and nuns and wiping out villages. He wore a well-cut dark suit to match his complexion, with an old Harrovian tie.

"For a start," Hakkab replied, "the handing over of the Crown Jewels. Then, the obliteration of Israel and South Africa, the sinking of the U.S. fleet and abolition of its air force, the execution of all judges and financiers and the blowing up of all banks. After that – "

Dr Bongola interrupted. "Do I hear correctly? You wish to blow up all banks?"

"Of course. Entirely. Eliminate all usurers. All banks."

"Including Swiss banks?"

"Especially Swiss banks."

"I cannot give support of the Freedom Fighters' Front to blow up Swiss banks. Our funds are there. In numbered accounts."

"Let us not quarrel amongst ourselves," the Reverend Amigale Pyle implored, "or the Lord will not bless our endeavours. First, we must secure the Crown Jewels."

"And before that, our prize," Angus added. "Within one month. Guaranteed. If all I ask for is provided. Such as the island of Phlogge,.."

"Phlogge?"

"Between Plugge and the Kyle of Ballyhoolish. A nice little island. Secluded. It has its own brand of sheep."

"How much?"

"A quarter of a million pounds."

"That is a lot of money."

"Worth one of the smaller diamonds on one of the minor pendants of the Crown Jewels."

Hakkab grunted, but wrote out the cheque before the meeting dispersed. It had not been a satisfactory meeting so far as he was concerned. No fault could be found with Angus McBean's credentials. A soldier of fortune of proved worth, but he seemed to Hakkab more like a serpent than a soldier. Evasive, secretive. Not to be trusted. But the stakes were high enough to rivet anyone, secretive or not, to the enterprise in hand. Within a month, the Alliance would have pulled off the greatest *coup* of modern times.

Angus had plenty of time to conclude negotiations for the island of Phlogge before setting forth down the motorway towards Shipton Wick. "I'm sure you'll find it a most satisfactory purchase," said the young man in Knight, Frank and Rutley's, concealing his surprise at receiving a cheque for the full price, one hundred thousand pounds, without argument and on the nail. "Excellent fishing of course. A breeding beach for seals I understand. Seabirds everywhere. The sheep have four horns."

"Any inhabitants?"

The young man looked through the folder. "Five. They speak Gaelic. You will find them, I'm sure, cooperative."

"Communications?"

"Ah, yes. A boat runs every fortnight in summer from the mainland to the neighbouring island of Yell. Weather permitting, of course. Phlogge has its own rowboat."

"And when the weather doesn't permit?"

"That's the beauty of these rugged, picturesque islands. You really get away from it all. No telephones, no telex, no stock exchange quotations. Right out of the rat race. Bargains like this don't often come on to the market. My congratulations, sir. You'll be getting the contract in day or two."

Angus left the office humming 'Over the Sea to Skye' under his breath. But the tune was too melancholy to suit his cheerful mood and he changed to an old favourite, 'Blue Skies.'

He had another reason for his cheerful mood. A meeting of the Shipton Wick and District Ecologists Group was to be held that evening at Lammas Cottage with a badger-watching session to follow, and Astrid would be there. He had taken to Astrid. A simple, fresh, outgoing country girl with whom a man engaged in dangerous and momentous enterprises might enjoy a little relaxation on the side. Besides, that young Daryll was an ass. Putting his nose out of joint would improve its shape.

It was dark when he reached Lammas cottage but he soon had the stove lit and potatoes in the oven. Meat-free sausages and baked spuds would be right, he thought, with mulled oak-leaf claret, one of the best; and afterwards thick lentil soup with rye-bread slices and polyunsaturated butterene, with home-brewed beer. His personal bottle of Scotch was handy in the larder behind the bread-bin.

Angus looked with satisfaction round his cottage. Built evidently for people of small stature, if not actually dwarfs, and of a mountaineering race – crampons were not essential to tackle the staircase, but they would be a help – he was able nevertheless to fit himself into it without too much discomfort. He'd got himself installed as tenant just in time. Even a Prince couldn't dislodge a protected tenant.

Astrid and Daryll were the first to arrive. With them came Judy Mustard, minus her riding crop but equipped with camera, binoculars, tape recorder and an infra-red spotlight with batteries.

Speculation about the state of the night sky was interrupted by the arrival of Charlotte Evers with a young man in tow: the vet, Sebastian Knibbleworth, a useful ally, it was hoped, in the battle of the badgers. He was a tall, thin, sandy-haired East Anglian brought up among dykes, ditches, coypus, wild mink and hand-reared pheasants and a variety of pets. Of these, the most beloved was Plutus who, raised from a tadpole, had grown into an amiable and portly toad. A visitor weighing fifteen stone had sat so heavily on Plutus, who was basking on a garden seat, that the local vet had been unable to save his life. There and then, the young Sebastian had decided to become a vet and to devote his life to the cause of animal welfare.

Angus greeted him warmly. ''Welcome to our group. We're delighted to have you on our side against the bureaucratic brutes who want to murder our badgers. Poison gas! It's they who should be gassed in their miserable warrens.''

''And all the members of the hunt torn to bits by wolves and their bones picked clean by vultures,'' Judy Mustard added with relish, accepting a mug of oak-leaf claret.

''Sebastian's making a study of foxes,'' Charlotte informed them. The vet had brought his dart-gun and a supply of the appropriate drugs in case any foxes should be encountered. ''He shoots darts into them and fixes on radio collars. Then they go about bleeping and he knows what they're up to.''

''Unkind, surely, to shoot darts into them,'' Daryll protested, ''If not actually cruel.''

"It's quite painless," said Sebastian. "They recover at once when the antidote's injected."

"And then go about bleeping? How would you like to go bleep bleep day and night wherever you were?"

"Awkward for wives and husbands in the wrong beds," Angus observed. Such facetiousness was not well received. Charlotte wrinkled her nose at the meatless sausages. Breadcrumbs, that was all, with herbs, bound with an egg. Her heart and soul weren't really with the Ecologists but she found Sebastian quite attractive, when he could be kept off foxes. On horses he was definitely sound, and his horizons were wider than those of Shipton Wick. He had travelled.

"Sebastian's work on porcupines has made history," she pronounced. "No one had suspected that porcupines stand on their heads and orchestrate a kind of tune with their quills as part of their mating ceremony until his pioneer work in the Lualangwa Wildlife Park in Zambia."

There was impressed silence as the sausages were munched. It was broken by Astrid, whose interest in porcupines was minimal.

"He's moved in," she announced. "The housekeeper came last week. Hoity-toity, mum says. Orders by phone from Shipton, London even, doesn't go down to the shops. Some of the carpets are down. Chose them himself, they say. Persian rugs in the lounge, cream and gold upstairs."

"Television cameras behind every bush I expect," said Judy. "Lot of waste of money. If I had my way – "

She was interrupted by the arrival of two unexpected badger-watchers: surprisingly, Jo, accompanied by Arthur. He was dressed for the occasion in a deerstalker hat, rough tweeds and waders, but his face, Daryll thought, bore a careworn expression.

"Delighted to welcome you, Jo. It's a braw nicht for our little excursion." Angus rolled his r's with a gusto reinforced by a good dollop of scotch in the oak-leaf claret.

"I'm running away," Jo gruffly stated.

"From the commune?"

"No, from the General."

"His attentions have rather been overwhelming" Arthur explained. "He's an impetuous fellow. First-rate commander, I've no doubt, in a cavalry charge."

The truth was, General Mkubwa had been leading Arthur what might be justly have been described as a dance. First of all there was the matter of his loaded revolver. A suggestion that he might care to be relieved of so cumbrous an object had been received with such disfavour that Arthur had feared for the safety of all within range at Cockscombe Castle. Mention of firearms had reminded the General of his bodyguards. What had become of them? The Hapanan Embassy had no suggestions to make. The General had been heard – and heard throughout the Castle and beyond – ordering his Ambassador to complain forthwith to the Queen, to call a press conference to announce the kidnapping of two honoured Hapanan citizens on an official visit, and to telephone the Hapanan President demanding that he should mobilise the army and break off diplomatic relations with the United Kingdom.

Pale and shaken, Arthur had got on to the Foreign Office, whose spokesman had made light of the affair. The Queen, he had pointed out, was away on a state visit to Iceland, and the telephone line to Hapana was out of order most of the time. "All right, I'd better send someone down to sort it out," he had languidly concluded, and hung up.

Nor had that been the end. The General had refused to sleep without a bodyguard beside his bedroom door and another outside his window. In this dilemma Mr Whackers had proposed that the British bobby, in whom the whole world placed (or had formerly placed) implicit confidence, should step into the breach. Sergeant Bullstrode would, in the course of duty, be available to sleep beside the General's bedroom door and W.P.C. Helen Wiggett, well wrapped up, could occupy a deck-chair beneath his window.

In a sudden change of mood the General had accepted the proposal, smiled expansively, and almost knocked out Lord Gwent with a clap on the back. "And tell that thin maiden, that Jo, that tomorrow she will come with me to see the Lots' Road Power Station," he had said. "I have wanted since a child to see the Lots' Road Power Station. My mother had a picture of it pinned to the wall.''

The problem of the General's armaments remained. A call to Scotland Yard had set in motion a chain of events which led to the arrival of an officer experienced in burglary techniques. The General's snores were reassuring and, when he girded on his belt and holster next morning, he remained unaware of the substitute of dummy bullets for the live variety.

Altogether, Arthur felt, matters had been handled pretty competently, and luck had held. But they were not out of the wood. Suppose the General were to try a little target practice on the garden statuary, or on one of the portraits of bygone Marquesses of Gwent in the hall? Suppose the line to Hapana had been repaired? Arthur listened with anxiety to the eight o'clock news. No mention yet of ruptured diplomatic relations.

Nor was that the only crisis he'd had to cope with. There was the matter of the badgers. A minor matter, but one pregnant with unpleasant possibilities. Under the Prevention of Contagious Bovine Diseases Act of 1970, the Ministry had power to enter, after due notice had been served, the property of those landowners or tenants (and even sub-tenants) believed to harbour badgers, for the purpose of their destruction in a humane and effective way. Such notice had been duly served in the correct fashion on the proprietor of the Cantilevre estate. Moreover, farmer Stubbins had angrily reported that badgers which had strayed on to his land from that of his royal neighbour were threatening the health of his attested accredited tuberculin-free pedigree herd whose matriarch, Cobberley's Bottom Jupiter's Runnymede Peascod IX, had three times won the championship at the Piddletrenthyde and Broughton Poggs annual show. The Lammas Wood badgers were evidently doomed.

But then – the Ecologists. They weren't going to take this lying down. And, the Prince's image. More than once, he'd spoken out in support of conservation, wildlife, the countryside, Britain's heritage. If the Ecologists fought back with no holds barred, they'd be able to represent him as a murderer of badgers, a callous landowner content to allow harmless creatures to be gassed to death in his woods and fields. A word to the press and there'd be an invasion of reporters and photographers, followed by pictures of dead badgers on the front pages of newspapers and on television screens. The Ecologists might carry matters further – sit-ins, lie-downs, demos, hunger strikes and so on. All this wouldn't help the Prince at all, just when he was preparing to get integrated with the life of Shipton Wick. It was Arthur's hope that by meeting the Ecologists informally and sharing their badger-watch he might, as it were, remove their sting – or, anyway, find out what was in the wind.

Visibility, when the Ecologists sallied forth into the night, was poor. Clouds obscured the full moon and a slight drizzle was falling. A gusty wind shook the branches of the trees and caused a faint coughing that reminded Astrid of the breathing of a sick animal hiding in the darkness. Eerie. She was quite glad when Angus, resolutely in the lead, took her hand. "Careful of the ruts," he warned. The ground was squelchy underfoot and slippery with fallen leaves. "Quietly does it," he added.

Lammas Wood clothed a gentle slope running uphill from the cottage, and the badgers had made their home about halfway up. After whispered directions, the party took up a position by a fallen tree-trunk whence, had there been light enough, they would have commanded a good view of the mouth of the sett. As it was, there was nothing to be seen. Something to be felt, though; Angus' hand, that had several times squeezed that of Astrid's was embarking on a more adventurous course. She wriggled, and heard Daryll breathing rather hard on her other side. An owl hooted.

"I think we're wasting our time," Daryll said.

"Quiet, everyone," Angus commanded. Daryll, in a rebellious mood, raised his voice.

"They're probably miles away by now. In farmer Stubbins' fields, passing on germs to his cows."

"Idiot!" hissed Judy Mustard. "It's the cows pass on the germs to the badgers."

"Which is right?" asked Arthur, appealing to Sebastian's veterinary knowledge. Sebastian, with scientific caution, answered: "Perhaps a two-way traffic."

What a lot of noises, Astrid thought, went on at night. Rustles, squeaks, swishes, snaps and just little sounds impossible to put a name to. Insects perhaps? Leaf brushing against leaf? Trees breathing and growing? Then came the faint faraway hum of a car's engine, then the moo of a cow. A twig snapped, or so it sounded. A footfall? Something moving in the wood? Astrid was glad of Angus' hand, now behaving with greater circumspection. Then an eerie screech, repeated several times.

"Dog fox," whispered Sebastian. The next quick, shrill call sounded nearer. "Anyone mind if I have a try?" he asked, dart-gun in hand, "Don't suppose I'll see him but. . ."

"Can't you leave the wretched animal alone?" Judy indignantly demanded.

"It doesn't do them any harm."

"So you say. You'll be saying next it's for their own good."

"Well, so it is. Behavioural studies. . ." Sebastian moved off, clasping his gun, in the direction of the noises.

"I'd like to fix a radio collar on to *him*" said Judy fiercely. Daryll felt obliged to defend the practice.

"Sometimes these studies lead to valuable discoveries. An American scientist found that porpoises must come up to breath every three minutes. Before that, people thought they could stay under for three-and-a-half."

Angus' patience was exhausted. They'd better get back to the baked spuds and home-brewed beer if they had as little self-discipline as this, chattering like a flock of rooks.

"I think we – " His words were cut short by a crash in the bushes near at hand, a startled cry and then a furious bellow, followed by Sebastian's horrified voice.

"I say, I'm awfully sorry, I didn't mean. . ."

Angus leapt forward and shone his torch in the direction of the commotion. The beam revealed a raincoated figure in the act of plucking a dart from his trouser leg. Sebastian materialised out of the darkness.

"I saw something moving. I'm terribly sorry – I'm sure you'll be all right. . ."

"Who do you think you are, shooting arrows or whatever they are at people in a private wood?"

"If you start feeling dizzy, I've got the antidote."

"Antidote be damned. What are you doing here?"

"Looking for badgers." Plucking up courage, Sebastian added: "What are *you* doing, come to that?"

The brim of the man's hat was pulled low over his face, but as he stood up Arthur's exclamation indicated recognition. "Good lord, old man, fancy running into you." Arthur's remark sounded as lame as his feelings. A torchlight beam sprung through the darkness into his face.

"I might say the same, Captain."

"Mr Whackers," Arthur said, adding in his best party-going tone: "Allow me to introduce you to the Shipton Wick Ecology Group."

"Pleased to meet you, I'm sure. And now you'd better bugger off before I have you all arrested for trespass, lurking with intent, conspiracy, malicious possession of lethal weapons and attempted murder." Under his breath he added several other accusations relating to unnatural practices with badgers.

It was a crestfallen little party that returned to Lammas Cottage, rye-bread sandwiches and home-brewed beer.

"Tell you what," Angus said, fortified by a quick swill at the whisky behind the bread-bin, "what we all need in a good hot mug of coffee."

"Made with acorns?" Judy dubiously enquired.

"No, no, the real stuff this time. Maxwell House."

"Who *is* this Mr Whackers?" Sebastian asked. Clearly the question fell to Arthur to answer. Ambiguity seemed advisable.

"I'm not absolutely sure."

Perversely, the moon had emerged from behind the clouds when the dampened party dispersed – an extra large moon, Angus noted, and tinged with orange. The hunters' moon, countryfolk called it. Well, the hunt would soon be up. The lights had gone out at Cantilevre Manor.

Judy Mustard was assembling her equipment preparatory to mounting her moped. "Where the hell is my zoom lens?"

"Be a good chap and fetch it for her," Angus said to Daryll. "On the table under the picture of The Farewell of the MacBean of MacBean on the Eve of Culloden."

Daryll reluctantly re-entered the cottage, catching an un-expected whiff of something meaty emanating from the stove. The hairy humbug, he thought. Angus was a swift mover. Astrid found her face enveloped in a bristly beard. Stifling, but something else as well – electrifying, intoxicating. It was almost with relief that she heard Daryll returning and announcing morosely: "I can't see any zoom lens." Angus had released her, but she was still tingling all over.

"Must have left it in the carrier," Judy said. "Well, goodnight all. No badgers this time but we're not defeated. On with our strategy for the Opening Meet!"

Angus waved them off, returned to the whisky bottle and savoured the smell of the beef stew simmering in the oven. In a rich bone stock done with carrots, onions, a stick of celery, paprika and a little red wine.

There was a gentle tap on the door, followed by several more taps. Angus ran a hand over his beard, put down his glass and raised the latch of the door. Reggie Whackers walked in.

Chapter Six

No one would have expected the launching of the world's first microchip toothbrush to be a simple matter. It was a challenge, and one that Peter was braced to meet.

The first hurdle had been to find the right name. He'd set his heart on bringing in the word Prince but by itself it wouldn't do. Too stark; besides, too many dogs and horses were called Prince. After trying and discarding many variations on the theme, he hit on the right answer in a flash, while cleaning his teeth. The White Prince. Simple, effective, punchy. Historical undertones, right associations, the royal connection all in one. Losing no time, he commissioned a top-ranking firm of designers to handle the packaging. Each White Prince would come reclining in a hygienic case stamped in gold with the name and the Prince of Wales' feathers, the words Buggins' Brushes in more discreet lettering underneath. When Cantilevre's new owner moved in, a specimen would be there to welcome him in every bathroom. Surely the Royal Warrant must follow after that.

Best of all, the Prince had agreed to launch the New Technology at Buggins' Brushes. The royal finger would press the button that would start the new product rolling off the line. This was to be his first public appearance in his new home town.

No sooner had one problem been dealt with than others reared their spikey heads. Hitherto, relations between management and workforce had been excellent, but the New Technology, it had to be admitted, had introduced a discordant note.

When all the silicon chips and computers had been brought into action, the whole factory could be run by two girls, one at a pinch, with possibly a third to make the tea, although this would be better done by a vending machine. That would reduce the work force to at most half a dozen, taking a generous view and keeping on old Uzell, who wandered round with a broom gathering debris into little heaps, until his retirement. That would cause some sixty-seven ladies from Shipton Wick and surrounding villages to become redundant.

Despite all that was said and written about the delights of leisure, opportunities to pursue hobbies, useful part-time work that could be performed at home, and the desirability of mothers spending more time with their children, the workforce had not displayed a favourable reaction. Not favourable at all. They had, of course, their union – seven unions in fact. One of these had five branch members and the other only two, one of whom was a Jehovah's Witness and regarded all unions as profane. So in practice, so far as management was concerned, it boiled down to relations with the Amalgamated Union of Workers in Applied Hygienic Equipment, and the Associated Workers in Industrial Progression and Chemical Tectonics. The factory's branch of the former mustered twenty-three members, of the latter, nineteen.

The convenor of AWAHE (known as Away), Mrs Sandboy from Poggleton, the wife of a member of the Council's Refuse Disposal Unit, it was true, proved stubborn, it might even have been thought cantankerous, over the installation of automatic towel-drying equipment in the ladies' rest-room. Her eldest son worked as assistant manager of the Poggleton, Shipton Wick and Little Chorlton Steam Laundry, who had the contract for Buggins' towels, and some pressure from that quarter was suspected. The temperament of AWIPCT's convenor, Mrs Sproggs' niece Elaine, was more inclined to concord than to contest. An enthusiastic member of the ballroom dancing group run by Mr Dangle, the Works Manager, she and her boyfriend Justin had attained their Bronze, were working towards their Silver and even indulged in daydreams of a Gold. Elaine was a conscientious convenor, but hitherto had felt that conscientiousness should not be allowed to cross over into the territory of officiousness.

So, by and large, things had gone along pretty smoothly at Buggins' Brushes. But now, The White Prince – behind that happy name, what seeds of disharmony might be about to germinate? Peter hoped that all could be managed in a friendly spirit, but could not deny that misgivings, like those nasty little root-worms that had devastated Donkin's young cauliflowers, were niggling away in his mind.

The die, however, had been cast. Painters had been busy in the workshop, bunting ordered, the date fixed, the invitation list drawn up – several invitation lists in fact, one after the other. This was Sybil's province. If everyone on her first list had accepted, Peter pointed out, the guests, packed shoulder to shoulder, would have stretched from Shipton Wick to Bristol and back again. Even after the first whittling, they would probably have got as far as Bath. The Lord Lieutenant would be there, the High Sheriff, the chairman of the County Council with a posse of senior officials, the Minister of State from the Department of Industry and his entourage, the Mayor and Town Council of Shipton Wick, and goodness knows who else besides.

While Sybil was coping with her usual *applomb*, a measure of disorganisation had crept into her writing room. Peter left her for the factory surrounded by scraps of paper, her desk littered with invitation cards, the telephone enjoying no rest and Heloise and Abelard in possession of the two principal easy chairs. At lunch time, a transformation greeted his return. The bits of paper were in tidy piles. The invitation cards, alphabetically arranged, were in their envelopes and Heloise and Abelard, looking resentful, were curled up together in their flopsy bed. Sybil looked a shade resentful too. Charlotte and her portable electric typewriter had been installed.

"Poor Sybil, a bit much for her to cope with all this single-handed." Charlotte smiled at him in a conspiratorial way. Clad in a polo-necked sweater and a neatly creased pair of navy trousers, her dark hair stylishly brushed, she put him in mind of the calm in the eye of the storm. "Sebastian's put a splint on Coca-cola, the next catering job isn't till Saturday, so luckily I've nothing urgent for a few days and can lend a hand."

"Very kind. Where's Jo?"

Sybil looked displeased. "Gone back to her commune, I'm sorry to say."

"Perhaps it's just as well. The General. . ."

"There are worse things than the General. More dangerous, anyway."

"You mean. . .?"

"We think, we fear, a bottle of deadly poison. Donkin reports that a bottle of his most potent pest-destroyer is missing from the garden shed.

"In God's name, why should Jo want a pest-destroyer?"

"She's been acting strangely lately. When Miss Cheer went in to wake her up this morning she was muttering in her sleep extra-ordinarily *sinister* things about someone, or something, that sounded like Queen Anne."

"Well, Jo can't do *her* any harm."

"There was a lot more muttering about poison, rats, sewers and that sort of thing, or that's what it sounded like Miss Cheer said. I hope she was wrong."

"I think we ought to warn the Munshi."

"I shouldn't worry, Peter," Charlotte said. "Jo's well able to look after herself. Now, about the opening ceremony. The Prince arrives sharp at eleven-thirty. Here's a draft of the time-table." She proffered a sheet of typing. "And here's the draft invitation lists, one for guests, the other for the media. National coverage of course, press and television. Foreign networks too. The Germans, French and Americans are sure to be interested, and I think the Japanese too."

Peter was taken back. Hitherto his ideas hadn't risen much above the *Star and Echo*, the *Wilts and Gloucestershire Standard*, possibly the *Bath Chronicle* and *Western Daily Press*, and slots in Points West and Report West. He felt rather as if a fondly nurtured pot-plant was burgeoning before his eyes into a great big forest tree.

"Copies to Arthur of course and Reggie Whackers," Charlotte added, "they'll be vetted for Security and then the cards can go out."

I wonder, Peter thought, whether Charlotte would consider a job as company secretary? Once The White Prince had got into its stride, he'd need someone to reorganise the office on more modern lines. Sybil, he feared, would not approve. "Got her eye on Arthur Longshott," Sybil had said. "Worming her way in." Charlotte seemed to have wormed her way into Hartley's all right, and anyone who could worm a way past Sybil deserved respect.

Leaving Charlotte and Sybil to complete the invitation lists, Peter returned to the factory to find the Works Manager looking harassed.

"What's the trouble?"

"Nicoletta. She's asked for her cards."

Nicoletta was the girl who had been selected, after much consideration, to operate the computer that would control The White Prince. She'd been sent away for training, come through with flying colours and had seemed all set to play her key role in the operation.

Peter was dismayed. "She can't do that. We've had her trained. Why?"

"Usual trouble. Got to get married."

"Good heavens, there's no hurry these days is there? Most vicars take them up to six months pregnant I believe, and sometimes the earlier children act as bridesmaids."

"It's not that. Income tax. Rebates if they marry before the end of the month and a better bracket."

Peter swore. "Today's the twenty-first."

"Yes. End of next week. And the big day's the week after."

"I'd like to boil her in oil. How soon can we train a successor?"

"It isn't difficult." Demetrious Dangle was a shortish, stubby man with wide shoulders, brawny arms and a small black moustache. Ballroom dancing would have sprung to few minds as his *métier*, but once on the floor, clad in a tight-fitting black suit with a white silk jabot, he was a different man. A model of Terpsichore, Muse of the Dance, in imitation bronze, won in partnership with his wife at an International Terpsichorean Festival in Boulogne, was the most valued treasure of the Dangle family.

"A crash course," Peter said. "Anyone in mind?"

Demetrious looked more glum than ever. "It's turned political. Unions. Mrs Sandboy wants the job for one of her AWAY members, and Elaine of AWIP has asked for it herself. Awkward situation."

"Why not give it to the union with two members?"

"Mandy's got arthritic fingers and Jayne's due for retirement in a month's time."

"Awkward, as you say." Really, Peter thought, I've had enough for one day. The invitation lists, Charlotte's bright ideas, Jo's extraordinary behaviour. "I'm sure you'll come up with the right answer, Dem. You always do."

He drove back to Hartley's worrying about Jo. A pest-destroyer. Why? To destroy a pest, presumably. Who? Could it be the Munshi? No, she thought the world of him. Was she even at the commune? Arthur, he recalled, had bullied her into promising to take the General to the Lot's Road Power Station, God knew why. Perhaps she was there. Perhaps the pest-destroyer was intended for the General, unlikely as it seemed. A weapon to repel his advances, should he be planning to carry her off to fatten her on sweet potatoes and monkeys and add her to his harem? More like Jo to welcome the prospect. He shook his head. His thoughts were getting out of control.

A call to Arthur established the fact that Jo hadn't accompanied the General on his sentimental journey. Lady Pandora had gone instead. Arthur, like Mr Dangle, sounded harassed, as indeed he had every cause to be. First of all there was the matter of the missing bodyguards. Their General had not forgotten them. The scowl on his face when he enquired, once more, as to their whereabouts reminded Arthur of an awesome indigo and purple bank of storm-clouds he had once seen breaking with thunderous menace over a peak in the Himalayas. Tact, he told himself, not naked cowardice, impelled him to keep the full truth hidden. The fact was that the bodyguards, Arthur trusted and believed, were by now safely back in their native land. A police car had taken them from The Goat and Compasses to Heathrow with instructions to the officer in charge to put them on the first plane bound in the direction of Mogadah, Hapana's capital.

"They've been recalled," he said. "Your president urgently requires their services. He sent a message through your Embassy. He hopes you'll do him a favour of releasing them. He'll send replacements soon."

"Replacements," the General said thoughtfully. His brow

had cleared as quickly as it had clouded over. You never could tell with the General. "Yes, replacements. I find my own replacements. The maiden with the little hat who sits outside my window. The hat is speckled like a guinea-fowl. She is thin like all your maidens. Her bosoms are small like sodom apples, but they may improve. She will do."

"Ah, yes, W.P.C. Wiggett. She belongs to our police force. I'm not sure. . ."

"I said, she will do." Storm-clouds began to reappear. "But she has no gun. You will get her a gun. Two guns, I think. She will come with me to the Lots' Road Power Station."

"Well . . . I'll see what I can do about getting W.P.C. Wiggett seconded for special duties."

W.P.C. Helen Wiggett had not been overjoyed. Nights were beginning to turn chilly, she had had enough of sleeping in a deck chair planted in a bed of withering asters. Her aunt Mildred, with whom she lodged, was on to her continually about damp and bronchitis, pneumonia, arthritis, piles and other ailments which would be visited upon her sure as God made little apples, and quite right too. It was no part of Helen's duties, aunt Mildred repeatedly said, to sleep like a Christian slave on the doormat of a heathen satrap, and it wouldn't end there, mark her words.

But Helen Wiggett was a conscientious girl and ever mindful of her Oath of Loyalty, which obliged her without fear or favour to render unto Our Sovereign Lady the Queen such homage, fealty and obedience as may be due to her, and without hesitation, demur, miscreance or laches to carry out such duties, missions, functions and exertions as may be entrusted or assigned to her by Her Majesty's lawful deputy, surrogate, minister, chamberlain, steward or seneschal, without demur, lentor, trepidation, irresolution, impropriety, truancy or dereliction, but with obedience, despatch, integrity and impartiality as befits a lawfully appointed guardian of the peace and loyal servant of Our Sovereign Lady the Queen. Besides, as she had remarked to her aunt Mildred, the General wasn't such a bad old sod underneath all that brass, though he did snore a treat. Probably a heart if not of gold, at least of bronze, was beating away beneath all those medals. He'd brought her a king-size ice cream sundae, saying that she looked underfed.

"Special duties," Sergeant Bullstrode said. "And what might they be, I'd like to know?"

"At the moment, inspection of the Lot's Road Power Station. Escort duties. Probably armed."

The Sergeant was disgusted. He was also perturbed. The subject of guns was a tender one. What with all the goings-on, the Security and Mr Whackers and footpaths and the checking up on foreigners and the question of a demo about badgers, the matter of the automatic weapons that Mrs Sweetapple had hidden in a shed behind The Goat and Compasses had momentarily slipped his mind. When he'd gone round to see about it, he'd received disturbing news.

"Colin Rumble's been round asking about them guns." Mrs Sweetapple told him. "Seemed to think they was important. Took photographs and all. First the guns, then the bin where they were hidden, even took the childrens' rabbits though what they've got to do with it I don't know."

"Those guns were forfeit, Mrs Sweetapple. Unlicensed. Illegal. Impounded. You had no right to show them to Mr Rumble or anyone else."

Shutting the stable door, he knew, when the horse was off and away, probably as far as Fleet Street by now. Colin Rumble was the *Star and Echo's* ace reporter (one of two). A decent enough chap, often rang the station to get a story; press and Constabulary worked well together. But Colin Rumble was a stringer for several of the London dailies that had no more scruples than a ferret loose in a pen of chicks.

Well, what of it? A couple of sub-machine-guns, if that was what they were, stowed out of harm's way behind a pub till they were impounded. They hadn't been fired at anyone, threatened anyone, been planted by the IRA. No interest to anyone, the Sergeant told himself. Colin Rumble had been wasting his time.

"Got a nice litter of Belgian hares," Mrs Sweetapple told him. "Like a couple for the kids?" The Sergeant declined, and took away the guns. Wicked looking things. Shipton had been a nice quiet place till all this bother came along. Loyal as he was to the Crown, no one loyaler, royalty like everyone else should keep to its proper place, and the proper place for Princes was in palaces, not turning upside down a nice quiet country town.

That troubles never come singly is a well-worn adage of whose truth Sergeant Bullstrode had long been aware. A second or a third trouble was to be expected, but that a whole avalanche should descend upon the heads of those attempting to preserve the peace in Shipton Wick was carrying things too far.

The first hint of trouble came on the eight o'clock news. "An aircraft of Casablanca Airways carrying 128 passengers has been highjacked over the Atlantic," said the melodious, unruffled voice of Pauline Bushnell. "The highjackers are believed to belong to an extremist North African group whose aims haven't yet been made clear, but probably include the release of about two thousand political prisoners held in Benghazi. The aircraft was on a flight for Heathrow to Bogatá but it is not yet known to which destination the highjackers are demanding to be flown. Here is our North African correspondent. . ."

Arthur, who had just finished shaving, turned the radio down but not off, hoping to catch later news of prospects for the game between Sheffield Wednesday and Manchester United. It was a nice morning, just a touch of frost in the air, and he looked forward to an untroubled day. The Prince was in the North, opening an X-ray and therapy unit at the Muggleton and District War Memorial Hospital and visiting the Hogsbottom Gujerat Society's social centre. Reggie Whacker had approved the invitation list for the Buggins' Brushes visit with one or two exceptions, and the cards would be going out today. A good job, he reflected, that Charlotte had taken on the arrangements. Sybil, left to herself, would probably have invited all the remaining crowned heads of Europe together with the Emperor of Japan. A sensible girl was Charlotte, head screwed on the right way. Possibly no raving beauty, but not so bad to look at either and neatly turned out. Quite a lot going for Charlotte. Arthur reflected. A good cook, too.

Meanwhile, there was breakfast. The turn of poached egg today. In the matter of breakfast, Arthur kept to a strict routine:

eggs – boiled, fried, poached, scrambled, in that order; then a break with sausages and bacon then off once more with boiled. Now and again, to avoid getting into a rut, he just had cereal. Turning up the radio, he carried it to the kitchenette, took the poacher off the saucepan rack, greased one of the cups and selected an egg. Good, fresh, old-fashioned eggs, bought off Mrs Collins, the cowman's wife at Cantilevre.

The news was ending with the latest on the highjacked plane. Two men, said Ms Bushnell, were involved, but their demands were still obscure. There was a language problem. The passengers were so far unhurt, the pilot had turned back and was coming down to re-fuel in the Azores. It was thought that the highjackers were demanding a plane to fly them to a destination which so far the pilot had been unable to identify. Which of a number of revolutionary groups they belonged to had yet to be ascertained.

As Arthur broke the egg, a thought struck him. 'Struck' seemed indeed to be the right word. The thought had the force of a blow. Hitherto the phrase 'his blood ran cold' had been merely a phrase. Now it seemed like a reality. He almost shivered. Police officers were not necessarily well versed in African geography, especially as the names of countries, not to mention capitals, quite often changed. Bogatá. Mogudah. . .

Arthur's egg had lost its savour, but by the time he had consumed his toast with Mrs Sproggs' home-made marmalade and drunk his coffee, his spirits had revived. That sudden thought was, of course, quite absurd. You couldn't highjack a plane without weapons. He remembered reading of highjackers with toy pistols, but in this case toy pistols were just as much out of the question as real ones. On with the days work. A decision was needed about the wallpaper for the housekeeper's room at Cantilevre. Should he worry the Prince about that? High time he got married. I might consult Charlotte. Arthur thought. Nothing wrong with her taste. The pupils at the infants' school wanted to present a bouquet of paper flowers cut from catalogues at the ceremony at Buggins'. Where should they be positioned when the Prince arrived? The plumber's bill – three times as large as the estimate. The telephone rang.

The assistant personal private secretary was on the line.

"For God's sake, Arthur, what's going on?"

Arthur glanced out of the window. The baker's van was coming up the drive.

"Nothing's going on here, old man. Quite a nice morning. But the plumber's bill. . ."

"What are you babbling about? Haven't you seen the papers?"

"Papers?"

"Newspapers, Arthur. Things with headlines a foot high. And photographs."

"Photographs," Arthur felt limp and cold all over, as if someone had plucked him out of a slimy, chilly swamp and wrung him dry. "Highjackers?"

"Pull yourself together, Arthur." There was a slight pause and a rustling of paper. Martin's voice came through deliberately and clearly. " 'Arms Cache Found Near Prince's Home'. 'Terrorist Hideout in Prince's Hometown'. 'Police Bungle Royal Security'. 'Deadly Weapons Find Threatens Prince'. And so on."

"Oh my God," said Arthur. "The Goat and Compasses. I thought Sergeant Bullstrode had collected those guns."

"Sergeant Bullstrode has. But too late. The media are on their way to you now."

The guns. The bodyguards. The General. Flight 368 to Bogatá. Everything was rushing headlong like an avalanche, out of control. "Get on to the General's Embassy. They must claim the guns. They'd better claim the bodyguards too, come to that. I think they've highjacked a plane."

"How can they have highjacked a plane?

"God knows how. But apparently they have. It's on its way to the Azores. Better get on to the Portuguese Embassy too."

The media were on their way. Only his military training and a long family tradition of service to the Crown held Arthur back from leaping into his car and heading for some distant race-meeting where the waters of forgetfulness could close over his head.

The day had started quietly at The Goat and Compasses, with

Sweetapple taking the labradors for a walk before opening time and Mrs Sweetapple feeding the hens and rabbits after getting the children off to school. It did not stay quiet for long. First, half a dozen cars disgorged reporters from the dailies. Then came a commanding blonde from a German magazine, closely followed by the BBC and ITN. Hot on their heels came a French television crew, jostled by representatives of American and Japanese networks and journals. In no time the bar of The Goat and Compasses was festooned with cables, cameras were peering from the ceiling, others poking through windows and some positioned on the roof.

"Dunno who they was," Jack Sweetapple was saying for the umpteenth time. "Battledress they was wearing, soldiers, I suppose."

"Irish accents?"

"Arabs?"

"Italians? Germans? Red Brigades?"

"Foreigners," said Jack Sweetapple firmly. "Didn't speak no English."

"Don't you go thinking we allows in customers with guns," Mrs Sweetapple asserted. "Dogs and guns strictly forbidden. They just walked in, couldn't stop 'em."

"How did you feel when you saw these armed men walk in?"

"Well, I don't know. They seemed friendly."

"They held you up at gun-point? Seized everyone as hostages? Bound you hand and foot?"

"Jabbered away, like. Not a word of sense in it. If it hadn't been for that policewoman, that Helen Wiggett, they'd of been here till closing time."

Representatives of the media, who had begun to suspect the story to be lacking in punch, perked up again, and the identity of W.P.C. Wiggett was soon established. Notebooks were snapped to, cameras de-positioned, cables ravelled, and the hunt for W.P.C. Wiggett was on. Heroic policemen were nothing new but heroic policewomen comparatively rare, especially one whose heroism had thwarted a terrorist attack on the person of the Heir.

W.P.C. Wiggett proved elusive. Sergeant Bullstrode disclaimed all knowledge of her whereabouts, it was out of his hands, but from his tone it was clear that he thought she was up to no good. Aunt Mildred's semi was bolted and barred, its occupant having gone out to visit relatives in Poggleton after feeding her budgies. Application to the Chief Constable's office produced a statement that she had been seconded for special duties, but what these duties were was unclear. The spokesman for the Chief Constable, who had never heard of W.P.C. Wiggett, managed to evoke a sense of mystery that, like the cries emitted by a huntsman to egg on his hounds, set the media with renewed vigour on their search for a trail. They fanned out in various directions, ears pricked and noses to the ground.

It was not long before one particularly sensitive nose picked up the scent, it would be hard to say just how, and the words Lots' Road Power Station, in an equally mysterious fashion, spread like a subtle odour among the seekers after truth. One by one, cars took off and headed for the motorway until there remained only a pair from *Paris Match* who, reckoning W.P.C. Wiggett to be something of a red herring, had decided to cast their nets wider in the hope of a more interesting haul. What ladies had been perceived to have paid recent visits to Cantilevre Manor? What advice was being sought, and from whom, on such matters as the choice of carpets and curtains? Who were the cleaners, plumbers, electricians, suppliers of light fittings, of wine, of linen, who had access to the Manor? Was there a nursery wing? Were the builders installing bidets, a necessity which, they had found to their dismay, most bathrooms of the barbarous English were without? There were more promising leads to be followed than that of a policewoman who had, for some obscure reason, disappeared in the direction of an obsolescent power station.

Chapter Seven

As THE object of an excursion, Lady Pandora had never given high marks to a power station in Fulham. Her first problem had been to get the General into the front seat of her open sports-car. The car was small and the General large, and not in the best of tempers. Still clad in his striking blue uniform he had, with difficulty, been persuaded temporarily to lay aside both his medals and his guns, on the grounds that the workers at the power station would come out on strike.

"I see no guns," he barked at W.P.C. Wiggett. "I ordered guns. You are my bodyguard. Bodyguards have guns."

"All guns strictly forbidden in power stations, sir." Helen Wigget was always deferential, but felt that she was beginning to get the General's measure.

"This push-cart, this market barrow, this worthless buggy – we go in this? This little wagon fit for poor mans' children?" If looks could kill, his would have killed Lady Pandora's vehicle. "Why is there no Mercedes? In my country I have four Mercedes. First goes one with servants, then General Mkubwa and his aides, then bodyguards and last come wives. And no roof – why is there no roof? No bullet-proof windows?"

Still grumbling, the General squeezed himself into the front seat, Helen Wiggett having clambered in behind. Lady Pandora was as slender as the General was large. Her tangle-toss hairdo had given way to a medieval pageboy style, simpler for Astrid to accomplish but not, in Astrid's opinion, so becoming. There was nothing to suggest the medieval in her patched levis and scarlet T-shirt inscribed over the bosom with the message, in six-inch letters, "Dracula Lives!" Not that the bosom beneath the inscription was seriously in evidence. "No melons," the General grunted as he settled himself in. "Not small melons even, Berries. That is all."

The day was fine, the sky blue, the fields a rich sepia-brown where stubble had been ploughed or vivid green where black-and-white cows or red steers with white faces grazed upon them. Tractors were busy, trees leafy, hedges here and there beginning to show autumn tints. A peaceful scene, but peace did not reign in the hearts of Lady Pandora's passengers. It was not long before W.P.C. Wigget observed that, far from heading towards Fulham, they were going in the opposite direction. Should she call the driver's attention to this? As custodian of the General's safety, undoubtedly she should, but with Lady Pandora at the wheel, and the speedometer needle approaching eighty on a B road, might such action not diminish rather than enchance the General's safety?

While she was pondering this, the General flung himself back in his seat and uttered a bellow which might well have split Helen Wiggett's ear-drums had not her hands, clutching her speckled-banded hat to keep in position, covered her ears. Peering over the General's shoulder, a movement in the glove compartment caught her eye. Amid a medley of tattered maps and dirty dusters she discerned, there was no mistaking it, a pair of small but bright and and piercing eyes.

The General's admirable command of the English language deserted him, but Helen had no difficulty in getting the message as delivered in his own tongue. The General wished the driver to stop in order that he might disembark. Lady Pandora slowed down a little, but more as a concession to a sharp bend in the road immediately ahead than to her passenger's request. The dusters in the glove compartment heaved and maps rustled. A pair of small pricked ears could be discerned, and a brown furry body.

"Mustard," Lady Pandora shouted as they rounded the bend. "Or possibly Cress."

Clearly the moment had come for W.P.C. Wiggett to intervene.

"Lady Pandora," she shouted, "kindly stop. The General – "

The furry creature leapt on to the General's lap. A second furry creature followed. So blood-curdling was the General's scream that several sheep resting in a field beside the road leapt to their feet and made off, flicking their tails.

"Mustard *and* Cress," said Lady Pandora.

A volcano in eruption, a major earthquake, a boiler blowing its top, all these are metaphors that might convey an idea of the upheaval in the passenger seat of Lady Pandora's car. The General heaved and roared, kicked and bellowed, writhed and yelled. Clearly it would be better now if the car *didn't* stop. Once the General had leapt out of it, as he undoubtedly would, nothing on earth would get him back in.

"Poor little things," Lady Pandora shouted. "You shouldn't frighten them. You *have* frightened them. And Cress is pregnant, I've reason to believe."

Mustard and Cress had taken refuge under the seat, but not before Helen Wiggett had caught a glimpse of them sufficiently clearly to enable her to identify their genus, if not their species. Rats, undoubtedly, but Black (*Rattus rattus*) or Brown (*Rattus norvegicus*)? The former, she recalled, had brought the Plague to Europe; the latter lived in sewers, ate corpses, spread typhus and bred so prolifically that the world held more of them, it had been said, even than of people. Clearly the General had reason for his dismay. He had been reduced to a state he could rarely have experienced, that of speechlessness. Lady Pandora took advantage of this silence to remark:

"They're timid little creatures, wouldn't hurt a fly. And so faithful. They sleep in my bed. I wouldn't say they're entirely house-trained yet, but they're learning. I'm taking them to see Mustard's parents. Cress's, I'm afraid, are dead. Sad they didn't live to see their grandchildren."

Helen Wiggett felt that the time had come to assert her authority.

"Lady Pandora, my instructions are to see the General safely to Fulham and back. Not to a rat farm. We are going in the opposite direction. I must order you to turn and go back."

"Here we are."

A twice life-sized wooden model of a pair of giraffes flanked the entrance to Little Goosey Safari Park. Glimpses of llamas, alpacas, barasinghas, guanacos, capybaras, manatees, nilgai, wombats and other creatures grazing, resting, burrowing or swimming (as the case might be) in their enclosures could be obtained as the visitors' vehicles wound their way to the car-park and centre of the complex, where they could replenish their supplies of teacloths, notelets, place-mats, mugs and paper napkins (all adorned with portraits of various beasts) and commemorate the occasion by purchasing little models of everything from crocodiles to Bambi fawns.

As Lady Pandora's car approached the park the reappearance of Mustard, or possibly Cress, who perched on his, or her, owner's shoulder, did nothing to improve the General's temper. His agility on extricating himself from the vehicle was considerably greater than it had been when getting in.

"Those are unclean," he protested, glowering at their owner. "Unclean, dirty, bad. Evil spirits get into them. They bring bad fortune. They are accursed. You put me with them in this poor man's wagon that flies like a hawk. For this you will suffer. You will be barren, or give birth to monsters. For this you will have boils all over, your feet will rot, your fingers swell and your bosoms wither. Already they are withered," he added ominously.

"Well, before the rest of it catches up with me we'd better find Torkel," Lady Pandora replied. Cress, or possibly Mustard, had emerged from beneath the seat and was perched upon it, preening his whiskers. Although he looked sleek, even quite appealing, Helen was firmly on the General's side. The germs of typhus and bubonic plague might indeed be described as devils who got into rats, and she felt it only too likely that they would bring misfortune.

Had she, she wondered fleetingly, the power to arrest them? On the face of it this appeared unlikely; she doubted whether she could even detain them to help the police with their enquiries. On the other hand, it seemed more than likely that they would cause a breach of the peace, in which case her powers would certainly stretch to arresting, or should it be impounding, Mustard and Cress. But if they, supported by their owner, were to resist arrest, or impounding, she had no way to summon reinforcements and the attempt might be a spark to set the General alight. On balance, it seemed best to let things ride, attempt to defuse the situation and hope to find a telephone and transmit a call for help.

Helen was right. As they proceeded through the park in quest of Torkel, whoever he might be, Mustard and Cress stowed away in the pockets of Lady Pandora's levis, the General gazed with increasing interest at the various animals, some of them doubtless familiar to him, that could be seen in or under the spreading trees.

"These animals," he enquired, "these you eat? Are they for the Prince's table?"

"No, no," Helen replied. "We don't eat them."

"Then why are they here?"

"Well, sir, people like to look at them."

"Why do they do that?"

Helen felt at a loss. Why, indeed? Groping in her memory, she recalled an essay on 'The Principles of Conservation and Preservation of Natural Resources: Only One Earth.' Its arguments were a bit hazy now, but she volunteered:

"Some of them are rare and endangered. In the wild, they may die out."

"The wild – where is that?"

"Where they come from, I suppose. Africa and places like that." A tactless remark, she immediately realised. "And Scotland", she added.

"In my country, we eat these animals, but if we do not like to eat them we die them out."

"How unkind," said Lady Pandora. They had reached a cage containing a pair of owls sitting side by side on a bough amid a few tired and withered leaves, motionless as rocks, their disc-like unfocused eyes staring into space. Lady Pandora held a hand against the cage with Mustard, or Cress, perched on her wrist. "Blink, stupids," she commanded. The owls paid no attention. "Overfed," she added. The General averted his eyes.

Fearing another explosion, Helen directed his attention to a happier sight, that provided by the adventure playground. Children of all ages, shapes and sizes were clambering up ladders, swinging on ropes, crawling through hollow logs, slithering down slides, running round the ramparts of mock-castles, digging in sandpits and using up surplus energy in other ways. Sounds of piping voices, shrill laughter and excited shouts filled the air. The General's broad face crinkled into a beaming smile. "Totos," he said. "This is a place for totos to play. That is good. Better than animals. But – " the grin faded and gave way to a scowl. "It is not the Lots' Road Power Station."

"Quite so, sir," Helen soothingly agreed. "I'm sure Lady Pandora will take us there next."

"Those unclean beasts – "

"If they weren't so exceptionally good-natured," Lady Pandora retorted, "they'd take offence at that remark. Now we will find Mustard's parents."

Perceiving a chink in the ominously lowering clouds, Helen quickly intervened. "Lady Pandora, I'm sure the General must be tired after the journey and might be spared an introduction to Mustard's parents. I suggest we rest on that bench over there while you go in search of your rats. You can pick us up when you've completed your business." A plan was forming in her mind. The General obviously enjoyed the children's company as much as he disliked that of the rats. Perhaps, with Lady Pandora out of the way, it would be safe to leave him in the playground while she made a dash for the nearest telephone.

"Mustard's father is a real character. Half his tail is missing from a fight with a baboon. Full of pluck. Mustard's mother's quieter, more the maternal type. They were the best of companions – I had them in my flat. Now Torkel's looking after them. They're much more affectionate than children. Well, have it your own way. Back soon."

The General watched her back-view with a sullen look and wrinkled brow. "No buttocks" he commented as she vanished into the crowd. Meanwhile, there was the maiden with the guinea-fowl hat. A useless bodyguard, but bosoms that at least showed a little promise. Larger than berries. Baby gourds perhaps.

A football landed at his feet and he returned it with a vigour that sent it soaring over the trees into a pen containing peccaries and wombats, who registered surprise and alarm and, in the case of the wombats, dived into their holes. The ball was retrieved to become the centre of a scrum in which the General's massive figure, lashing out with unrestrained ebullience, towered above his playmates. Delighted shouts mingled with periodic roars. This was her chance. Sprinting towards the cafeteria, Helen glanced over her shoulder to see the General, having kicked the ball into a pond occupied by sea-lions, disappearing head-first into a hollow log. "My God, he'll stick!" she cried, and sped on.

The telephone was un-cooperative. First a honeyed voice informed her that all lines to Bristol, Gloucester, Cheltenham, Chippenham and Frome were engaged, adding seductively "Please try later." Then there was a series of cackles, followed by high-pitched buzzing sounds, interrupted by a faint and adenoidal voice saying: "That's just what I told Madge, I wouldn't stand for it I said, with Derek's moving over there with Hilary leaving Chris with the baby, as I said to Madge, Julia's got enough on her plate what with sore feet and now there's talk of gallstones, if I were her. . ." Helen tried again with increasing desperation, picturing the General stuck in the hollow log and dying of asphyxiation or burst blood vessels. At long last, the Sergeant's manly voice came through.

"Sergeant Bullstrode, Shipton Wick police station."

"W.P.C. Wiggett speaking. I'm at the – "

"W.P.C. Wiggett!" The manly voice rose by several pitches and took on an outraged tone. "You have absconded! Absent without leave! Dereliction of duty! You are NOT at the Lots' Road Power Station."

"I know I'm not. I'm at the – "

"Do you understand that half the media of the free world are looking for you? That they've over-run the Lots' Road Station and caused a power cut? That my phone's never given me a moments rest, the Chief Constable's got his dander up and General whats-is-name you're supposed to be looking after, he's scarpered and his Embassy or whatever it is is in a muck sweat and pestering the life out of everyone – you've made a nice mess of things I must say. You'll be for it, W.P.C. Wiggett, when you give yourself up and no mistake! Where *are* you, anyway?"

"I'm trying to tell you. I'm at – " Pip, pip, pip, pip, Helen searched desperately in her pocket for another 10p. Fifty, no good, one p, no good either, two half-pence even less so. Frenziedly, she shouted into the receiver: "I'm at the Little Goosey Safari Park. With the General. And Lady Pandora. For God's sake send a car." Had she been in time? No way of knowing. She didn't dare start the process all over again with the General probably dead, or half dead at best, by now. Back to the adventure playground. The hollow logs were empty, or populated by small, lithe children who popped in and out like ferrets. No General. Where was he? Gone after the ball to be savaged by the sea-lions and probably drowned? Borne away in an ambulance? Enjoying a ride on the Little Goosey Trans-continental Express, whose carriages could be seen winding their way among trees and shrubs and past white rhinos, mountain goats, Soay sheep and Siberian tigers?

The next half-hour was about the worst Helen could remember since she'd been lost in a supermarket as a child, lost in a terrifying forest of wire trolleys, adults on the move, and stacks of bottles, jars and packets that seemed to extend to eternity. It was scarcely possible that anyone so conspicious as the General should become invisible in an English park. Or perhaps he was no longer in that English park? Could Lady Pandora have somehow enticed him back into her car and driven him off at ninety miles an hour to an unknown destination?

At last, she found him. There he was, standing quite quietly, pensively even, gazing up into the branches of a tree. The tree stood on an island surrounded by a moat designed to keep the monkeys who inhabited its branches on one side and the public on the other. It hadn't worked that way. The General was on the island with the monkeys, having, Helen surmised, leapt the moat.

"General," she called across to him, "please come back."

He turned to face her with a smile so beaming it was positively seraphic. "Monkeys," he said.

"Yes, I see. Please come back. We'll find the manager and he'll get us transport back to Shipton Wick."

Matters more important to the General now occupied his mind. "Monkeys. Young, fat monkeys. I did not know you have monkeys in your country. Food for chiefs, food for emperors, food for Generals. This General!'' His fist smote his chest and he roared with laughter. ''Stewed with groundnuts, roast with honey, fried in coconut oil. You see, I understand cooking monkeys. We take these monkeys. When the Prince comes – and why is the Prince so long in coming?'' His face clouded over and Helen feared another outburst, but a monkey swinging in the branches overhead restored his spirits. ''When the prince comes, he shall have a banquet. A feast of monkeys!''

''I'm sure he'll appreciate it. But we must find the manager first.''

''Who is this manager?''

''He owns the monkeys. And a car. To get home.''

''These monkeys belong to him?''

''More or less.''

''Then I will order him to catch me monkeys.''

With a farewell glance in the direction of the succulent dinners swinging in the tree, the General picked up a plank lying on the grass, laid it over the moat and walked across, replacing it in some shrubs where the keepers had half-concealed it. Always a mistake, Helen thought, to under-rate the General. Not for nothing had he reached the top of his particular tree.

The manager proved elusive. The first individual Helen questioned didn't know who he, or she, was. A man raking leaves thought it was Mr Callahan who might be feeding the flamingos. A woman selling ice-cream said it was Syd who had gone to Alaska. By stages, they worked their way back to the entrance. Helen was pursuing her enquiries in the souvenir shop when a great welcoming shout reverberated through shop and garden centre, cafeteria and toilet block, to reach the pens and cages beyond and evoke an answering cry from a macaw.

''Arthur!''

Arthur slid out of the driving seat of his car and braced himself to receive the General's friendly pat on the shoulder. Helen breathed a deep sigh. So her message had got through.

Arthur's relief at locating the General was as great as Helen's at being located. His day so far had been a nightmare, and it had not ended. The invasion of the media; the discovery of the arms cache; calls from the Palace, the White House, the heads of thirty-two Commonwealth countries and even more friendly nations seeking reassurance as to the Prince's safety; the breaching of security at Cantilevre Manor by two representatives of *Paris Match* who got rolled up in a carpet (to be unrolled, to their chagrin, not in the master bedroom as they had expected but downstairs in the cook's sitting room); all these blows had rained down upon his head while he was endeavouring at the same time to pick up the latest bulletin on the highjacked flight from Heathrow to Bogatá.

The aircraft, he learned, had landed safely in the Azores. Gendarmes were ringing the airport, ambulances and fire-engines standing by, troops on the alert and a dialogue had started between the pilot on the one hand and the Portuguese authorities on the other. The pilot, Captain Muspratt, spoke in puzzled tones.

"I can't understand a word they're saying and what they keep repeating doesn't make sense. Where they want to fly to, I mean."

"Cuba? Libya? Iraq?"

"No. Somewhere that *sounds* like Buckingham Palace."

Arthur, listening with a hollow stomach to Robin Day introducing fifty minutes of news, and comment, this Tuesday lunchtime, learned that confusion continued to surround the highjackers' demands. The Libyan government had denied all knowledge of their identity and so far no revolutionary group had claimed their allegiance. The plane was re-fuelling and food and medical supplies were being taken on board. The high-jackers, it was believed, were armed with hand grenades. The plane would be returning to Heathrow where preparations were being made for its reception.

It was not without emotion that Arthur heard the story unfold. As a former serving soldier, loyalty to one's officers and devotion to duty regardless of personal risk came high on his list of virtues. Here was loyalty displayed in a most touching manner. Regardless of personal considerations, knowing their place to be at their General's side, the bodyguards had gone to all lengths to be reunited with the chief from whom they had been so unwillingly parted. Not only was their loyalty touching, their ingenuity was commendable. Hand grenades. All the fuss about the automatic weapons, and all the time the bodyguards were hung about like Christmas trees with hand grenades under their tunics. It was a wonder they hadn't used them in the skittles alley of The Goat and Compasses.

Members of the World Revolutionary Council were following events with equally keen attention, mixed with some degree of puzzlement. The highjackers had brought off a *coup* in the best revolutionary tradition, but to which group did they belong? "Not yours, are they?" Hakkab of the Levantine Liberation League enquired of a colleague who spoke for Partisans of Peace. "Not that I know of," the authority replied, "but you can never be sure of what they're up to in Kamchatskya. Always starting hares up there and telling no one. Try the Scarlet Brotherhood."

The Scarlet Brotherhood must have changed their number; an aggrieved voice said that he was speaking for the Kleenatrice Towel Service and what the hell were they on about. Hakkab eliminated from his enquiries the World Congress of Churches and Womens' Rights Worldwide, but when he tried the Freedom Fighters' Front a gleam of light came through.

In the modest offices of the Excelsior Trading Company above an off-licence in the Clapham Road, where Dr Daniel Dongola conducted his multifarious affairs, there had been some hard thinking since the eight o'clock news. Of late the FFF had not figured prominently in the news. While big things were brewing, there was a temporary lull. An opportunity to keep the FFF in the forefront of the public's mind should not be overlooked. At any rate, there could be no harm in livening things up a bit. 'Keep the kettle on the boil,' as Dr Bongola's old teacher at the Idaho Pentacostal College had been wont to say. He got through to the editor of the *Evening Excess*.

"This is the Freedom Fighters' Front. Two of our comrades are concerned in the incident involving the Casablanca Airways plane, flight 368 to Bogatá."

"You mean the plane that's been highjacked?"

"That's the one."

"Are you claiming responsibility?"

"You might put it that way."

"Well, either you are or you aren't. Where are you speaking from?"

"Addis Ababa. If their demands are not met imediately, they will blow up the plane."

"What *are* their demands?"

Dr Bongola had not so far formulated them, but he was a quick thinker. "Release of all political prisoners in South Africa, South America and Siberia. Dr Botha's public trial and execution. Handing over all gold, diamond and uranium mines to the Organisation of African Unity. Fifty million dollars ransome. Oh, and freedom of the Laxative Islands." Dr Bongola rang off. An hour or so later a special edition of the newspaper was on the street with the exclusive story, together with a *résumé* of the recent activities of the Freedom Fighters' Front.

Hakkab, meanwhile, had been visited by second thoughts. Why should the Freedom Fighters' Front get away with all this free publicity? Hakkab didn't like to admit it, but he had been slow off the mark on behalf of the Levantine Liberation League. Well, it was not too late. Less than couple of hours later, a special edition of the *Daily Planet* was on sale with the exclusive story, together with a *résumé* of the aims of the Levantine Liberation League together with a picture of their most recent achievement, the bombing of a cinema in Aleppo in which one hundred and eighty-five people had been burnt to death.

The highjacked plane, meanwhile, was approaching Heathrow. A detachment of the SAS had already arrived, the runway allocated to the plane sealed off, an operations room set up, fire engines from as far away as Deptford assembled, and the Chief Commissioner of the Metropolitan Police, in close contact with the GOC Southern Command, was monitoring the crisis minute by minute.

Arthur in his car was speeding towards Shipton Wick, the General at his side and W.P.C. Wiggett in the back seat. He switched off the radio as Robin Day passed on to lesser matters. "I think", he said, "that we must go to Heathrow." He turned on to the motorway.

It was not, as he had expected, an easy matter to penetrate the barriers of security that had been thrown up around the airport and to reach, after much persuasion and production of proofs of identity, the operations centre in the VIP lounge. The military were being kept under wraps, more or less; crouching figures in battle fatigues could be glimpsed here and there behind luggage trolleys, rubbish bins and doorways into lavatories. A softly-softly technique had been decided on, and the VIP lounge was crowded with professors of psychology, practising psychiatrists, consultants from mental hospitals, lecturers from the Centre for Strategic Studies, experts on terrorist techniques, and specialists in various other fields. A team from the school of Oriental and African Studies, covering a wide spectrum of vernacular dialects, was standing by to translate.

Tension mounted as the minutes ticked by. The airport lay in unaccustomed silence; no planes were taking off or landing, no trucks or other vehicles weaving about, no figures moving on the tarmac.

"Why all these people here?" enquired the General.

"They've come to welcome back your bodyguards."

"My bodyguards need no welcoming back. They need reprimands. They have deserted."

"Unintentionally."

At last the aircraft could be seen overhead. Rifles were cradled, firemen took up their stations, television cameras were poised at the ready. The plane touched down and taxied to a halt.

"Captain Muspratt, can you hear me? Captain Muspratt?"

"Here."

"Where are the highjackers? What are their demands?"

"They're drinking tea. Their demands don't seem to have changed."

"Particularise."

"They keep on about Buckingham Palace."

The experts had already given this phrase their consideration. A word in a dialect spoken in Lesoto meaning earwig, and another in Fulani meaning the after-birth of a three-year-old cow, might be correlated with Buckingham. One school of thought held that Palace was Intended for Alice in Central Australia, suggesting a link with activists of Aboriginese protection movements. Another opted for Harris in the Outer Hebrides, indicating perhaps a revival of the Tartan Brigade. Paris; a region in Bolivia that sounded somewhat the same; and Dallas, Texas, were other possibilities.

"Get them to the microphone."

There was a pause. "They don't seem anxious to come."

"What are they doing?"

"One of them's, well, shall we say getting familiar with one of the stewardesses. The other's shouting for a General, it sounds like. General and then some foreign word."

The occupants of the VIP lounge were startled by a deep roar. Before anyone could make a move, General Mkubwa had shot out of the lounge and on to the tarmac apron, waving his arms and bawling at the top of his powerful voice: "Moja! Mbili! Salamia!"

Two grinning faces appeared at a window. Safety catches on levelled rifles were released, cannisters of CS gas gripped ready for propulsion, a military helicopter hovered overhead. The only other sound was the whirring of television cameras. You could almost hear everyone holding his breath.

The plane's rear door opened and two men in battle-dress burst out with arms upraised – not, however, in a gesture of surrender, but the better to greet their General, who with open arms returned their embrace. It was a moving reunion. Thoughts of disciplinary action had evidently been cast aside. Moja and Mbili were friends as well as bodyguards. One was, in fact, the General's sister's husband's brother's nephew, the other his father's ninth wife's brother's son.

The drive back to Shipton Wick was boisterous and, for Arthur, somewhat nerve-racking. The General, sitting in front, was in an exuberant mood and had put his recent frustrations out of his mind. The bodyguards, sitting behind with W.P.C. Wiggett sandwiched in the middle, had much to relate about their experiences. Discipline, while no doubt strictly enforced when on duty, was relaxed, and the bonds of kinship allowed to replace the protocol of military rank.

The General, though as yet he did not know it, had in the space of a few minutes become a national, indeed an international, hero. The story, relayed by satellite, had soon spread round the world. Alone, unarmed, unprotected, this General from the New Commonwealth, attached to the Prince's staff, had advanced unflinchingly upon the highjacked aircraft with its armed desperados belonging to a ruthless terrorist group – or possibly to two ruthless terrorist groups – and disarmed them. Over-awed by his mere presence, they had given themselves up without a struggle; the safety of the hostages was assured and the ransom money, tied in packages, remained in its suitcase undisturbed. Already there was talk of the George Cross, a knighthood, the Freedom of the City of London and other awards.

Everything had ended happily except that both General and highjackers had disappeared. Agents of the media were hot on the trail of the former, the forces of law and order of the latter. Meanwhile, there was splendid television coverage of the General on the tarmac, the terrorists leaping from the plane, their unconditional surrender. That morning, all that the media had expected had been a heroic policewoman; by evening they had a story which, if less spectacular, was almost as gripping as that of the Entebbe raid.

Darkness was falling by the time Arthur and his passengers approached Shipton Wick. Cockscombe Castle, he feared, might already be under seige. A quick call to Reggie Whackers from a service station on the motorway had given warning of his predicament. "Leave it to me," Reggie Whackers had said. "Use the back door."

"No key."

"I'll leave it under the dustbin. Look out for dogs."

The General, Arthur reckoned, might just be coped with; anyway, he couldn't be let out of sight. But the bodyguards . . . Three ebullient members of the Hapanan army under the Gwent's roof would be too much. They could never be kept concealed. They would not wish to be concealed. And the police, presumably, were after them with no holds barred. Incubi permanently lodged on Arthur's shoulders, that was what the bodyguard had become.

"I'm afraid," he warned the General, "that you and your faithful, loyal fellow-countrymen must again be separated. Only for a short time you understand. Perhaps just for the night. They'll be close by and well looked after. But there's no room at Cockscombe Castle I'm afraid."

"No room?"

The Gwents have filled the castle with their guests."

"The bodyguards sleep in my room. By the bottom of my bed."

"I'm afraid not. The Prince doesn't allow it."

"Why does the Prince refuse my bodyguards to sleep at the bottom of my bed?"

This was indeed a poser. "He wouldn't consider it fitting. Rules of hospitality. Every guest must have a room to himself. I expect it's the same in your country, a great chief wouldn't share sleeping accommodation with his slaves."

"Where does the Prince order my bodyguards to sleep?" the General demanded ferociously. Where indeed? Poser after poser. They were entering Shipton Wick. From the back seat, Helen Wiggett gave a deprecatory cough.

"If I may, sir, I have a suggestion."

"You may indeed. Proceed."

"My aunt Mildred takes in lodgers now and then. She has a nice front room at present vacant, twin beds, facing south, electric heater, use of bathroom, heat, light and laundry included with breakfast and an evening meal. No lunch. She keeps her charges reasonable. These gentlemen might like to, well, rest there for a few days."

If W.P.C. Wiggett hadn't been in the back seat, Arthur would have flung his arms around her sturdy shoulders and kissed her amiable face. Hers might not be the perfect solution – Moja and Mbili did not seem to be the resting type – but it would do for the night.

"Marvellous," he exclaimed. "But – " The same thought was in both their minds. Helen had distinctly felt something hard and knobbly on both sides while sharing the back seat with Moja and Mbili. Lodgers were one thing, lodgers with hand grenades another.

"I'll see what I can do," Arthur said. The General's revolvers had been successfully dealt with; why should the same method not work with hand grenades? Whether Scotland Yard could lay hands on dummy ones at such short notice was a question, but one for them to answer, not him. Directed by Helen, he drove to her aunt's residence on the outskirts of the town. It proved to be a well-kept semi faced in reconstituted stone with a neat front garden (bird-bath, but no gnomes), a small aviary with budgies, and a vegetable plot behind.

"I'm sure you'll be comfortable here," he told the body-guards. "You must be worn out. A good meal, then a good rest." He and Helen exhanged glances. Although she looked a healthy girl, few people nowadays hadn't at some time or other procured sleeping pills from their doctor, and kept half-emptied bottles in a drawer. Even if Helen herself slept like a top, Aunt Mildred, with all the worries of taking in lodgers, must surely have suffered from bouts of insomnia.

"A hot meal first," he suggested, "then a nightcap."

"Yes, sir. There's a bit of stew left over in the fridge. And then a nightcap." One eyelid flickered in the ghost of a wink.

Night had fallen by the time Arthur and the General reached Cockscombe Castle and drove around to the back. Trees were black shapes against a black moonless sky, statuary in the sunken garden seemed like grey ghosts in the darkness. Was that a gleam from a tangle of shrubs beyond the lawn? A canine eye, a human movement? The dogs were doubtless somewhere in the darkness, he hoped under strict control. Thank God, the media didn't seem to have arrived. The Castle's bachelor wing was dark and silent, but at the back lights showed through curtained windows. Evidently the Gwents were at home.

Arthur found his torch and shone it on the back door, flanked on each side by a lidded dustbin. The General's former good humour had given way to a resentful mood. No doubt he was tired and hungry and missed the companionship of Moja and Mbili.

"We'll both feel better," Arthur told him, "After a good stiff drink."

Something about the dustbins looked not quite right. Like many of their kind, each was equipped with two metal clips that, pressed down upon the lid, held it in place. Now the clips were not clamped down but folded back. Careless, Arthur thought; cats might dislodge the lids and scavenge, or sudden gales blow them right off. On impulse, he lifted the lid of the nearest dustbin. Inside, coiled up in a most uncomfortable position, was a young woman in jeans and a tee-shirt with dark hair done in a pony-tail, clasping an expensive camera. The lid of the other dustbin flew off and from it erupted a young man uttering a startled gallic cry. Both fled into the darkness with more gallic cries. There was an ominous woof-woof from behind the statuary in the sunken garden.

"Ah! *Paris Match*," Arthur said.

He found the key and led the General past the old, disused kitchen quarters, through the former servants' hall, stained now with damp, through the wine-cellars, the buttery, the stillroom, the butlers' pantry, the laundry, all lifeless and void. But light came from an open doorway at the foot of the back stairs. In what had been the housekeeper's retreat, a cosy little room the Marquess sat beside a small electric heater with a spotlight focused on his embroidery frame. There was a colour television, two arm-chairs, a work-table and several interesting old Italian prints of dragons on the wall.

"I hope we're not disturbing you, sir."

"No, no, my dear boy. I'm sorry that Mary is out – the Institute, I think, or it may be the Council for the Preservation of Bronze Age Long Barrows. She was made a patron the other day. Another ten quid, I'm afraid." He added stitches to his kneeler. "You are staying here, I think? I hope you are comfortable."

"Couldn't be more so." Taking the General by the sleeve, he quickly led him, too confused to protest, up the back stairs and through a labyrinth of passages to reach the bachelor's wing. Drawing the curtains as tightly as he could, he took a whisky bottle from a cupboard and poured two stiff drinks.

"My stomach cries," the General stated. "Where is food?"

Where indeed? Arthur opened the door of the fridge. The

remains of half a cooked chicken, an opened tin of sardines, a carton of yoghurt, a little left-over kedgeree, half a cucumber. Could he take the General to a pub? No, of course not. No falling into the lap of the media.

Food, Charlotte. Somehow, this formed a natural equation. Surely she must keep snacks, more than snacks perhaps, in the freezer. A resourceful girl. Charlotte answered the telephone.

"Arthur! Where are you? Everyone's been after you."

"They're after me now. I've got the General with me and we're both famished. Could you – "

"Come along right away. Mummy's just put a casserole in the oven. So you've got the General! He's vanished. The news is on about it all the time."

"I'll tell you all about it. We might need two casseroles."

"Don't worry, come along straight away."

Arthur left the receiver off its hook, but, a moment later, the other telephone rang. He looked at it with apprehension. The direct line to the Palace.

"Hello, yes?" His voice changed. "Yes, sir, he's here." He handed the receiver to the General.

"I am wanted?"

"By the Prince."

The General beamed, and strode to the telephone. His beam widened as his master's voice spoke into his ear. He hung up with a flourish. "The Prince congratulates me. He says that I am brave and fine and full of resources. He speaks of medals. He has sent a message to our great leader, our good shepherd, Field-Marshal Dudu. I am the Prince's good friend. I will report for duty at Buckingham Palace on Monday morning."

"Splendid, old man. Super."

The General nodded. "At last, I start my duties. I take my bodyguards."

"By all means. You do just that. Now, food."

"Ah! Food."

"I'm taking you out to some friends of mine. There's a maiden there, a good cook."

"Ah, maidens."

His voice, Arthur thought, had lost it fine edge of enthusiasm when it came to English maidens. A touch of disillusionment, perhaps, had crept in. Still, there was always W.P.C. Wiggett batting for the side. "This one is Charlotte, the one with the dark hair. Quite tall, slim figure."

The General made a grimace. "All thin. Now food. My stomach cries."

"We must hope for the best from the casserole."

Chapter Eight

COUNCILLOR Mrs Hussey had naturally assumed that the programme drawn up for the Prince's visit to Buggins' Brushes would include a performance by the silver band. Any thought to the contrary had not entered her mind. It therefore came as a surprise when Councillor Peter Paxton, never backward at coming forward, remarked, after casting his eye over the proposed plan:

"With respect, madam chairman, I feel we're not striking the right note with all this high-jinkery. This isn't supposed to be a sort of jamboree or carnival. The Prince is coming to open a significant chapter in the story of British industrial progress. Up to date, forward-looking, in tune with the New Age. A silver band, now – not the right image. Not at all."

"I don't know what you mean about image. The silver band follows in one of Shipton's most respected traditions."

"Exactly! Traditions. What we're doing now at Buggins' is to get away from traditions. Leave them behind. March with progress – silicon chips, laser beams, space satellites, you name it. Dispel the fuddy-duddy image of hidebound old Britain. I feel sure – "

"I *beg* your parden" said Councillor Rufford in aggrieved tones.

"What d'you mean, fuddy-duddy image?" asked Councillor Mavis Pellett, who kept the Health Food shop at the bottom of the High Street, just where it curled round to go over Packmule Bridge. A prevalence of double yellow lines, plus a steep climb to reach the car park, had virtually restricted her clientèle to those who possessed, or could borrow or steal, a Disabled Driver sign, or to athletes in training. As an ardent student of Shipton's long history she had, with some reluctance, allowed her name to go forward for election to the Council in the hope that she might speak up for that side of life relating to the town's culture and amenities. This latter word, she had soon found out, covered a number of matters only loosely related to culture, such as the upkeep of public conveniences, street cleaning, the swimming pool and the annual carnival. On the credit side, she had persuaded the relevant committee of the County Council to authorise the acceptance by the Museum of a collection of coins bearing the imprint of the Emperor Tiberius, found during excavations for a sewer near York.

"Fuddy-duddy image!" she repeated. "May I remind you that the record of Shipton Wick, as of other ancient market towns, is one of constant adaption to change. After the Romans – "

"That's just my point," Peter interrupted. "Here we are adapting to the electronic age. A silver band – "

"The Silver Band, if not in its present form, is one of our most ancient and historic institutions. The name is a corruption of course – 'silvern band' should be the true designation. From the Latin silva, meaning woodland, under the protection of Sylvanus, the god of woods and fields and flocks. Flutes were no doubt the original instruments. One can visualise a small band of flautists under the greenwood tree – "

"Serenading the first microchip toothbrush no doubt." Councillor Snape spoke in his usual sour tone. "I agree with Councillor Paxton for once. Lot of flimflam if you ask me. Cut the cackle and leave out the silver band."

"That would cause a great deal of offence," the Mayor objected. "The silver band has always performed on occasions of this kind. The members would feel a sense of grievance."

"Let them," said Councillor Snape shortly.

The Mayor knew perfectly well what lay behind Councillor Snape's objection. Mrs Snape's carryings-on with Syd, the swimming pool attendant, was nothing less than a public scandal; and Syd was the trombonist of the silver band. There was no talking him over; he must be out-voted. Robert Rufford, an influential member, was on her side. Certainly, he considered, the Prince should be greeted in a joyful spirit, a bit of glitter, something to uplift everyone's spirits; but he wasn't sure about drum majorettes who were also on the programme. An

American invention, alien surely to the spirit of Shipton Wick. *Too* modern.

"There you are," Peter said brusquely. "Modern, so you condemn drum majorettes out of hand. We should *welcome* modern things. Some, anyway." Too late, he realised that he had fallen into a trap. The last thing he wanted to see was a team of tarted-up young ladies with short skirts and white boots tossing batons about.

"We don't want drum majorettes," said Councillor Snape, now, inadvertently, an ally.

"Want them or not, we really must have them," the Mayor said firmly. "This is a political issue, I'm afraid."

"Political?" Sir Hubert Evers had been doodling on his pad, his mind on the higher gastropods of tropical oceans and the problems their morphology posed for the biologist. The ominous word political brought him back to his present surroundings. "Surely . . ."

"Although there's never been any question about Shipton being Cantilevre's market town, I needn't remind you of the attitude taken up by Poggleton. Or some Poggletonians, anyway. Their town is larger than ours, we all agree, and though they're five miles further from Cantilevre than we are there's been a certain amount of resentment, entirely unjustified of course, about Shipton, as they put it, hogging the limelight."

"Sheer jealousy," Councillor Rufford put in.

"Ridiculous."

"Petty."

"Just because they've got a mainline railway station – "

"I don't see where their drum majorettes come in," said Councillor Snape.

"You won't have forgotten that we had a meeting with elements of their Council to discuss co-ordination. They feel they are entitled to a say, a minor one of course. They think the Prince will be making use of Poggleton on occasion. The station for one thing. And Westmacott's cheeses in the market on Fridays are world famous. Well-known all over Gloucestershire."

"You don't suggest the Prince will be nipping over to

Poggleton to buy a slice of cheese?''

"I wasn't at that meeting" Councillor Snape's tone was belligerent. "It was held behind closed doors. Undemocratic. A betrayal of Open Government. What you're saying is you did a secret deal with Poggleton."

"Not at all," the Mayor retorted with some heat. "I hope the Councillor is not accusing me of duplicity. There was no secret deal as you put it. Merely an amicable arrangement to co-operate, to some extent, in public functions held to demonstrate our loyalty to the Crown. Surely Councillor Snape can't object to that. Besides, they offered to contribute to expenses.''

"How much?"

"No precise figure was agreed. As I said, this was just a general friendly meeting. I'm sure – ''

"And in return for a vague promise of an unspecified sum, the Council's been committed to these drum majorettes I suppose. Are we permitted to ask what other secret agreements were reached?''

"Really, Councillor, we're getting off the point," the Mayor protested. "The drum majorettes will do us no harm. On the contrary. Don't forget the television and press photographers, something to liven up the scene. Poggleton will pay all their expenses, and something extra towards the bunting and so on. All we've got to settle now is about the silver band. I should have thought it would give deep offence to many of our steadiest rate-payers to leave it out.''

"You all seem to forget this isn't a civic reception," Peter persisted. "The Prince is coming to launch the New Technology in *my factory*.''

"We'd better take a vote," the chairman decided.

The vote came out at even numbers. A draw, with one abstention.

"Sir Hubert, may we have your vote?''

Still Sir Hubert hesitated. There was much to be said on both sides. On the one hand, he quite saw Paxton's point. This should be a dignified, workmanlike occasion without a lot of fuss and razzamatazz (if he'd got the word right.) He'd grappled with a similar problem before, over the matter of traditional dancing on the Queen's Birthday. Traditional dancing, once unleashed, was liable to continue for three days at least, and to involve both the mass deflowering of virgins (very young virgins at that) by newly circumcised warriors, and ritual copulations among their elders to ensure a favourable harvest.

While conceding that traditional dancing, with all its spontaneity and vigour, was a valued part of the islanders' culture, he had never considered it to be a suitable way to celebrate the Queen's Birthday. He had expressed his opinion in a file submitted to the Colonial Office with a request for guidance on this delicate matter. Delicate, because Queen Chotonopohaggis and her advisors would undoubtedly take a poor view of any attempt by the Governor-General to tamper with these ancient rites. The Colonial Office had kept Sir Hubert's file for five years and by the time it re-appeared on the island, engorged by many learned opinions, Sir Hubert himself was on his way home to an honourable retirement. It was unreasonable, he considered, to expect a snap decision on a question which, while admittedly parochial, had, like the matter of traditional dancing and the Queen's Birthday, much to be said on both sides. He looked at his watch.

"Madam Chairman, it is now ten minutes to one. May I suggest that we adjourn for lunch, and take the final vote on our re-assembly at half-past two?"

Although he held in high esteem his wife's good sense and proven discretion, Sir Hubert made a point of not revealing to her the secrets of the Town Council's discussions. True, he was no longer bound by the Official Secrets Act, but the habit of a lifetime prevailed.

But now he was bothered. He had been placed in a false position. It was not for him alone to make up the mind of the Town Council. The uncongenial role of a dictator, he felt, had been foisted upon him. There was only one satisfactory way to settle questions on which opinion was evenly balanced, and that was by referring them to precedent. Somewhere or other, he felt sure – although he was bound to admit that he did not know where – a precedent must exist that would offer guidance as to whether the opening by royalty of a new manufacturing process should be celebrated by a silver band, or indeed by any other kind of orchestra. (The drum majorettes seemed to have slipped through.) But to search for such a precedent would take time, and a conclusion must be reached by half-past-two. It was very worrying. He needed advice.

In this dilemma, a lifetime's rule might perhaps be bent a little. Marjorie, he was sure, would let the matter go no further. He laid the problem before his wife over a pilaf of chicken livers. He had never really liked chicken livers, but there it was.

"I don't see why they shouldn't have their band if they want it," she said.

"The point is, some want it and some don't."

"Who doesn't?"

"Paxton for one. He thinks it strikes the wrong note."

"Well, if I know anything about silver bands it probably will. Does it matter?"

"We're not celebrating a jubilee or any other royal occasion."

"Think what went on on the Islands on the Queen's Birthday."

"I'd rather not . . . It looks a bit like rain." Marjorie glanced out of the window and Sir Hubert slipped a bit of chicken liver to Cherub under the table. The dog merely sniffed at the morsel, simultaneously wagging his tail.

"Lie down, Cherub," his mistress commanded. "You know he's not allowed to beg at table, Hubert."

"Yes, indeed. Some of the other Councillors are against the band too. That fellow Snape, for instance. I don't trust him."

"Snape in the grass." Of late, Sir Hubert had noticed a certain change in Marjorie's manner. Nothing you could put your finger on, but he seemed to detect an element of, well, levity, which had certainly not been in evidence at Government House.

"Of course I can rely absolutely on your discretion, my dear." If she had not been quite as helpful as he had hoped, nevertheless putting the issues before her had clarified the position. It was plain that there was something to be said on both sides. At twenty-past-two he set out on foot for the Civic Centre, still in a troubled frame of mind.

Half an hour later Marjorie set out for the Salon Marie-Louise to enjoy her fortnightly shampoo and set. Astrid was persuading her to try a different style – a bit more relaxed, a softer line.

"Busy, I expect?" she enquired.

"Fantastic." Astrid secured the strings of the pink robe around Marjorie's neck. "It's only to start some new machinery or something at the factory but the way everyone's going on about it, you'd think it was the Hunt Ball. They say Mrs Paxton's taken on a social secretary and sent out so many invitations there'll be a queue right down to the bottom of the High Street. Where are all the cars going to park, that's what I'd like to know."

Marjorie lent her head back, closed her eyes and prepared to enjoy the soothing application to her scalp of Astrid's firm and soapy fingers.

"The latest is, they're going to turn the pigsties at Cantilevre into a police station manned night and day, with television cameras in the forks of trees. Did you hear about those French journalists?"

Astrid deftly wrapped a towel round Marjorie's dripping locks and escorted her to the setting table. With head thrown back and soap getting into her ears, the customer was at a disadvantage; under the drier, she was silenced; in between, during the setting process, she had her chance.

"The French can be relied upon to give trouble. I remember how in the Condominium – "

"Curls over the ears this time, Lady Evers, or would you rather swept back over the temples?"

"Swept back I think. The French Ágent Gèneral – "

"They say he's been seen about with a new girl now, quite young, and titled, but the papers think up a new one every week, don't they, keeps up sales I suppose. There's been all that talk about him and Lady Pandora. I don't know what he'd say to pet rats. Brought them in to the Salon, she did, some of our clients didn't like it one bit."

Pink and blue curlers were sprouting all over Marjorie's head. Abandoning the Condominium for the moment, she began:

"Rats can be quite intelligent I believe. I remember once – "

"They were quite well behaved, that I will say. The rats I

mean. Now she's making a collection. Collecting something's all the rage, she says. You know, candlesticks, old prams, gate fastenings, postcards, bottle-tops, anything. So she's started a collection. You'll never guess what.''

"My husband had an excellent collection of gastropods. Pickled in alcohol. Unfortunately – ''

"Olive stones. Quite original, no one else collected them till Lady Pandora started but now it's taken on. The thing is, they must be spat out by a celebrity. She's got one spat out by Princess Margaret, another by Terry Wogan, one by Dirk Bogarde, then there's Mohamed Ali and one by Iggy Pop''.

"Who's Iggy Pop?''

"To tell the truth, I don't know, but he must be a celebrity or Lady Pandora wouldn't have collected his olive stone. Gets them from waiters at cocktail parties. They fluctuate in value all the time, she says. She paid a lot for one of President Carter's, but now it's worthless. On the other hand some that you can pick up for a song double their value overnight if you're a good talent-spotter.''

"I must tell Charlotte. But – '' There were only a few more curlers to go, time was running out. She'd had enough of Lady Pandora.

"I only hope the big event goes off all right. It would be disaster if the Prince's first public appearance in Shipton were to be spoiled by stupid rows in the Town Council.''

Marjorie had, she could see, successfully claimed Astrid's attention. "Yes, I fear there's a serious disagreement about the way the whole reception should be handled. A split down the middle. Of course, I shouldn't be saying this.''

Indeed she shouldn't. Years and years of discretion had forced her into a mould. Now the mould was broken, the Official Secrets Act a dragon slain, freedom of speech had alighted upon her like a sort of Holy Spirit, if that wasn't profane. She felt liberated, drunk with the heady wine of freedom.

"Yes, split down the middle. One side saying keep it sober, businesslike, dignified – a bit dull I think. The others all for bunting, bands and fun and games – drum majorettes even. If the Council goes on like that, nothing will be settled and the whole event fall flat on its face. Personally, I think they should consult the Prince, but he's away in the Isle of Man opening the House of Keys, or perhaps shutting it, I can't remember which, I've *heard* he's got his eye on a very pretty girl up there, a daughter of the Clerk of General Gaol Delivery. And there's a mad African general chasing about all over the place looking for escaped monkeys who's supposed to be one of his equerries. I do think the security people should do something about it."

"Good heavens," Astrid said. "I'm all for royalty, but it does seem to be putting things about in poor old Shipton."

Marjorie took her place under the drier, well satisfied. She could rely on Astrid. More, she feared, with a spasm of guilt but not remorse, than Hubert could, any longer, rely on her.

Her confidence in Astrid's news-imparting skills was not misplaced. Before the day was out, it was all over Shipton Wick that a blazing row erupting in the Town Council had led to the resignation of the Mayor and the arrest of Councillor Rufford for embezzlement; that Councillor Mrs Pellett had suffered a heart attack; that the Prince's visit had been postponed or cancelled, Councillor Paxton had closed down the factory and attempted suicide, and a mad African general had commandeered an aeroplane to fly to the Isle of Man where the Prince had rescued a famous film star who had been wrongly incarcerated in the island's jail. Colin Rumble of the *Star and Echo* felt like a spaniel distracted by half a dozen enticing odours as he followed up the stories, one after the other. Long experience had armoured him against the blows of disappointment. One by one the leads led back to the Salon Marie-Rose and quite soon he gave up.

Something to tell Daryll about, anyway, Astrid thought as she made her way for a brief lunch-time break to Ernie's Place, where she and Daryll sometimes shared a table for a coffee and a salad, or now and again a slice of quiche or a wholemeal sandwich with tomato and cottage cheese. They didn't have a regular assignment; Astrid fitted in her lunch-break with her appointments, and Daryll could never be quite sure when Tony Borrowdale might send for him. Now and again, more often of late, he was entrusted with a mission to show a property to a client. Not an important property of course, one of the less saleable terraces perhaps or a crumbled cottage consisting of little more than a heap of lichen-encrusted stones, ripe for renovation and situated in unspoiled rural surroundings.

Something to tell Daryll about would start the conversation off on the right lines. Truth to tell, now and again there were moments when her attention was not entirely rivetted by badgers, or even whales, and lately porpoises in Japan, or rather in Japanese territorial waters. Daryll was a poppet, but like everyone else he had his prejudices, and by now she was well apprised of a certain failure of communication between him and Judy Mustard, and a noticeable lack of appreciation of the virtues of Angus MacBean.

There was no sign of Daryll in Ernie's Place. Astrid settled herself down with a cheese salad and a paperback about the adventures of a Regency buck. She had almost finished the chapter and her coffee when Daryll appeared. She could see at once from his manner that something of more than everyday interest had occurred. Her suspicions were confirmed when he collected a poached egg on spinach. Raw food bulging with vitamins was Daryll's dietary imperative. Astrid wished that he would eat less sparingly, something more solid – even, though she hadn't like to mention it, meat now and then. Vegetarian food was all very well in its way but, as her mother often said, it didn't build muscle.

"Extraordinary thing," Daryll remarked as he broached his egg. "You know that old place off the Dudgrove Turville road, turn left by The Duke of York, Shuddering Park they call it. Been on the books a long time and no wonder. Rising damp, falling lintels, half the roof caved in. Belonged to a family called Pagan I believe. The last owner hanged himself in the buttery, the one before that baked his wife in the bread-oven, bells ring though there aren't any bells and there's supposed to be a ghost in the attic that smells of carbolic."

"Well, it sounds nice, I must say."

"As you can imagine, not an easy place to flog. Mr Borrowdale thought it might do for Princess Margaret, on account of its seclusion and the view. 'Needs money spent on it of course,' he said, 'but that wouldn't be a problem. Easy reach of Cantilevre.' That fell through.''

"Not surprising."

"Well, today Tony Borrowdale sent for me and said he'd got a client looking for something in the neighbourhood right off the road, secluded, sheltered from the public with a bit of ground to go with it. 'Some sort of religious outfit' Mr Borrowdale said. 'They want to meditate. Shuddering Park's just the job for meditation and I daresay they've got minds above rising damp. Take him out there, Daryll old man,' he said, 'and pitch it into him good and strong – historic old manor, not listed (through an oversight) so they can monkey about with it as much as they please, marvellous view, going cheap for a quick sale, a real bargain – though not so much of one,' he added, 'since the Prince bought Cantilevre and doubled property values in the district, bless him. But in the case of Shuddering Park we're prepared to be flexible'. So off I went, picked up this chap at Poggleton station and took him out to see the property. Queer sort of fellow, a reverend, American, it beats me where these cranky orders or whatever they are get the money."

"Not the Moonies, are they?"

"Something like that I shouldn't wonder. Want to start a sort of college, he said, a meditation centre. Plenty to meditate about, I said, destruction of the planet, world pollution, genocide of whales. As a matter of fact you could make a splendid little nature reserve up at Shuddering Park. The woods have been let go just right for badgers, there's a pond with mallards and a nice little colony of bats in the roof."

"Well, I must be going. Mrs Satterthwaite at two fifteen. Did the Reverend buy it?"

"That's the extraordinary part. As a matter of fact, he did."

"Super, Daryll. Mr Borrowdale's sure to give you a rise for that."

"Of course you never know till contracts are exchanged. He didn't seem to mind fungi on the walls or smell of dry-rot. 'Our thoughts are on the transcendental,' he said, or something on those lines. 'The manifestations of divinity lie all about us,' he said. 'The hand of God shaped the humble cockroach as it shaped the mighty king.' I got Mr Borrowdale back from lunch and this chap forked out the deposit there and then. Queer sort of name – Reverend Amigale Pyle. Queer sort of business altogether if you ask me.''

"Well, they sound harmless enough. So long, Daryll. Be seeing you.''

"At the meeting tonight I hope. Usual place and time.''

"Yes, of course, only I'm not absolutely sure . . .''

The glow of interest and, indeed, excitement that had suffused Daryll's countenance faded, to be replaced by an expression that was almost a scowl. "It's important. Judy wants to organise this badger demo as you know, when the Prince comes to Buggins' Brushes. So do certain other members who think they run the show. I'm going to oppose it.''

"Are you really? Angus says . . .''

"Angus can say what he likes.'' Definitely, Astrid thought, a scowl. "There's a time and a place for everything, including demos. The first public appearance of the Prince – though I must say I don't think the occasion's been well chosen – and what do we do? Wave banners at him protesting about badgers. Enough to set him against us for the rest of his life. Counterproductive. The time for the demo is at the Opening Meet.''

"The publicity – ''

"Publicity can cut both ways. I mean to speak out. Please come, Astrid.''

"Oh well, of course, if you feel like that – '' She gave him one of those dimply smiles that did something painful yet delightful to the pit of his stomach. "Heavens, I must fly or I'll be late for Mrs Satterthwaite.'' She fled.

Light as a bird, Daryll thought. He stood himself a second cup of coffee. The proprietor of Ernie's Place, a Cypriot from Bermondsey, kept a tin of his caffeine-free blend especially for him.

Mrs Satterthwaite was being kept in play by Tracey who was extolling the virtues of a new restructurant. "Does wonders, Mrs Satterthwaite. Gives body to the filaments, nourishes the follicles, the whole effect almost you might say sets the hair aflame.'' Tracey was coming along nicely; she had all the making of a good stylist.

''You're looking well today, Mrs Satterthwaite.'' Astrid made heroic efforts to control her breathing after running up the stairs. ''How's David liking his first term at college? Did Debbie enjoy her trip to Italy? Now what are we having today? There's Honey Gold of course or what about a lovely new shade, Nordic Blonde?''

Chapter Nine

THE MEETING of the Shipton Wick and District Ecology Group was held at Sunkist Orchard, Judy Mustard's cottage off the Poggleton road. Certainly the place had character. A low-ceilinged, stone-flagged hall strewn about with dog baskets, wellingtons, riding crops and tins of dog-food; a fire burning (if only just) in an open grate with wrought-iron fire-dogs in the sitting room; leaded window panes, worn rugs, worm-eaten beams, a spinning wheel; a copper cauldron hanging by a rusty chain above the log fire. Much cosier than St Ursula's Hall but, for Astrid, less easy to reach – too far to cycle on a wet evening.

Angus solved the problem by his offer of a lift; he almost passed her door. Angus ran a small yellow builder's van with a ladder on top and a legend painted on the side: 'Instant Erections. Service with a Smile. Cladding, Lagging, Facing, Guttering, Pointing, etc. Satisfaction Guaranteed.' More serviceable than smart, perhaps, but better than the bike.

Angus was a puzzle. He was interested of course, wanted a bit of a canoodle as they all did, and she couldn't deny that he exercised a sort of magnetism. Powerful, masculine, a tweedy smell. That beard . . . But then, who was Angus really? What was he after? She wouldn't put it past him to have a wife and family somewhere in the North. One or two feelers, not exactly questions, had met with evasive replies. She liked to know where she was with people. Whereas with Angus . . . Still, there was no harm in his taking her to the meeting, whatever Daryll might say.

A warm greeting awaited them at Sunkist Orchard, where the other members of the Group were already installed.

"Come in, come in, our honourable Chairman. It's a braw bricht nicht the nicht, come in and toast your toes and warm up with a glass of punch. A base of parsnip with beetroot, and three guesses as to the flavour." Judy was dispensing the wine.

"Lovage?"

"Bladderwort?"

"Stinking hellebore?"

"You're all wrong. Try again." She passed round pottery mugs decorated with wavy lines, and proposed a toast. "To Brock, God bless him, and damnation to his enemies! It's Purging Buckthorn."

"Oh. In that case I'm not sure – " Daryll was not the only member to put his mug down on the nearest shelf or table. He was scowling again, Astrid observed. There had been no mistaking his look of reproach when she'd come in with Angus. The expression in his eyes had put her in mind of a labrador deprived of its bone.

"Nothing to worry about, Daryll, I promise you. Berries crushed with a few pine kernels and bollases. The medicinal properties are in the bark."

"Plenty of bite, anyway," Angus said, draining his mug. "Congratulations, Judy. If we could get the badgers on to this there wouldn't be a murdering vet dare go near them with his gassing apparatus. Now, to business. Our big chance is coming up, comrades-in-arms. Our chance to get the plight of badgers on the front page of every newspaper and right there on all those television screens at peak viewing time. The strategy's agreed. Now for tactics. Judy, how far have we got with the plans?"

Daryll opened his minute-book and cleared a space on a table among mugs, dog-whistles, seed catalogues and a jacket Judy was knitting for a friend's whippet. Not that she approved of mollycoddling, but it was the friend's dog, not hers.

"I'd better read the minutes first," Daryll said.

"Of course, Daryll, Go ahead."

"There's nothing in them to say the strategy's been agreed."

Angus clasped his beard in gnarled fingers and frowned. No kilt tonight, instead baggy breeches, a rough Harris tweed jacket, a red tie and a sheathed hunting knife stuck into the top of a stocking. Flamboyant as usual, Daryll thought. He had seen with suppressed anger the dimply smile Astrid had bestowed upon him as they had come through the door together.

"Come on now Daryll, we were all agreed. A smashing big

demo outside Buggins' Brushes when the Prince arrives. Ten times life-size plywood badger and everyone to have a replica twice life-size, held aloft. Then banners. 'Save Our Badgers'. 'Royal Badgers Look to You'. All quite respectful of course. But hard-hitting.''

''I don't agree with a demo when the Prince comes. He's Shipton's guest. The time for a demo is at the Opening Meet.''

''Of course we'll have a demo at the Opening Meet. But that's to be for whales.''

''We can have whales *and* badgers.''

''Why stop at whales and badgers? How about porpoises, black rhinos, gorillas, eagles, parrots, Siberian cranes, marmosets?''

''Why stop at the Opening Meet? Why not *all* the meets?''

''Why not picket Cantilevre Manor?''

''What about the Amazonian forests?''

''What about orang-utans?

Namibian bush-babies . . . Madagascan lemurs . . . rape of the krill . . . dwindling mineral resources . . . advance of the desert . . . horse-shoe bats . . . Clearly strategy was not yet fully agreed. Clear, too, that the Shipton Wick and District Ecology Group contained an active, caring bunch of members.

''Order, order, fellow members. Order please.''

There was no doubt either that the Chairman had authority, qualities of leadership, carried weight. Even Judy Mustard deferred to his commands. Fleetingly, Astrid wondered whether, one day in the future perhaps if not now, he would rate an olive stone in Lady Pandora's collection.

When order was restored, opinion proved to be almost equally divided. Daryll knew himself to be no orator, but conviction sharpened his words. No one felt more passionately than he about the future of the badgers; the question was, would that cause be helped or damaged by welcoming the Prince with placards, petitions and perhaps disturbances. Anti-demo, hence anti-badger, feelings would be aroused.

If Daryll was no orator, Judy was. Her eyes sparkled, her words boomed, before she'd finished she had the pulses of her audience quickening, their minds lifted to the plane of action, a trumpet-call sounding in their ears. To save the badgers was indeed a noble cause. As with soldiers marching into battle, here was no room for the falterer, the doubter, the faint of heart – could one even say the traitor to the cause? Talk of tact, fears of opposition, doubts about timing – what was all that but weak-kneed fear, chicken-livered cowardice? A betrayal of the badgers' cause.

The pro-demo faction won by a substantial majority. Daryll entered the result in his minute book with a shaking hand. To be called a traitor, weak-kneed, chicken-hearted, stung him to the quick. It was he and his few supporters who were the true champions of the badgers, not the tub-thumping, publicity-seeking Judy and her lot.

Worse was to come. Daryll didn't rate a company car, but there was a Ford Escort kept for general use which he quite often drove, in theory when he went out on a job. In practice, Tony Borrowdale didn't mind him using it privately now and then. Daryll had come along in it tonight.

"I'll drive you home," he said to Astrid when the meeting was over. Judy was handing round mugs of weak instant coffee and squares of goats' milk cheese. Daryll didn't feel like staying on to natter away as if everything was lovely in the garden. A traitor to the cause! He'd choke on Judy's cheese, be poisoned by her nasty coffee. "We might stop somewhere and get a bite to eat," he added.

"That would be lovely, Daryll, only – "

"Only I'm running Astrid back." Angus had somehow sneaked up behind them – if anyone so bulky as Angus could sneak – and laid a massive hand on Daryll's shoulder. "Don't you bother, Daryll old man, it's not a yard out of my way. And Mrs Sproggs has promised me a slice of her Boiled Devon Treacle cake."

"But Astrid said – "

"I know you'll want to write up the minutes while they're fresh in your mind. You do such a super job as Hon. Sec., pity to lower the standard by letting things get stale. I'll run her back tonight – can't miss that treacle cake. Your turn next time."

"That's for Astrid to say."

Astrid looked as if she wanted to curl up like a hedgehog or withdraw into her shell like a snail. "Oh Daryll, well, it's awfully kind, you see I did more or less say to Angus – " Without another word, Daryll picked up his minute book and strode – if anyone so spidery could stride – out of the room.

A volcano seemed to have erupted in his breast, a turmoil of smoke and flames and molten lava, an explosion of hatred and malice, murder and mayhem. Visions of boiling oil, thumb-screws and stakes, hurling from battlements, severed heads, lashing to chariot wheels and other savage images flooded into his mind. Later, looking back when relative calm had been restored, he couldn't believe that emotions so foreign to his nature could have overwhelmed him. It came as a surprise to realise that feelings which, in greater men, could alter the course of history and form the stuff of the world's great tragedies could surge as fiercely through his own modest breast.

To go back to his lodgings would be intolerable. Either one or the other of his landladies – there were two, widowed sisters – would waylay him and deliver a long spiel about (in the case of Mrs Hubble) the plight of Zoroastrian refugees in Patagonia or (in the case of Mrs Earp) the necessity of neutering cats in cities, or he must face the solitude of his room with its collection of nature transparencies, its small but valued library of cassettes and half-finished homework for lesson eight of a correspondence course in Comparative World Religions which he hoped would broaden his mind.

In the company of birds and beasts, even though slumbering, of trees and grasses, 'of sun moon and stars, brother, all sweet things, likewise a wind on the heath' – in these lay his only salvation. Lammas Wood – his mind recoiled; that wood was forever tainted by its association with the cottage and its nauseous tenant. An idea germinated. Shuddering Park – where better? Wild tangled woods, owls hooting in hollow trees, damp and darkness, smells of leafmould and spotted fungi, the creaking of boughs, the rustle of falling leaves, stars glimpsed through a whispering tracery of twigs and foliage – Shuddering Park would be the perfect anodyne.

The gates to the pot-holed drive had long since rotted away.

Daryll ran his car a little way off the track, as it had become, got out and walked towards the house. The night was dark and rather windy, with occasional glimpses of a half moon. The gravel underfoot was damp with dew. Yes, that was a fox – people called it barking but it was more of a howl. One of Sebastian's perhaps? Daryll hoped it hadn't been inflicted with a collar and condemned to go about bleeping. An invasion of privacy if ever there was one. Now Sebastian had incarcerated several of his study animals in a pen. Quite a roomy one, admittedly, but still a prison.

From foxes, Daryll's mind turned to bats. Bats hanging from worm-eaten beams in the roof were a virtual certainty. Pipistrelles, for sure, but what if there should be, amongst them, a sub-colony of Greater Horseshoes? Now an endangered species and found in less than half a dozen British sites. To make such a discovery would indeed be a momentous event. Absurd, of course, even to imagine such a happening; local naturalists would long have found the site and kept it under observation. Still, no harm in having a quick look round.

The volcano in Daryll's bosom had, if not actually subsided, simmered down. Raging fires still raged, but more fitfully. If only he could concentrate on bats, the raging torment might be reduced to a dull ache. And one could live with a dull ache, after a fashion.

The house, square and tall – late seventeenth-century, he recalled from the prospectus – loomed blackly in the darkness. Beyond a lawn, level still but tangled with gone-to-seed grasses, was a portico, then a flight of steps. Daryll made his way round to the back. One of the back doors, he remembered, lacked a lock, or the lock had rusted in an unlocked position. The Reverend Pyle hadn't noticed it, or if he had, he'd made no comment. Daryll pushed against the door, which yielded, after a struggle, with a creak that pierced the silence with a sound like all the banshees in the bogs of Ireland screeching together.

Black as the pit, and smelling mustily of mould and dry-rot. Daryll's footsteps sounded on the bare boards like an army marching and, when he halted, silence flowed back to envelop him like a mountain mist. He groped his way along a wall in the direction, if he remembered rightly, of a broad staircase, struggling at the same time to subdue waves of panic. Suppose he lost his way in all this blackness? Crept round and round unable to locate the door? Imprisoned here till morning? What unknown creatures lurked in corners, under floors – giant rats, man-eating foxes, even escaped wolves?

And ghosts. Daryll did not, most emphatically did not, believe in ghosts. Of course there was no ghost in the attic smelling of carbolic. The woman who'd been baked in the bread-oven, the man found dangling from a rafter – dead and gone, leaving no soul in torment to haunt the scene of their grisly end. Of course. Yet what was that noise coming faintly to his ears – a muted moan, a hissing kind of whisper, a tortured sigh? It was coming closer. Hair standing on end, blood running cold – these seemed no longer metaphors but accurate descriptions. He halted and the sounds ceased. Then came a tapping from above, gentle, uneven – a sound that might be made by the feet of a dangling corpse, shaken by the wind, knocking against a wall. And to his nostrils came the faintest odour, the mere wisp of an odour, of carbolic. Easy to talk of dismissing thoughts. He dismissed them, but they wouldn't go.

Gradually, as his eyes adjusted, blackness turned to charcoal grey and shapes emerged. Through uncurtained windows, light filtered in to suffuse the encircling gloom. Not much light, only what a half-moon partially obscured by cloud could offer, but sufficient to enable Daryll to perceive the staircase ahead. Part of the bannister, he recalled, had rotted away and he made his way up with extreme caution, trying to fix his mind on bats and marvelling at his own temerity.

It seemed as if the stairway was thronged with silent, unseen presences watching his progress, pressing in upon him yet invisible, intangible, incorporeal. From below came a sound that induced almost total paralysis. A sort of scuffling, a dry moving sound. Perhaps rats. To be expected. Quite harmless. A vision filled his mind of giant rodents with long, pointed, bloodstained fangs. Gripping the bannister, calling on his last reserve of resolution, he proceeded up the stairs.

Halfway up, a different sort of sound altogether brought him to a halt. A real sound this time, real and no mistake. The sound of the engine of a car coming up the drive. Somehow this was more chilling than all the other noises, real or imaginary, that had affrighted Daryll hitherto. Who could be approaching Shuddering Park at this hour of the night? Only people engaged, surely, on some unholy mission. Was Shuddering Park the secret rendezvous of a conventicle of devil-worshippers, an orgiastic sect, a coven of witches?

The sound of the car's engine ceased. A silent pause seemed to go on forever. Then came a thump, creak, bump, resulting from the opening of a heavy door. The front door. Whoever it was had a key.

Perhaps, after all, only the Reverend, returned to inspect his property – though why should he do so in the middle of the night? And the key. It should still be in the office, to be handed over on completion. Footsteps were crossing the hall and a beam of torchlight flickered below. Then voices. Male, guttural – sharp, unfamiliar voices, awaking echoes from cobwebbed walls.

Daryll was cornered, stuck halfway up the stairs for perhaps the rest of the night. The least move, a sneeze, a creaking board, would betray his presence and then? A knife-thrust in the ribs, a slit throat, slow strangulation, strung up by a rope to a beam? His knees jellified. Those desperadoes down below must surely hear the thumping of his heart. Be still, my heart, he commanded. His heart paid no attention. Indeed, his whole body was out of control. To his anguish, he heard a loud rumble from his empty stomach. If only he'd eaten some of Judy's goatsmilk cheese . . .

Perhaps only burglars. But what was there to burgle? All he had noted in the way of furnishings were a couple of rusty, broken iron bedsteads on the first floor, a disintegrated dog-basket in the dining-room, a worm-eaten cheese-press in a cellar and a vat for mixing pigswill in what had evidently been a kitchen.

Not burglars: they were bringing something in, not taking anything away. Something that sounded heavy as they dumped it on the floorboards. With extreme caution, he lent over the bannister and peered into the hall.

Below were three black shapes lit fitfully by a torch held by one of the trio. They had carried in some kind of box or crate. One was giving orders to the others. Not in English. Foreigners. Daryll lent a little further over the bannister. There was a creak that sounded like a bullet shot, then a noise of splintering and the bannister gave way.

Daryll could remember little of subsequent events. He landed on something that, while hard, gave way a little. An agonising pain shot through him like the thrust of a spear. Broken bones or no, he scrambled to his feet and sprinted for the square of light that marked the open doorway. Shouts filled his ears as he reached the driveway and pelted down it, dodging pot-holes and tussocks, as if the wings of Mercury had been fitted to his heels. Shouts behind him, then silence. No sound of following runners, nor of an engine starting. One shoulder hurt abominably but he ran on, stumbling and recovering, towards the sanctuary of his car. The gods were with him. Safe, he thought, I've made it, as he leaned, gasping for breath, against the side of his Escort.

Headlights were coming at him from the other direction, where the drive turned into the main road. Another vehicle was on its way to Shuddering Park. Bushes, bent grasses, boles of trees, rutted gravel sprang to life in the headlight's beams. Daryll shrank back, uttering a silent prayer. Would the headlights pick up his Escort, half-hidden in the trees? It seemed inevitable. A fallen branch lay in the path of the approaching vehicle. The lights swung away from him as the driver took evasive action. Its tyres crunched on gravel as they rolled on.

Daryll's eyes followed the vehicle as it proceeded up the drive. It had slowed down, and its rear lights illuminated a familiar shape. A van. A yellow van, with a ladder on top.

Chapter Ten

IT WOULD have been pleasing to report that the great day had dawned bright, clear and sunny, but it had not. It dawned cloudy, grey and with a slight drizzle. But a weak front over the Pennines retreating towards the Skarrerat gave grounds for hope that bright intervals might occur later in the day. Harry Sproggs favoured older and, in his view, more reliable forecasting methods.

"Farmer Stubbins' cows was lying down all together, not one standing up. Sure sign of rain." On the other hand, he'd noticed several spiders' webs on a disused hayrack and gnats had been about the previous evening, equally sure signs of fine weather. Summing up, he quoted an old West Country saying:

> If Luke's day dawn bright
> Rain come afore night.
> If cloud wraps holy saint
> Sunshine be faint.

"Don't see as it matters really," he added, "seeing as it's all indoors nowadays." He finished his second cup of tea and went out to instal himself in the cab of his tractor, secure from the caprices of the weather.

"Well I must be off," Mrs Sproggs said, cleaning up the sink. "Crates of champagne they got down at Buggins', turned the packing room into a buffet. It's a wonder how they puts away all the food they do, the royals I mean, or all that's put before them anyway. *And* the drink."

"He's very abstemious so they say. You ought to get a super view, mum, will you be handing the champagne round do you suppose?"

"Washing up glasses. Poky little wash-room at the back. Elaine, now, *she's* the one to get the view."

"Elaine?"

"Right beside her he'll stand. Next to the computer."

"Elaine doesn't work the computer."

"Well I never, haven't you heard? Nicoletta packed it in, something to do with income tax, they had to find a substitute, there was a lot of argy-bargy and in the end Mr Dangle picked Elaine."

"She doesn't know how to work a computer any more than I do."

"Crash course, picked it up quick as a flash Mr Paxton said. So when the Prince presses the button or whatever it is starts off the machinery, there he'll be standing close to her as I am to the door, I shouldn't wonder. Well, I'll be off now. Dinner's in the oven, will you switch it on when dad gets back."

"Okay, Mum. Fancy Elaine." She'd never thought a lot of her cousin, amiable enough but not what you'd call a live wire. Now she'd got a boyfriend Justin, percussionist in the Rabid Rattlesnakes group, they'd performed in all sorts of places and there'd even been talk of a recording. Astrid wondered sometimes what Justin saw in Elaine, but that was his business and things seemed to work out all right. Elaine lived in Dudgrove Turville and had a Yorkshire terrier Moppet she was potty about. Silly little dog, Astrid thought. And now Elaine was going to work the computer. Couldn't be a difficult job.

Mrs Sproggs arrived at Hartley's to find the air tense with expectation and preparations well advanced. The champagne and snacks – *petites bouches écossaises*, salmon dreams, stuffed olives, salted almonds, *kartoffelstangen* – were already set out in Buggins' packing room, now swept and garnished with streamers and flags. Although Sybil's list of guests had been pared down to its final state, the telephone was still busy. What the cost of it all would be, Peter shuddered to think.

"Publicity, Peter. We must have the top Fleet Street men."

"I don't know whether the top Fleet Street men – "

Sybil dialled a number written on her pad. "Get me Mr Rupert Murdoch."

"Really, Sybil, I hardly think – "

"Not available? Why Not? In Australia? Well, he must have a number in Australia. Yes. One Moment. 010612 . . ."

"All this fuss," said Miss Cheer, entering with Sybil's bag and gloves. "What good it will do anyone I'm sure I don't know, and it's properly upset Heloise and Abelard. Abelard's been sick in the kitchen. Am I to make up Jo's bed?"

"I've no idea whether Jo's coming. Yes. Is that Mr Murdoch's Sydney office? Gone to Melbourne? The number please . . . Yes, Mr Murdoch in person. Of course it's urgent. Don't like to disturb him? Why not? The middle of the night? That should make no difference. The press never sleeps . . . Good Evening . . . Night then . . . The Prince would *not* be pleased if, by some mischance, or shall we say faulty organisation, your newspapers failed to give due prominence to . . . Yes, of course . . . Immediately, not a moment to lose . . . Yes, your very *top* man . . ."

At Buggins' Brushes, engineers had been at work all night to check and re-check the installations that would, at the flick of a switch, transform the factory from an old-fashioned sort of place full of chattering ladies indulging in tea-breaks into a shining example of the New Technology. At one side of the shop floor stood the computer, draped in a Union Jack. If a plump girl could be said to hover, Elaine was hovering round it, kneading a handkerchief and wishing fervently that it was all over and she was back in Dudgrove Turville having tea. Just her luck, her pains were coming on and they always made her feel like death warmed up.

"I know I'll do the wrong thing," she said to Dem Dangle.

"You don't have to do anything. It's all programmed. Just sit there, press the switch to turn on the current, then the Prince presses the button and the chips do the rest."

"You make it all sound so easy. As if I didn't really have to be here at all."

"That's about the size of it." Dem Dangle patted her shoulder in a fatherly way. "Don't you worry, Elaine. Just give the Prince one of your nicest smiles, he'll start it all up, then one of the kids from the Mums and Tots Wednesday Playgroup comes forward with a bouquet, then Mr Paxton says a few words – I hope just a few – and everyone shakes hands and the silver band strikes up 'He's a Jolly Good Fellow' and it's off to the buffet and the booze. Easy as pie.''

All very well for him to say that, Elaine thought, he's the manager, I do all the work. Though exactly what work, come to think of it, she found it hard to say. Who, she wondered, was the Jolly Good Fellow? The Prince, Mr Paxton, or perhaps the silicon chip? She'd had more of her share of worries lately with Justin, who'd stood her up on Tuesday which was ballroom dancing evening saying his group had got to play in Bath when all the time, so a well-wisher had told her, he was at a disco in Poggleton with one of the drum majorettes.

Security had proved to be a problem. Buggins' Brushes, established long before factories had been banished to the Industrial Estate by the old station yard, lay off a narrow lane running steeply from the High Street down to the river. The lane, called Maltings Way, had been sealed off at both ends by officers drafted in from neighbouring divisions to reinforce the police. Traffic had been diverted from the High Street, plain clothes men posted at strategic points. The question was, which points *were* strategic in the jumble of narrow twisting streets, irregular rooftops, unexpected alleyways, back gardens, potting sheds, rear premises of shops, crumbling walls, rubbish heaps and whatever, that had grown up over the ages around the site, whose actual location was a matter for dispute, of St Ninian's Well. Reggie Whackers had more or less given up the struggle.

"Intelligence," he said to Sergeant Bullstrode. "We must rely on that. Up to a point.''

"Yes, sir.''

"Any strangers seen about, acting suspiciously. Or just seen about. Reports of unusual events. That sort of thing.''

"Yes, sir.''

"Well?''

Sergeant Bullstrode pondered. Since the place had been turned upside down like it had, it was impossible to keep tabs in a sensible way on what was going on. Though he wouldn't admit it, the descent of the media had shaken his nerve. That and the matter of the guns and W.P.C. Wiggett and the crazy general, and people coming and going night and day trying to get a glimpse of Cantilevre and parking their cars on the roadside to photograph its chimneys. No sense to it. He made an effort to direct his thoughts into constructive channels.

"Well, sir, there's a bunch of foreigners come three days ago looking round, taking photographs too. Staying at The Red Lion."

"What sort of foreigners?"

"German, sir. Come about twins."

"Twins?"

"Yes, sir. It's the Council's idea but they say Mr Rufford's behind it. Got a brother in the Forces that married a German girl."

"You mean they had twins?"

"No, sir. Not as far as I know. It's Shipton that's to be a twin. With some German town." The Sergeant's voice expressed disapproval.

"I see. We can check on them. Anything else?"

"There was some Frenchies came a few weeks ago. Singing."

"Patriotic songs?"

"Religious, sir. Exchanged."

"You mean you've been exchanging singers?"

"That's right, sir. The Shipton Singers. Under the vicar, but Mrs Moake out at Turville is really behind it. The Mrs Moake that walks the hound puppies. Went to France last year in a coach. Got back safely," the Sergeant added, not sounding too pleased.

"Quite a cosmopolitan town."

"Yes, sir. There was a religious gentleman come to enquire about property in the neighbourhood, so I heard. American. One of those cranky churches I daresay."

"Plenty of those about. Anything else?"

"Not as you could take down in writing, sir. Rumours, mostly."

"Such as?"

"I heard it said, a young gentleman that works for Mr Borrowdale got bitten in the neck by a ghost out at Shuddering Park. No evidence, not as I'm aware of."

"Hard to get evidence in such a case that would stand up in

court."

"Yes, sir. He's one of the Eggologists, cranky lot. There's to be a badger demo when the Prince arrives."

"We'll see about that."

The planning of the demo had called for a degree of resourcefulnes that would have made the reputation of a Commander-in-Chief. It was no good supposing that the supporters could simply march along the High Street, turn down Maltings Lane and line up at the entrance to Buggins'. Everything was sealed off, re-routed, controlled by uniformed men.

"Harassment, that's what it amounts to," Judy Mustard complained. "Coppers all over the place acting aggressively, provoking peaceful citizens. Denying us our constitutional rights. They'll have a riot on their hands if they go on like that."

Angus was soothing. "Don't you worry, Judy. We'll find a way round."

This was to be taken literally. By assembling in the old station yard, crossing the river by Abbot's Bridge and into Silver Street (the territory of Shipton's prostitutes in medieval times), skirting the Jubilee Gardens and The Red Lion's stable yard, the marchers could arrive at the car park at the back of Buggins' Brushes, which was overlooked by the windows of the packing room. Here, while the distinguished guests nibbled their snacks and quaffed champagne, the marchers could make their protest and could not fail to be seen.

"Now then, comrades, time for action! Up and awa'!" It was a day of the kilt for Angus. "Over the river and up the hill to save our badgers in the name of Queen and Country! All together now to the tune of 'John Brown's Body'. Judy, you lead the way."

"Brave Brock's body lies a-mouldering in the grave, Brave Brock's body lies a-mouldering . . . ." The sound swelled as the group of twenty or so members carrying banners and a ten-foot-long model of a badger wound its way over Abbots' Bridge, up Silver Street and along towards Buggins' car park at the factory's rear.

The same idea about the car park had come to others. The

drum majorettes were already paraded in the section marked Vans and Lorries, resplendent in white boots and batons, red caps and saucy uniforms, but unable to manoeuvre because the silver band, in the section marked Staff Only, was letting go on 'Pomp and Circumstance' to such effect that the majorettes own musicians, poised to strike up the 'Teddy Bear's Picnic', were overwhelmed. Members of the Mums and Tots Wednesday Playgroup, assembled in the section marked No Parking, were looking bemused.

Judy was not one to take that sort of thing lying down. Advancing on the drum major, she asserted the claim of Ecologists to a territory from which those engaged merely on cheap entertainment must be expelled. The major did not see it in that light at all. In her opinion, the importance of drum majorettes, a disciplined force whose part in keeping up the morale of the nation could not be over-estimated, had a prior claim over those concerned merely to preserve badgers, and diseased badgers at that. Fortunately, perhaps, for the preservation of the Queen's peace in Shipton Wick, the music of the silver band drowned the voices of the champions on both sides.

Unexpectedly, the band stopped playing. Angus again. Blessed as he was with robust lungs, his message "Free drinks all round" managed to reach the conductor's ears.

"What, now?" asked the conductor.

"At the end of the show. Meanwhile, give our demo a break and play 'John Brown's Body' when we line up under the windows when the Prince comes."

"Thirsty work, you know."

"Two rounds, then."

"A deal."

Meanwhile, something like confusion reigned in Maltings Lane. Up the High Street came an ox-drawn dray decorated with branches and bearing an enormous painting executed in magenta, puce, purple, burnt sienna and yellow ochre, of a subject hard to identify. In front walked white-clad figures with skulls and crossbones daubed in black on their robes, playing flutes. The dray was manned by youths and maidens clad in sacks and sandals, all with blood-red hands. Behind walked a figure in a monk's habit tolling a bell, and behind him attendants holding up a banner bearing the legend "Victims of Inhuman Cruelty – Liberate Laboratory Animals Now". On the obverse was another message: "The Right to Live for Mice and Men".

Two policemen stepped in front of the oxen and raised their arms. The oxen, which were large with spreading horns, plodded on. "Hey, stop those bullocks!" Neither the bullocks nor the passengers on the dray paid any attention. One of the policemen laid his hands on a pair of horns and attempted to turn the animal's head. The ox paid no attention. Someone, somehow, had evidently got the message across to them that they were to proceed down Maltings Lane. They proceeded. Truncheons were clearly ineffective in such a predicament. Sharpshooters there might be, hidden behind chimney-stacks, but sharp-shooting the oxen seemed to offer no solution. Walkie-talkie sets pleaded in vain for instructions. The oxen plodded down Maltings Lane and, directed it seemed by some mysterious telepathy, halted outside the factory gates. The gates through which, at any moment, the royal car would turn.

Peter Paxton, standing near the entrance with a cluster of notables in attitudes of expectant deference, looked upon the scene with horror. The equipage he recognised; it belonged to the commune; was Jo there upon the dray? Or was she fluting? The painting was in only too familiar a vein. Simon . . . Jo . . . the Prince . . . the police . . . Peter felt the earth crumbling beneath his feet.

Sybil in her wheel-chair, with Charlotte beside her, was equally distraught. "Quickly, quickly, *do* something!" she cried as her hand went out to seize a telephone that wasn't there. "The Director of Veterinary Services, the Meat Marketing Board . . ."

"Charlotte," Lady Evers said to her daughter in urgent tones. "Remember that time at Kota Kinabaul when the water buffalo . . .?

A light sprang into Charlotte's eyes. "Of course. But Cherub . . ."

"Sybil left Heloise and Abelard in her car. Just over there, on double yellow lines."

Without another word Charlotte sprinted through the factory gates and into Maltings Lane. There was Sybil's Mini Metro half on the pavement, unlocked. (Sybil never locked her car, taking the view that protection of her property was the task of the police.) Heloise and Abelard were miffed, to put it mildly. Left, deserted, on the back seat, a nasty little boy had made faces at them through the window and they hadn't been able to bite back. Charlotte swept them up – a further indignity – and, with inciting noises, deposited them beside the dray.

Dogs may be divided into two classes: those who are merely afraid of cattle and those who can't abide them. Heloise and Abelard belonged to the latter class. A hackle-raising bovine smell came to their nostrils. Yapping furiously, they charged.

Few cattle are at ease with dogs. Either they rush at them, hoping to put them to flight or even trample them underfoot, or they take evasive action. These oxen fell into the latter class. With balls of fluff impelled by fury and armed with small but pointed teeth at their heels, they fled. The dray rumbled at speed down Maltings Lane. The flutes were stilled. The policemen wiped their brows and straightened their helmets. Charlotte resumed her place by Sybil's side. "That water buffalo would have knocked us over," Marjorie Evers said to her husband *sotto voce*, "if it hadn't been for the ADC's pointer. Young Piers Fortesque. I always thought that he and Charlotte . . ."

"Ssh, my dear. Here he comes."

The royal car turned through the gates and the great moment had come. There were introductions, smiles, congratulations, affability all round. The Lord Lieutenant said a few words, the Prince made a graceful reply.

Everything was going as Peter would have wished. Business-like. Brisk. True, the silver band was there, also the drum majorettes, but they had been kept out of sight and might even strike a festive note not inappropriate to the occasion when the ceremony was over and the champagne flowed.

On the shop floor, anticipation electrified the air. Members of the workforce had been busy the evening before with shampoo and curlers, washing powders and irons, and were looking their best. The floor was almost shiny from repeated applications of old Uzell's brush. The first to be presented was Dem Dangle, scarcely recognisable in a stiff brown suit and button-hole of white heather. Then came the shop-stewards in order of precedence, Mrs Sandboy first; six others should have followed but Mandy of the USGSCW (the one with two branch members) had gone to the top of Silbury Hill to greet the Second Coming, and Jayne was at home with a cold, so there were only five.

And there stood the computer, swathed in its flag with Elaine standing beside it, nervous as a dozen kittens. Her nasty nagging pain wouldn't go away. Justin had been abrupt, in fact quite cross, when she'd brought up the subject of the disco in Poggleton and, to crown it all, Moppet had a bad go of worms. She found it hard to concentrate on the computer, and the crash course had left her with only the haziest idea of what it was all about.

Escorted by Peter and Dem Dangle, with half a dozen followers in tow, the Prince approached. They came to a halt. Mr Paxton said a few words and the Prince made a brief reply: pleasure to perform this function, all to be congratulated, historic occasion, Shipton Wick his future home leading the way, opportunities for youth, rewards for enterprise, socially desirable, whiter teeth, health and beauty – some sort of joke there, but Elaine was too distraught to take it in.

A sign from Mr Dangle and she gripped the corners of the flag with sweating hands, jerked it off, pressed the switch, hoping to God it was the right one, stepped back, got entangled in the flag and nearly fell, and stood panting with her hair awry and her face red with embarassment. She'd be a laughing stock when all this was over.

At last, over it was. The Prince stepped forward to press the key that Mr Dangle indicated. With satisfaction Peter heard his machinery starting to hum, shafts to rotate, wheels to revolve, capstans to thump, ratchets to engage, dies to be punched, all with flawless order, harmony and smoothness, perfect discipline. No false notes, no ragged errors, no clumsy human blundering like that silly girl whom Dangle had put on the computer.

Here was harmony and order, Peter thought, such as may be

found in the motions of the universe, the rotation of planets, the wheeling of galaxies, the remote and unchanging progression of the stars. For a moment, he felt strangely uplifted. Here was poetry, here was romance, here was the excitement of creation. His own creation, and all these shafts and wheels and cogs and jigs and all the rest were dancing to the tune of those silent, invisible chips. Was God himself a silicon chip? All this is going to my head, he thought, I must come down to earth. The climax has come. The moment to unveil to the world the first White Prince.

With measured steps Peter walked across the floor to where the cameras were grouped around the birthplace of The White Prince. In his hand he held the leather case embossed in gold letters in which it was to be swaddled for presentation to the royal guest. A whirr, a click, and the first one dropped neatly into place from an endless belt which would beat away its multitudinous successors to the packing room. Gleaming white, created without human touch, the child of the silicon chip. Peter held it up, almost too moved to speak.

"To mark the honour of Your Royal Highness's visit, I name this toothbrush The White Prince."

Only then, in the glare of many flashlights, did he see it clearly. At such moments, only tried and trusted clichés can fit the occasion. He stood as if turned to stone. He felt as if turned to stone. The White Prince was not as other toothbrushes. The firstborn of the chip was deformed. The bristles were there all right, but not at one end of the handle. The bristles were neatly grouped in the middle.

It is at such moments, also, that a man is tested and tried. Most will sink beneath the cruel waves of calamity, seeking only oblivion. Amid the ruins of their hopes and dreams they will succumb, the spirit beaten out of them, the waves closing over their heads. But the few, the chosen few, firm as granite, resilient as rubber, will from the nettle of disaster snatch the flower of victory. Not for nothing had Peter risen from humble origins, built up a business, controlled a workforce, earned respect and esteem, survived setbacks and failures, sustained rebuffs – in short, become a successful business man. His mind worked almost as swiftly as the silicon chip.

"Your Royal Highness my Lords, ladies and gentlemen: now you see revealed the secret so closely guarded in our small community until this moment. Not only is The White Prince the world's first microchip toothbrush, it is made to an entirely new design, the product of years of research by our finest designers and of prolonged experiment. A breakthrough in technology, and here I must pay tribute to our workforce, who have not only toiled without complaint to increase their productivity, but kept the secret hugged to their breasts. The bristles of old-fashioned toothbrushes were, as you know, positioned at one end of the handle, thus failing to utilise the full potential of the product. This has, for all these years, posed awkward problems for the left-handed, not to mention the disabled."

Peter paused; there was a round of clapping; a murmur of "hear, hear".

"Your Royal Highness, my Lords, ladies and gentlemen, with this new design we have solved these problems. By using *both* hands, considerably greater pressure can be brought to bear, the motion is more regular, the teeth will be brighter, the time spent on this necessary function will be less. A number of our leading dental surgeons have enthusiastically endorsed the new design. I think I may justly claim, your Royal Highness, my Lords, ladies and gentlemen, that with this revolutionary development, fraught with possibilities for good in the shape of greatly improved hygiene especially in the Third World, that Britain, our poor battered old Britain, still has the brains, the energy, the inventiveness, the skill and expertise, to lead the world!"

The round of clapping became a roll of sound, hear-hears resounded over the shop floor and if everyone had not already been standing, Peter would have received a standing ovation. Someone struck up 'For He's a Jolly Good Fellow', and a small girl from the Mums and Tots Wednesday Playgroup was propelled forward clasping a squashed bouquet. In the distance, the silver band burst into the national anthem, drowning the shouts of 'Save our badgers' and the lowing of oxen, which had eventually been coaxed into the car park. It was a moment of universal euphoria.

"Your Royal Highness, my Lords, ladies and gentlemen, refreshments await us all in the buffet and please be good enough to come this way." Peter shepherded his guests into the packing room, saying in tones of urgency to his helpers "For God's sake take round the champagne quickly and lash it out, keep all the glasses filled." There was a scramble as members of the press rushed out to telephone their stories, and television crews to load their reels into fast cars. The crew from Nippon Television was bound for Heathrow and soon news of Britain's latest break-through in technology would be known in Tokyo.

As the royal party moved towards the buffet, Peter caught Dem Dangle's eye. It had the look one might expect to find in the eye of a tortured sheep. The only decent thing, Peter felt, would be to put him out of his misery.

"That silly bitch Elaine", he said, "I shall boil her in oil."

"With bristles in the middle", Dem pointed out, "you can't get the brush into the sides of your mouth."

"The same thought had occurred to me."

"So only your front teeth can be brushed."

"Only your front teeth show."

"You seem to take it very lightly."

"What else can I do?"

"I've stopped the plant, of course. But not before a whole run has come off the line. What are we to do with them?"

"Treasure them. They'll be period pieces, valuable, like faulty stamps."

Dem Dangle shrugged his shoulders. The ultimate disaster seemed to have destroyed the boss's reason. But he, Dem, would have to face the music from the girls next day. Not, if you came to think of it, that they'd be there much longer to make music or anything else. Only while they worked out their notices. Well, it was an ill wind he supposed. Redundancy might do a bit of good to attendancies at the ballroom dancing classes. He hoped that Elaine wouldn't try and throw herself under a bus.

Out of the windows, the drum majorettes could be seen marching to and fro with the Major swinging her baton while the silver band played the 'Teddy Bear's Picnic'. Badger placards were waving about and the would-be liberators of laboratory animals were holding hands and dancing round in circles, chanting a dirge. Sybil was talking with delighted animation to the Prince, Arthur Longshott was looking at his watch and wondering whether the time had come to go, Lady Pandora was offering the Prince a plate of snacks. "*Please* take an olive, sir," Peter heard her say. The Prince smiled and selected a salted almond. Lady Pandora looked furious. "I *must* have the Prince's olive-stone," she said to Arthur. "I must, I must."

"They're stuffed olives," he replied.

Chapter Eleven

DR EDWARD POMFRET of 127 Eastern Avenue, Pittsburgh, U.S.A. – or so he appeared on the register of The Golden Fleece in Poggleton – was displeased. He sat in his bedroom with a glass of mineral water by his side, a small, neat suitcase at his feet and a shiny black briefcase on the table, and glared at Angus. His hair was frizzy, his eyes onyx-black, his suit well-pressed, his true name Hakkab, and his life dedicated to forwarding the aims of the Levantine Liberation League.

"I buy the guns," he said, "Sten guns, bren guns, patchett guns, big guns and little guns, the best. And time-bombs, very good time-bombs, very expensive. I have them packed, labelled – I have the labels specially printed, Toothsome Pet Foods. The mansion is bought, the guns are packed, Giuseppe takes them to this empty mansion hidden in a forest – tucked away you said as if it were a baby in a cot. All is arranged. And then what happens?"

"That's just the question," Angus said. "What exactly did?"

"Giuseppe says that he was attacked by a ghost."

"Giuseppe was a little, shall we say, over-excited."

"And the guns. You ordered them to be thrown into a lake."

"A pond. Giuseppe assured me that the crates are water-tight."

"That is true. They are in sealed containers. But they will not achieve our object at the bottom of a lake."

"We shall retrieve them from the bottom of the pond, not lake. It's quite shallow, popular with nesting ducks. But if Giuseppe's ghost talks about his latest haunting, we must expect a pretty thorough search of Shudding Park. We must hope they won't drag the pond."

"Hope is not enough."

Angus nodded, and poured the beer that Dr Pomfret, alias

Hakkab, had, with some reluctance, ordered for his guest. Hakkab had not intended to come personally to the scene of action. His part was in the background, directing and controlling events. But already, in the carefully planned run-up to the operation, there had been a slip, a human failing. Giuseppe of the Scarlet Brotherhood had panicked. "How could I tell there was a ghost?" he had demanded. Idiotic Italians, imagining things, giving way to impulses, unreliable. He should have insisted on Turks. Turks would not have talked nonsense about ghosts.

"Very well," he said curtly. "The guns are in the lake and can be recovered. The empty house is in our hands. Guiseppe and his men are in this town. In hiding."

"In a YMCA hostel. Delegates to an ecumenical conference in Cheltenham." Angus took a good swig at his beer, and added: "You've heard of Achilles?"

"Achilles Kyriakydes? Who had successfully scuppered three of his vessels before the Scarlet Brotherhood caught him on his island? Fifty million dollar rap, I think it was."

"There was another Achilles. Bullet-proofed all over except for one heel."

"You are talking nonsense."

"An Achilles heel is the vulnerable spot. Everyone has one and that is the basis of our plan."

Hakkab fiddled irritably with his glass. He should never have allowed himself to be mixed up with such idiots. In his own world, things were straightforward. Their basis was the gun, not riddles. Here, all talk and no action. "You speak in riddles. I do not like riddles. Speak plainly."

"Our man is closely guarded day and night. Trained marksmen always nearby. Bodyguards always on duty. But the bodyguards need to know just where the Prince is going to be. If they do not . . ." Angus drained the rest of his beer. Hakkab had ordered only one can. No spark of geniality in those onyx eyes. People devoted to the brotherhood of man, he had noted, were never brotherly.

"You say there is a vulnerable spot. Identify."

"The hunting field."

Hakkab frowned. His visage was, so far as Angus could see,

permanently dour. Doubtless life was dour when refreshment was confined to mineral water. Perhaps a harem? It seemed unlikely, but you never knew. He expounded.

"The Prince goes hunting. With dogs and horses. The dogs chase the quarry, the Prince follows, mounted on a horse. He goes where the quarry leads him and not to a place his guards know in advance. Perhaps the marksmen follow, but not at his side. He's vulnerable."

"So what does that avail? The bodyguards do not know the direction in which the Prince will go. Nor do we."

"There is a way."

"Explain."

"It's called a bag fox. You put the fox into a sack, you drag the sack along the ground and the dogs will follow the scent."

"Scent? These foxes are perfumed?"

"You could say that. Not with the perfume of Arabia, but they have their own. Look at this map."

Angus drew from his pocket an enlarged section of an Ordnance Survey map and spread it on the table. Hakkab eyed it with distrust. This man was mad. Dogs, foxes, scent, lunatic talk. How could the World Revolutionary Council have been taken in? Angus was prodding a finger at the map.

"Here's Cantilevre, see? The hounds meet here. The Opening Meet. A long tradition. They proceed to Lammas Wood to seek their fox. When the dogs find it, they give tongue – bark, that means – the huntsman blows his horn and away they go. In this direction."

Lammas Wood was bounded on the north side by a minor road, whence a gate gave access to the wood. Beside the gate was an old shed, disused but still intact. Angus traced a line with his finger through the wood and to the gate beside the shed. "This is the way we have dragged our fox. The dogs follow, then the riders, towards that gate into the road. Two of our men are in the shed, another is in the wood concealed in undergrowth. He has a gun."

"Of course."

"It is a special kind of gun. It doesn't fire a bullet. It fires a syringe that contains a drug. The syringe hits the horse. Within a hundred yards or so, the horse's legs start to wobble, then it collapses. Its rider stands beside it, confused, wondering what has happened. There has been no shot to cause alarm. Giuseppe and his colleague burst from the shed, they seize the Prince swift as lightning, in a flash they are in our fast car waiting in the road. Many cars will be there, ours is not conspicuous and with a bit of luck it will be away before anyone can block it or take its number."

"A bit of luck. In our enterprises, luck is not included. Only planning, skill, speed and faultless execution."

"Speed is the essence. Speed and timing. Local knowledge. The element of surprise. All there, you'll see."

"Yes, we shall see." Hakkab did not sound enthusiastic.

"In three weeks, the Crown Jewels will be ours in all their glory. Not to mention an obliterated Israel, a black government in South Africa, a united Ireland, the abolition of all banks, judges and the American navy, a black woman Pope and free trade unions in Ecuador."

"And freedom for the Laxative Islands," Hakkab added automatically. Angus folded his map and said: "The plan is ripening. You will see."

As he closed the door Hakkab picked up the telephone, dialled a number and said: "Valhalla Funeral Parlour here. Two dozen carnations on Friday week." "Any message?" asked a voice. "Immediate condolences."

Angus emerged into the bottom end of Poggleton's busy market place and headed for the car park, whistling a tune. A few moments later a dark-complexioned lady in a tight-fitting T-shirt, jeans and red-heeled shoes sallied forth from The Pincushion, a small emporium displaying embroidery kits and skeins of wool. She followed in his wake, swinging on her shoulder a green airline bag. A shop window displaying cakes, buns, eclairs, pies and other eatables caught Angus' attention. Pausing to feast his eye, he glanced back until that eye came to rest upon the dark-complexioned lady, who was examining an assortment of shoes. Angus entered the cake shop, bought half a dozen doughnuts and sauntered out by a back door leading into a passage which in turn led into a street, along which the car park could be approached by way of a yard containing garden implements and the loading area of a wine shop. In a few minutes he was on his way to Shipton Wick.

Hakkab had barely started on his second bottle of mineral water when the telephone rang. "Floral Fancies here. Unfortunately we have sold out of carnations. Will daisies do?" "They will not. Obtain carnations." Hakkab put down the receiver sharply, a deeper scowl than ever on his face. More blunders.

Angus, bowling along the Shipton road in his yellow van with a ladder on top, was in a more sanguine mood. His was, indeed, a sanguine nature. The pieces were fitting together, things moving in the right directions. Sebastian, conveniently, had three study foxes in a pen, and a map of Lammas Wood showing every foxes' earth and very nearly every tree. He had gladly given Angus lessons in the use of his dart-gun, with a view to a future joint study of red deer in Scotland. Now, home to tea and doughnuts.

He stopped his van outside the Sproggs' cottage, knocked and entered. Mrs Sproggs was frying sausages. "Smell delicious," Angus said. "Taste delicious too, I bet. Like your Boiled Devon Treacle Cake."

Mrs Sproggs turned the sausages. "Boil you another if you like when things settle down. If they ever do. Builders all over the place turning the pig-sties into a police station, passes you've got to have to get where you've always been and you can't walk along the High Street without getting tangled up in all them cables the telly people trail about. And now there's talk of Princess Margaret coming to the district on top of Princess Anne. Where's it going to stop, that's what I'd like to know?"

"Troubles never come singly."

"That's what Harry's said time and again. Mr Paxton, now, he's got his troubles and no mistake."

"Toothbrushes again?"

"No, Jo again. Over at that commune of hers. That Moonshit or whatever he's called rang up for Mr Paxton to come quick, said she's got hold of poison and someone's died but who it was I couldn't hear on the phone. Took the message. Mr Paxton went off in a fair tizzy."

Astrid came in before she could enlarge upon this pregnant theme. Angus, adopting a courtly old-world style, kissed her hand.

"Come off it, Angus," she said, not exactly bridling but not looking displeased. Mrs Sproggs said pointedly: "Well, now, Astrid, you'll be wanting your tea. If Mr MacBean will excuse us." She couldn't help having a bit of a soft spot for Mr MacBean, always a cheerful word, yet there was something about him . . . interested in Astrid, that stood out a mile, and of that she could *not* approve. Too old for one thing, and who was he anyway? Where was his family? Might have a wife, several wives if it came to that, in Scotland or some such foreign place.

"I'll be off, then," Angus said. "Brought you some doughnuts for your tea." He presented them with a flourish. "Don't forget the meeting tomorrow evening to mull over plans for the demo at the Opening Meet."

"Demos . . . Well, I don't know."

"New brew of elder-flower hock. Super. We're counting on you." He kissed her hand again. "See you tomorrow."

"What's *he* after I'd like to know," Mrs Sproggs remarked as he closed the door. "You look out, Astrid, fine words butter no parsnips, nor those foreign ways neither, anyone can see he's sweet on you."

"Oh, come off it, mum, it's just his way." Astrid busied herself with cups and plates and other utensils needed for tea. "Daryll may come by later. Got a bad shoulder. Tripped over something at that old place that's haunted, Shuddering Park."

"Well, I never. Dad's late."

"Latest is, there's Germans coming to Shipton, to do with twinning. We're to be twinned with some German town."

Mrs Sproggs disapproved, a view shared by others among her fellow citizens. A majority in the Town Council, however, had come down in favour of the project, advanced in the first instance by Councillor Bob Rufford. Shipton, they recognised, must not be left behind by the wave of twinning that appeared to be sweeping the country, or at any rate that part of it in which Shipton was situated. Poggleton had twinned already with a French town. If Shipton Wick held back, it would be in danger of presenting to the world the image of an out-of-date, backward-looking little hick town still under the shadow of Ethelbald the Elder, ill suited to the age of microchips.

Councillor Snape had led the opposition. "Free trips to Hunland, that's what it's all about," he had said in his usual high-pitched, snarky voice. "High jinks and holidays on the ratepayers, especially for those with relatives in that direction. Such as brothers. Then over come the Jerries back to Shipton and there's wining and dining and all that tommyrot and who pays? How about enlargement of the sewage works? Cleaning up the toilets which are a disgrace? No money for all that but plenty for high jinks and shenanigans with a lot of Jerries. Throw it out."

Councillor Snape had been over-ruled. Like it or not, Shipton Wick was now front page news and couldn't risk being held up to ridicule for lagging behind. One of the younger Councillors had even put forward the suggestion that Shipton Wick should lead the way by twinning not with a German but with a Third World town, thus proving itself to be not only forward-looking, but anti-racist as well. The problem had been to distinguish from an atlas which names were those of towns and which of rivers, hills, swamps, deserts, forests, lakes, tribal territories and other features, indeed which of the dotted lines were international boundaries and which were roads, district divisions, contours or footpaths. General Mkubwa, who might have advised the Council, was absent in Northumberland on manoeuvres involving the WRAC and WRNS, having been appointed Military Adviser to H.M. Forces (Womens' Section) in order to instruct commando units in jungle warfare, bush deployment and guerrilla tactics. He already had a unit of canoeists in training on the river Tyne and coming along, it was reported, very nicely, although a plan to dam the river and construct a series of rapids had run up against objections from the Department of the Environment. A public enquiry, likely to last three or four years, was about to begin.

Peter Paxton was, as a rule, a regular attendant at Council meetings, but on this occasion he had sent his apologies. In a state of considerable agitation he had driven hurriedly to the commune, wondering whether Jo had already been taken off in handcuffs to face a murder charge.

His fears deepened when he parked his car as near as possible to the Temple of the Sun. All was silent and deserted. That should have been reassuring, but it was not. The silence of the dead. An air of mourning hung like a miasma over the sheds, huts and temples. Donkin's strongest pest destroyer . . . Jo's savage mutterings about someone whose name sounded like Queen Anne . . . the message Mrs Sproggs had relayed, unclearly, from someone she called the Moonshit . . . Where was everyone? Jo, her fellow devotees, the Munshi himself?

A distant keening caught his ear. Not exactly keening, but a subdued wailing with a vaguely Eastern cadence. Presently a small procession came into view from behind the ablution block. The mourners were in a single file, two of them bearing something covered by a blanket on a stretcher. A bier. A small bier, noted Peter, by now weak-kneed with apprehension and clammy with cold sweat. A child perhaps.

A portly figure in a sackcloth robe, bearded, hook-nosed, his hands folded before him devoutly and a belt of jingly bangles round his waist, brought up the rear. The procession wound its way into the Temple of the Sun, the votaries fixing their eyes steadfastly upon the ground. The Munshi detached himself from the column, approached Peter and bowed gravely. Peter's throat was dry.

"Jo," he began, "is she – I hope – is something wrong?"

"There is no wrong that cannot be righted, if the emanations of the ethos can be tuned to the infinite centrality of the transcendental nirvana," the Munshi replied, in an Oriental kind of sing-song. "But it is true that, on our base earthly plane, there has been a sorry tragedy."

Peter steadied himself by resting a hand on the mudguard of his car. "Have the police . . .?"

The Munshi shook his head. His hair was long and black, his beard fuzzy, his eyes keen behind tinted spectacles. Peter felt himself to be in the presence of a mask. He didn't think he wanted to know what lay behind it.

"Where is Jo?"

"Jo has left us. We shall direct our meditations towards her re-integration into the community of Khama."

"Yes, indeed. But where is she *now*?"

"On the way, I believe, to Bootle."

"*Bootle*?" Peter's thoughts were reeling. "This seems to be a mad-house, not a commune. Who, or what, is on that bier?"

The Munshi cast his eyes down and looked mournful. "The earthly remains of our treasured Krishna, whose essence has mingled with the pneuma of his ancestors on the path to nirvana."

Peter recalled the size and apparent weight of the object under the blanket. "A child?"

"A goat."

There was a pause while Peter endeavoured to adjust his thoughts to this revelation.

"A sacred goat," the Munshi repeated, "whose spiritual value is beyond calculation. But on our base earthly plane a sacred goat, white and spotless, has a value that can be quantified. As I am sure you will understand."

The conversation, like the sacred goat, had now descended to an earthly plane on which Peter felt less at sea. "I'm sorry about your goat, but it's got nothing to do with me."

"There I must disagree. Krishna's innocent life, an impulse in the field of the eternal sensorium, was snatched from him in his prime by the action, prompted I fear by unspiritual motives, of your daughter."

"You mean she killed the goat?"

"I do."

"Why in God's name should Jo kill a goat?"

"The crime was committed with a fruit-spray intended to inflict serious injury, perhaps worse, on one of our most sincere votaries. Some of the deadly liquid fell upon the grass. The grass withered. Krishna ate of the poisoned herb and surrendered his earthly shell to Vishna. His spirit lives on."

Light was beginning to dawn. "What was the name of the votary Jo sprayed with an insecticide?"

"Roseanne."

"Ah, yes. I see."

"Perhaps you do not see with unclouded vision." The Munshi's voice took on a sharper note. "On the spiritual plane, Jo allowed the evil of jealousy to poison her psyche. On the earthly plane, she has poisoned a valuable animal. Our earthly plane is ruled by laws which provide for compensation."

Munshi or not, thought Peter, he's a pretty clued-up old sod. "In that case, there must be a post-mortem. The goat may have died of heart failure, over-eating, or old age."

"Krishna died of poison. One thousand pounds."

Peter recoiled as if shot. "You must be crazy! Not a penny without a veterinary report. And even then," he added hastily, "I admit no liability. Jo's over eighteen."

The Munshi bowed his head. His glinting glasses, his untamed black beard were faintly menacing. A dolorous wail came from the Temple of the Sun. "In that case, it would be impossible to prevent the sorry tale from coming to the attention of the media."

"The media would not be interested in the death of your goat."

"The media, Mr Paxton, will be very interested in a serious criminal charge brought against the daughter of a prominent citizen of Shipton Wick, a town on which their interest is focused already."

"What the blazes do you mean by a serious criminal charge?"

"Attempted murder."

Peter found himself speechless and shaking with rage, his heart pounding, his throat constricted. He needed all his self-control to prevent himself from hitting out at this absurd, and now threatening, tubby figure in a sack-cloth robe.

"Blackmail!" He positively spat out the word.

"There are witnesses."

"I shall call the police."

"I shall call the *News of the World*."

"Jo never . . . . . It's not attempted murder to use an insecticide . . . . ." But he could see the headlines. A *crime passionel*, certainly *passionel* if not actually *crime* – or was it? Assault and battery? Actual bodily harm? Possessing an offensive weapon? The local Bench would make a meal of it, Jo would be a laughing stock and as for Sybil . . . "Not a penny more than fifty, and even that's absurd."

"One thousand."

Five minutes later, Peter drew out his cheque-book. The fires of fury raged in his bosom as he wrote out a cheque for five hundred pounds.

He found Sybil in her writing-room, sipping tea. In his absence, Jo had come and gone, collecting *en route* a pair of jeans, a couple of sweaters, a mackintosh, several charms and a nasty looking carved image whose function in cabbalistic rites observed by a secret society in Nigeria could only be guessed at. Evidently Jo's trial of strength with Roseanne had not ended with the demise of Krishna. Peter outlined the situation to his wife, omitting the painful matter of the cheque.

"I can see that Jo has overstayed her welcome at the commune," Sybil remarked. "But where, why and what is Bootle?"

"In Lancashire. Why, God knows."

"A young man," Sybil concluded.

"Called Simon. Gone to Bootle, with Jo in hot pursuit as the military say."

"I wonder why Simon went to Bootle."

"Probably to escape from Jo," Peter suggested. He'll find it difficult, he was thinking. Like mother, like daughter. A chip off the old block. "Who would have daughters?" he said.

Chapter Twelve

THE SEASON of the year was advancing. A gale had swept many leaves, as yet barely yellowed, off the trees, and toppled over dustbins; rainstorms had bedraggled Michaelmas daisies and filled gateways with squelchy mud. Onions and apples had been harvested, blackberries were over. In sepulchral tones, people informed each other that days were drawing in, another summer over, man's time was about to revert to God's and soon it would be lights on for tea and electricity going up again. Old Donkin had dug the first leeks and sprayed the winter cauliflowers for the last time. At The Goat and Compasses, the Sweetapples' tortoise had vanished to hibernate under a heap of straw in the corner of a shed. In the chilly waters of the river Tyne the WRNS crack Canoe Commandoes had overturned their vessel and the General was transferring the unit to the river Tamar in Cornwall. The Prince still hadn't moved into Cantilevre but his horses were in the stables and it was said on good authority that he would be installed in time for the Opening Meet.

The good authority was Charlotte, whom Arthur Longshott was finding more helpful than ever. She had volunteered to cook him a little dinner for his birthday and had turned out a meal he could only describe as memorable. Soon his duties would keep him no longer at Cockscombe Castle and a pleasant little interlude would be over. He felt quite sad. The Castle was a comfortable billet, the Gwents unexacting and as a rule invisible hosts. The Marquess, on the rare occasions when Arthur encountered him, smiled politely and said: "I believe you are staying here? I hope you are comfortable." Lady Gwent was nearly always out on some business or other, whether Brownies, Mothers' Union, Bell-ringers, Parochial Church Council, Shipton Singers or one of many other bodies contributing to the good of the community. What with all these meetings and other matters such as organising the collection of clothes for refugees, milk bottle tops for the hospital and unwanted spectacle frames for Oxfam, it was seldom that she had an evening off but, when she did, Arthur was invited to play a game of Scrabble. Lady Gwent was a previous holder of the County Championship and might have gone far on the national level had not pressure of work stood in the way.

Never a dull moment, Arthur reflected, in Shipton Wick. And now, as if all that wasn't enough, there was to be a sponsored Bed Race. Sponsored walks had become so much a part of Shipton's lifestyle that their cutting edge, it was felt, had been somewhat blunted. A fresh approach was needed if cash was to be enticed from the public's pocket to the aid of the many good causes holding out their begging bowls.

It was Bob Rufford, chairman of the Lions, who had come up with the Bed Race suggestion. It was not original. A race at Poggleton the year before had been quite successful, although lack of definition of the rules had caused some confusion. First past the post had been a camp bed carried by its team, disqualified because the rules required beds to be pushed on castors. One of each team had to be carried on the bed, but nothing in the rules prescribed his, or her, clothing. A team whose bed had borne Miss Poggleton 1981 clad in nothing but a pair of panties could not, therefore, be disqualified but its victory, reluctantly conceded by the judges, had aroused a controversy that had continued for months in the columns of the *Star and Echo* and even been referred to from the pulpit.

"Mustn't have that sort of thing happening here," Bob Rufford told his fellow members of the Lions' committee. "We must make our rules absolutely watertight. Beds to be on their own castors. Not more than four feet wide including decorations if any. Five to a team, one to be carried on the bed *fully clothed*. Five miles course starting at the Town Hall, through Hurstbourne Tarrant, past The Gwent Arms and back to the Town Hall for the finish."

Rules were finalised, a date fixed, charities chosen, notifications drawn up to the Police and A.A. The Lions, were a business-like bunch on the whole. Already committee members were making up their teams. Although there were dissenters, by and large the Bed Race caught on.

Peter had not, at first, welcomed the idea, but soon found himself swept up by a tide of enthusiasm for the event among his workforce. Since the computer had taken over at Buggins' – The White Prince had been shaped to a more conventional design – the employees had had little, if anything, to do, at least connected with the factory's product. But they had not been idle. There was a flourishing bridge group; Lady Gwent was giving lessons in Scrabble; Dem Dangle's ballroom dancing classes were packed; nature rambles attracted outdoor types; devotees of drama were rehearsing *The Pirates of Penzance*. No one could say that the redundant ladies of Buggins' just sat around and moped.

Peter was relying on natural wastage, early retirement, retraining and similar measures to run down the workforce, but the ladies of Buggins' seemed a healthy lot, slow to appreciate the delights of early retirement and reluctant to retrain. Stirring exhortations by Government Ministers and captains of industry about over-manning, slimming down and higher productivity appeared to pass over their heads. The best solution would have been for the workforce to go on strike for an indefinite period. This was considered by the shop stewards, but turned down flat on the shop floor. Winter was coming on and the workforce couldn't see themselves paying for heating at home when they could stay nice and warm in the factory at their employer's expense.

Beds: 'What sort of bed?' became the question of the day. While a good, strong bed was more likely to stand up to the arduous conditions of the race, it might never again provide a comfortable couch for its owner, whereas an old crock could be consigned to the scrap-heap when the race had been run. Baynes and Buckle put on special offer half a dozen unusual beds that had failed to catch the public's fancy. A carved head and neck of a swan, painted white with golden wingtips, arched over the head of the recumbent user, creating the illusion that he was being lulled to sleep on the breast of the great bird. Retrieved from a warehouse, these elegant beds were cleaned up, a specimen was displayed in the window, space taken in the *Star and Echo* and within a week all had found buyers.

The Gwents, though not themselves taking part, offered to provide an elaborately carved and decorated French number said to have been slept in by Marie Antoinette. It had been brought to Cockscombe Castle by a scion of the family who had found it, while making the Grand Tour, in a junk shop in Louvain. Ever since it had reposed in an attic, and Lady Gwent felt that the time had come for it to make its contribution to charitable causes. A four-poster, she admitted, was unlikely to show a good turn of speed, but would add a note of stylishness to the field.

Charlotte had agreed to be Arthur's passenger, but her parents, rather at the last moment, entered a bed and invited her to make up a team. Like the Cockscombe entry it had been slept in by royalty, by none other than Queen Chotonopohaggis during her term in protective custody at Government House. As Her Majesty weighed twenty-one stone, Sir Hubert had caused the bed to be reinforced with heavy local timbers which, while adding to its weight and cumbrousness, also added to its durability and, Marjorie believed, might enable it to stay the course while lighter and more brittle beds shook to bits.

While the rules stipulated that every bed must be fitted with castors, nothing was said about their size or make. Taking note of this, Ernest Snape consulted catalogues and found that castors came in a variety of shapes and sizes, some solid metal balls, others miniature wheels. It occurred to him that the larger the castors, the faster would the bed proceed. As luck would have it, his brother-in-law owned a small engineering firm in Bristol. Thither he went. Designs were sketched, sums were done and a rush order placed for a set of solid, strong and very large castors.

Sybil had, in the beginning, spurned the event. It was not the sort of frolic she could see the Lord Lieutenant taking part in. But, as the day grew nearer, even Hartley's became infected with bed-fever.

"We must enter a team," she pronounced.

"You and I, my dear, plus Miss Cheer, old Donkin and perhaps Mrs Sproggs would have, shall we say, limited push-power."

"There are plenty of people willing to push. It just needs organisation."

"And a bed."

Sybil looked thoughtful. "I don't think any of ours would do. Now that the Prince is part of our community, I think he should provide a bed. He must have plenty."

"I don't see why. Presumably he only needs one."

"What Royalty needs and what they have are two different matters". Sybil's hand reached for the telephone. "Buckingham Palace? The housekeeper, please." An hour later she announced: "They're sending one from Sandringham immediately. A plain, strong, useful bed provided for bachelor guests at shooting parties. Nothing fancy. Now we must collect a team. Miss Cheer can be the passenger. For pushers . . ." Peter left her with a thought-furrowed brow. As he passed her writing-room on his way out he heard her say: "Knightsbridge barracks? The Commanding Officer, please."

A pity Jo would miss the fun (if fun it should turn out to be), he thought, as he made his way back to the factory. Even Sybil had failed to locate her in Bootle. The Mayor had proved unhelpful, the Town Clerk, or more properly the Principal Administrative Officer, incomprehensible, the Chief Constable unget-at-able and the editor of the local newspaper rude. "Northern bluntness," Sybil diagnosed.

Northern bluntness, or at any rate bluntness, was a quality in which Miss Cheer took some pride. She perused her daily newspaper with care, and retailed to her employers those items, generally disquieting ones, that took her fancy. Her employers were accustomed to her bulletins, and did not always pay strict attention to their purport. But she captured Sybil's immediate interest when, putting down a tea-tray, she announced with relish: "Jo's bringing all the dustmen out on strike."

"Good heavens," Sybil said. "What dustmen? Where? Why?"

"In Bootle for a start. It's spreading. Dustmen everywhere coming out in sympathy. Now we shall have all those plastic bags piling up again. Insanitary. Rats I shouldn't wonder."

"Would you kindly explain, Miss Cheer, just *how* Jo has

brought the dustmen of Bootle out on strike?''

''I'll fetch the paper.'' Miss Cheer did so, folding it to expose the relevant page.

ARTS COUNCIL CLASH WITH UNIONS

A grant by the Arts Council to a young artist threatens to halt refuse collection throughout Britain and lead to rubbish piling up at every door. Appointed Artist-in-Residence in Bootle, Lancs., two weeks ago, Simon Stiggins commenced his duties by sweeping refuse from Bootle's back streets into piles on Bootle's pavements. ''To get art out of mausoleums and to the people'' is how he described his mission. ''Art should be living, changing, beating to the pulse of the common man. I mean to show the people of Bootle how dynamic, meaningful patterns can emerge from the materials of daily life.

''Discarded sardine tins, plastic bags, ice cream cartons, cigarette packs, dead flies, bottle tops, dog shit – that's life, truth, reality.''

Bootle's dustmen have reacted vigorously. Failing to secure from the Arts Council the young artist's instant dismissal, shop stewards decided on industrial action and if their demands are not met by midnight, dustmen in all parts of the country will come out on strike. ''We have no alternative,'' said a NUPE spokesman. ''This is an intolerable violation of human rights.''

Simon said it was all a misunderstanding. ''As a member of the Workers' Revolutionary Party I threaten no one's job. I don't remove the rubbish, only re-arrange it in meaningful patterns. In this way I hope to bring home the obscenity of nuclear weapons to the future victims of American imperialism.''

Sybil put down the newspaper. ''Poor boy. Sweeping streets in Bootle! Though I daresay it's quite a healthy out-door job. But where does Jo come in?''

Miss Cheer took the newspaper from Sybil's hand, turned the page and submitted another item for perusal.

SIMON'S GIRLFRIEND CHAMPIONS DUSTBIN ARTIST.

''I'm behind him every inch of the way,'' said golden-haired, lithe-limbed Jo (18) in Bootle today. ''Simon is dedicated to his art and to the liberation of the under-privileged, exploited victims of multi-national capitalism by awakening them to a greater awareness of their predicament. Simon wouldn't hurt a fly, let alone a dustman.'' And who is Jo? The slim, sexy, up-trodden, un-oppressed daughter of a millionaire industrial magnate with multi-national interests who's given up a life of luxury to follow her boyfriend into the industrial jungles of our inner cities. "Where Simon goes, I go," she said. "He's great. He has a great message for the people of Bootle. We hope to carry the message also to the people of the Third World."

"Dear me," Sybil commented. "He seems to be a young man of ideas. I've sometimes thought a statue on the terrace, beside those lilac bushes, would add interest to that corner. We might commission him."

"He'd be more at home showing old Uzell how to sweep the rubbish on the factory floor into meaningful patterns," said Peter. "It's nice to know Jo's still alive."

"It's nice to know," Miss Cheer pronounced icily, "that one is working for a millionaire industrial magnate. In that case, the salary is woefully inadequate to say the least."

"One must allow for the Press's habit of exaggeration, Miss Cheer."

"And for the habit of employers to be secretive and stingy. Obviously there's no need for me to make up Jo's bed."

It had been Bob Rufford's idea that a team from Shipton's twin town should be invited to enter for the race. He telephoned the invitation to the Burgomeister. It was difficult, he found, to explain the nature of a Bed Race over the telephone. Herr Kesselburger spoke excellent English, but was inclined to speculate as to whether the word bed had other meanings beside the familiar one, the English language being renowned for its synonyms and wealth of idiom.

"That's right, things you sleep on," Bob Rufford explained. "Only we're not going to sleep on them, we're going to push them."

"Push?"

"Yes, you know – shove. Along the road."

"You push beds along the road?"

"For charity."

There was a pause. Bob could almost hear Herr Kesselburger thinking "mad dogs and Englishmen." Without weighing his words he added: "No mid-day sun. A kind of joke."

The pause deepened. At last Herr Kesselburger rallied, further explanations followed and it was agreed that Bad Schweinfaart would field a team, mixed sexes, bringing their own bed. Bob Rufford rang off satisfied that a significant gesture had been made which could do nothing but good to international relations, and might even re-kindle a noticeably lagging enthusiasm in Shipton Wick and its environs for the EEC.

The city fathers of Bad Schweinfaart discussed the project at length, and with considerable puzzlement. It was, Herr Kesselburger explained, a kind of joke. An English joke, to do with beds. Ah, beds! A sex joke no doubt. The well-known English prudery had given way, as everyone knew, to an attitude more in keeping with the 1980s. Sex was the order of the day. To show that they did not lag behind, Bad Schweinfaart must join unreservedly in the joke. But their opposite numbers in Shipton Wick had put serious obstacles in the way of achieving their own aims. The rules of the race laid down that the solitary passenger must be fully clad. It was difficult to understand how a single person, fully clad, could be very sexy.

It must be in the bed's decorations, on which no restrictions were imposed, that the sexiness was to be made manifest. Cartoons, blown-up photographs, models, adjuncts such as boots and whips, in these must lie the answer. Bad Schweinfaart, it had to be admitted, was not as up-to-date as perhaps it should have been in these matters. There was not even a sex shop. Two of the younger councillors were deputed to visit Frankfurt and return with original ideas for suitable decorations. Funny sex decorations. The appointed delegates set off in high spirits for Frankfurt, disappointed only in the refusal of the treasurer to sanction a visit to Copenhagen.

The councillors returned with many new and stimulating, not to say bizarre, ideas. Working at full stretch, the carpenters and painters of Bad Schweinfaart in a remarkably short space of time transformed the Burgomeister's grand-mother's solid, serviceable bed into a voluptuous couch on which Venus herself would not have spurned to lie in the arms of Bacchus, or perhaps Adonis, surrounded by mirrors reflecting several curious postures and scenes. A twice-life-size figure of Priapus stood at the fore of the bed, Europa seated on a very masculine bull at the rear. Altogether it was felt that the citizens of Bad Schweinfaart had entered with élan and credit into the spirit of the English joke.

The Burgomeister and his wife were naturally to be the guests of Shipton Wick's Mayor. The German entry, carefully crated, was delivered to the Mayor's front garden the day before the race was to take place. Here members of the team uncrated it, rejoicing in the pleasure they would give their hosts in delivering a bed whose decorations were so fully in keeping with the spirit of the joke.

Councillor Mrs Hussey's front garden faced on to Church Walk, a quiet yet well-frequented street. When the bed had been unveiled and all was ready, Herr Kesselburger, a well-dressed, tidy man with spectacles, fetched his hostess from the house to admire his townsfolk's handiwork. He observed with pleasure that a number of passers-by had halted and were gazing at the bed with evident interest and, it would appear, astonishment. No wonder. Shipton Wick was fortunate indeed to have twinned with such an enterprising, inventive, up-to-date town as Bad Schweinfaart.

Councillor Mrs Hussey's reaction was, in one respect, all that he had expected. Undoubtedly the bed kindled her interest. But admiration? Her expression seemed to Herr Kesselburger to be more as if she had been confronted by a spitting cobra than a work of art of originality and humour.

"This bed," she began, sounding as if she was being strangled, "this bed, these, ah, paintings, models, mirrors – you mean to push these through the streets tomorrow?"

"Indeed yes. That is for the joke."

"The joke?"

"The English joke. We have made a good joke, yes? Gone to town, I think you say."

"You certainly have. But – "

The Burgomeister looked his question. "But – well, for one thing, we have asked the Prince to present the prizes."

The Burgomeister beamed. "That will be a great honour. I think the Prince will enjoy these decorations, no?"

"No."

"No? The Prince is not a young man who enjoys a joke?"

"It depends upon the joke."

"This is not a good joke?"

"Please don't misunderstand me, Herr Kesselburger. I'm sure this is a very funny joke indeed but we shall have press and television coverage tomorrow and this bed would certainly create a national scandal and probably land us all in jail."

It was the Burgomeister's turn to register astonishment. "I do not understand. Mr Rufford said . . ."

"I will get Mr Rufford to explain. Meanwhile, would you *please* cover up the bed again? As you see, there's a crowd collecting and . . ."

The Burgomeister's manner had become decidedly stiff. "This crowd perhaps appreciates an artistic masterpiece and enjoys a good joke."

"Also it obstructs the highway. And the police . . ." She had caught sight of the police, in the shape of Sergeant Bullstrode, advancing at a leisurely pace from the far end of Church Walk. The next few moments were perhaps the worst she had experienced since she had been wrongly accused, in front of the whole class, of stealing Morna's diary from her locker together with a signed photo of Elvis Presley and a ten shilling note. Visions of headlines in the *Star and Echo*, even in the *Mirror* and *Express*, floated through her distracted mind. "Mayor Held on Obscenity Charge," "Love-Bed in Mayor's Front Garden," "Porn Rampant in Town Hall." The press, the police, prose-cution, persecution, ruin . . . Rushing into the house, she took the stairs two at a time, tore off a bedspread, dashed back to the garden and thrust it into the Burgomeister's arms. "Quickly, please!" Sergeant Bullstrode had fortunately been detained halfway along Church Walk by a woman with a dog. Reluct-antly, but obediently, the Burgomeister and his companions draped the offending contraption with Councillor Mrs Hussey's crimson candlewick bedspread. Let Sergeant Bullstode make what he liked of that, she thought, as she shepherded her guests indoors, telephoned Bob Rufford and handed the Burgomeister a corkscrew to open the German wine laid in for the occasion. An object of peculiar shape draped in a crimson bedspread and standing in the Mayor's front garden would no doubt wrinkle the Sergeant's puzzled brow, but it couldn't constitute a criminal offence.

Bob Rufford started this and Bob must sort it out, she thought as she uttered compliments about the wine, Frau Kesselburger's dress, the German character, Wagner and anything else she could think of (which wasn't much) about the Federal Republic. Glumly, but with efficiency, the bed was dismantled; cartoons, mirrors, models and other stimulants to passion were carefully packed away; and there the bed stood in its nakedness, just a plain, ordinary bed. The team from Shipton's twin town regarded it in silence and something akin to despair.

"We withdraw," the Burgomeister said. "We cancel."

"All we need is a different motif," Bob Rufford said. He alone retained his habitual optimism. Bob, his fellow business men considered, had something of the Midas touch. His enterprises flourished, his finger was in many pies. "A different motif," he repeated. "Got it! We name the bed the Spirit of West Germany and take it from there."

The members of the Bad Schweinfaart team were unimpressed. They doubted whether the Spirit of West Germany could be adequately represented by an unadorned bed.

"Give me half an hour," Bob said. He was back within the specified time with an armful of photographs blown up to poster size. One of his enterprises was a travel agency, and in its store-room reposed stacks of photographs depicting the more attractive features of the countries to which tours were directed. Not long since his agency had advertised a German tour by means of poster-pictures of laughing girls plucking grapes in Moselle vineyards, ornate baroque churches in Bavaria and joyful-looking tourists in colourful garb against a background of castles on the Rhine. These photographs, Bob suggested, would serve very happily to illustrate the Spirit of West Germany.

It cannot be said that the members of the Bad Schweinfaart team were impressed. But they were guests, and guests must accept without cavil the whims of their hosts. Nor could they risk inflicting damage on the tender plant of European unity. Using the tourist photographs, they re-mantled their bed.

Chapter Thirteen

SHIPTON Wick's Town Hall stood perched on pillars at one end of the Market Square. It had been built in medieval times on the very site where Ethelbald the Elder had held his first moot, thus planting in the Hundred of Sheepes-weke that seedling of democracy that was to burgeon into so sturdy a tree. Nowadays the city fathers deliberated in the Civic Centre, a modern building with accommodation for receptions, banquets, wine and cheeses, the crowning of Miss Shipton Wick with her attendant Maids of Honour, craft fayres, jumble sales, economy lunches on behalf of Christian Aid and many other functions. But the Town Hall remained a cherished part of Shipton's heritage and a perennial tourist attraction. It was here, at eleven o'clock on a Saturday morning, that the race was to start and, in due course, end.

Competitors started to assemble well before the appointed hour. Ernest Snape's entry, propelled as unobstrusively as possible into the Market Square, attracted immediate attention. Its castors were about twice the size of a regulation football and it leapt immediately into the position of hot favourite. Ernest had already placed his bet at ten to one. Sinking, for the moment, his personal feelings, he had enlisted the brawny swimming pool attendant Syd as one of his pushers. Syd had in turn called upon a robust young man employed as life-saver at the pool, and upon his nephew, a police cadet who had passed out of his training course with the junior boxing championship to his credit. Mrs Emmeline Snape, a small and shapely lady with a shock of ash-blonde hair, reclined upon her husband's entry clad in a fetching pair of cerise pyjamas.

The bed from Cockscombe Castle was a centre of attraction on account of its size and dignity, though its chances were rated very low. With its carved posts, brocade canopy and embroidered curtains, it was an object of beauty but scarcely of speed;

and its castors, unscrewed from a former maid's bed in the attic and attached to the stout legs of Marie-Antoinette's four-poster, did not look up to the job. Moreover its pushers were something of a scratch lot. Arthur had as his colleagues Mrs Merryweather, president of the Womens' Institute, a brawny lady it was true but not in her first youth; the Vicar, well accustomed to pushing since the churchyard was large and its mower antique, but also getting on in years; and Basil Crump, one of the churchwardens, a retired farmer who bred ornamental pigeons and, as a conscientious bell-ringer, had, it was hoped, kept his muscles in good trim by pulling ropes. Its passenger was W.P.C. Helen Wiggett, fortunately off-duty on the day of the race.

Colonel Martingale, Master of Foxhounds, was starter and judge. He surveyed the motley crowd with some disapproval. A lot of poppycock, in his opinion. With the Opening Meet only a week away, attention should be focused on more important matters than racing beds. It was right, of course, that money should be raised for charitable causes but in their choice of causes the Lions' committee had gone badly astray. Now that the Prince was to become a regular follower of the Hunt – Cantilevre lay in the heart of the Friday country – the need to show good sport had become more imperative than ever. Good sport could be shown only when good working conditions for hound and horse alike had been provided. Good working conditions for the hounds demanded a new, rat-proof, hygienic mixing room and store for their food. If ever there was a good cause, in Colonel Martingale's opinion, this was it. Yet the committee had considered that tree-planting in the car park where the trees, if they survived all the fumes, would get in everybody's way, and a tour of West Berlin by the Comprehensive's steel band, to be worthier objects of charity.

Still, the Colonel was all for a bit of good clean fun and would have overlooked the committee's decision had it not been for their inexcusable behaviour in regard to the Ecologists. That bunch of subversive, disloyal, unprincipled layabouts, instead of being cold-shouldered as they deserved, if possible banned, had been given every encouragement not only to take part in the race, but to flaunt their banners and disgraceful slogans as if this had been one of those idiotic demos that were all the rage.

No one could be keener on the preservation of the countryside that he was – an active member of the Country Landowners Association, on the committee of the Council for the Protection of Rural England – but behind the mask of preservers, the so-called Ecologists were destroyers and sabateurs, every one. In Russian pay, likely as not, recruited by those Cambridge traitors who'd taken over what used to be called the Secret Service. Soviet Service, he called it. Stop the Hunt, indeed. Bring chaos to the hunting field and disrupt the finest of all sports. The sport of our ancestors. More than likely that Ethelbald the Elder had sallied forth from this very spot with his wolf-hounds in pursuit of wolves, or boar-hounds seeking wild boars.

And there was the Ecologists' bed, parading its placards about badgers, which caused TB in cattle as everyone knew. There was that awful Judy Mustard with her fat behind and red complexion and hair all over the place – a vision of her hideous person tied to a stake and gnawed by ravenous foxes momentarily soothed his mind. And that red-bearded bounder from the wilds of Scotland, no doubt descended from a long line of Jacobites and midnight hags. He should be sent back whence he came, North Britain as it used to be called when it consisted of grouse moors, deer forests and salmon rivers instead of football hooligans, oil rigs and foreign tourists as it did now.

On the stroke of eleven the Colonel cracked his hunting crop, a cry of "they're off!" came through the loud-hailer, television cameras whirred, a cheer went up from the crowd and the pushers went into action. Hartley's serviceable bed, bearing Miss Cheer and propelled by four stalwart, clean-limbed young men in running shorts and vests on loan from the Blues and Royals, got away to a good start and soon took the lead. Lying back, biding its time, and moving lightly as an autumn leaf, rolled on the favourite. Not far behind, the plywood badger dipped and rose and banners fluttered as the Ecologists' entry, pushed with unstinted vigour, wove its way up the hill beyond the bridge accompanied by yelps from Judy and heave-ho's from Angus.

Daryll and Sebastian pushed doggedly, saving their breath, with Astrid as their passenger.

On the hill beyond the bridge the Snape entry rolled into the lead on its massive shiny castors while Emmeline, reclining seductively on velvet cushions, waved a hand adorned with crimson nails at rivals toiling painfully up the hill. Syd was pushing like Sisyphus eternally propelling his mighty boulder to the top of the hill. Ernest congratulated himself on his magnanimity in overlooking, at least for the duration of the race, the insolent attentions that Syd was in the habit of bestowing on Mrs Snape. It really looked as if victory couldn't be denied.

Sadly, dropping ever further to the rear, came Marie Antoinette's bed from Cockscombe Castle. Beauty of design was proving to be no substitute for lightness, manoeuvrability and efficient castors. Feelings of guilt overcame Helen Wiggett as she lay at ease while Arthur, Mrs Merryweather, the Vicar and Basil Crump heaved and shoved like so many willing but superannuated cart-horses. It was all wrong, she was the youngest and fittest. Leaping from her place when the pushers paused for breath she insisted on heaving Mrs Merryweather on to the bed and taking her place with the pushers, wondering at the same time whether she had made the right choice. The Vicar and Mr Crump seemed just as out of breath as Mrs Merryweather and were older, and weighed less.

By the time the beds formerly graced by Marie Antoinette and Queen Chotonopohaggis had struggled up the hill and on to the level stretch by Mrs Glugg's bungalow, farmer Westmacott's barns and the paddock grazed by Miss Buncombe's British Alpine goats, Ernest Snape's entry, with the Spirit of West Germany not far behind, was nearly half-way to the Gwent Arms. Here the first serious contretemps occurred. Traffic had been diverted, but the A.A.'s yellow signs and arrows carried no message to Farmer Westmacott's sheep. A flock of sheep coming towards you presents no problem; you simply stop and let the fleecy wave flow by. A flock of sheep going the same way is another matter, the fleecy wave becomes a bleating barrier.

The Snape bed slowed to walking pace and then halted. Rivals began to close the gap. Fuming, Ernest addressed himself to the lanky lad who, wheeling his bicycle, walked behind the flock to the accompaniment of discordant noises emanating from a radio concealed about his person.

"Get the bloody sheep off the road," Ernest commanded.

"I be taking them to Furzebush cut, mister."

"And where the hell is Furzebush cut?"

"Down past Butterfield's Bottom."

"Get them off the road, for God's sake!"

The boy looked round and, after a pause, enquired "Where to?"

Where, indeed? On both sides a narrow verge, a ditch and then a stiff hedge bounded the road. The hedge had been lately trimmed and offered no gaps. There was no gateway in sight. The Spirit of West Germany had caught up, Hartley's bed was close behind and, in the distance, the banners of the Ecologists could be seen. A massive pile-up like that to be seen on a motorway in fog seemed imminent. A light drizzle had begun to fall.

It was fortunate that, in this impasse, Colonel Martingale drove up in his Land Rover, having taken on the duty of keeping the course clear and dealing with emergencies. Leaning out, he enquired: "Well, Brian, can't you get your bleeding sheep off the road?"

"Not till I get to Furzebush cut, I can't."

"You're buggering up the race. Turn them into Sodom's."

"Sodom's been wired up since Frank's bull got in among them stirks. Fair up-and-downer, that was."

"Well then, put them in the old quarry by Adder's Copse."

"Council's moved in caravans since Friday, didn't you know? Re-housing overspill."

Colonel Martingale swore. The leader of the German team, a sports master from the secondary school, approached and said:

"Excuse me, sir, I see there is a problem."

"Observant of you."

"To all problems, there are solutions."

"Shoot the sheep."

"That will not be necessary. Turn them round."

The Colonel gazed reflectively at the schoolmaster and nodded. "I see what you mean."

"When they have passed, the race proceeds." The Colonel grunted.

It took a little time to put the sheep into reverse and all the beds were halted until the flock had passed the last competitor, the entry from Cockscombe Castle. "The Gwent Arms will have run dry by the time we get there," Arthur gloomily remarked. "Always get a nice cup of tea," Mrs Merryweather said consolingly. Basil Crump alone gave way to a measure of defeatism. "She's a heavy bed," he said, "and castors no larger than a bee's balls, begging your pardon, Mrs Merryweather." The word castor was an emotive one. "Outright cheating, that's what it is, that Snape with castors bigger than footballs," Mrs Merryweather complained. "They aren't actually against the rules," Arthur pointed out. "Well they ought to be." "The race is not always to the swift," said the Vicar.

All thoughts were now centred on The Gwent Arms. The rules allowed for twenty minutes rest with drinks on the house, before the beds took off again on the last lap. The Snape bed, the Spirit of West Germany and the Hartley's team, after running neck and neck in the lead, were completing their rest and preparing to depart when the last competitor, the bedraggled team from Cockscombe Castle, lumbered into the car park, dumped their bed and limped into the bar. The Vicar's feet were almost raw, Mrs Merryweather had contracted hiccups from the jolting and even Arthur was showing signs of wear.

"Where's Charlotte?" Arthur enquired, looking round the bar. No member of the Evers team was to be seen. "I fear they must have come to grief," the Vicar opined. He was right. The tropical timbers used to reinforce the royal couch (mangrove poles lashed together with wild sisal twine) had not proved equal to the strain. The bed had disintegrated. The debris had been loaded into a support vehicle provided to deal with just such a contingency, and Charlotte and her team had walked back to the town to spend a congenial hour or so in the bar of The Red Lion.

In the bar of The Gwent Arms, the twenty minutes of repose flew by all too quickly. "On your marks," called the Lion posted there to time each team and set it on its way. The

Cockscombe quintet rose wearily to their feet and made their way to the car-park, reflecting sadly that by now the leading teams must be more than half-way to the Town Hall.

"There's more downhill than up on the way back," said Mrs Merryweather. "It's clearing up a bit," said the Vicar. "All together then," said Arthur. "Heave ho and a bottle of rum as Long John Silver said if that's who it was." At least one bottle, he thought, as he took his corner.

As they emerged from the car-park a pugnacious military vehicle, heavily camouflaged, bore down upon them at a ferocious speed. Missing them by inches, with a skirl of brakes it slithered round to a halt. Fleetingly, Arthur wondered whether the third war was starting and general mobilisation had been called. From the vehicle a bulky uniformed figure emerged and strode towards them, followed by two men of lesser rank. Helen gave a little yelp, Arthur an excited exclamation and the bulkier figure a tremendous roar.

"Arthur, greetings! Salaam, jambo, salutations, may Allah bless you with a thousand children and ten thousand concubines! And here I see the maiden with the guinea-fowl hat! What is this you carry as if you were donkeys or women?"

"The General!" Arthur and Helen spoke in unison. Their greeting was as warm, if not as uproarious, as his. There were salutations all round. The Vicar, in addition to his sore feet, had to put up with a mangled hand.

Explanations followed. After a successful exercise on the river Tamar in which the General's crack commando unit of female canoeists had blown up the bridge then uniting, but now severing, Devon and Cornwall, manoeuvres had been suspended for the winter and the General was returning to his duties as equerry. Finding Cockscombe Castle temporarily deserted he had gone in search of Arthur, attended by his henchmen, Moja and Mbili. And now, here they were.

Arthur found his current activities harder to summarise. Bed Races did not lie within the General's experience. His look of puzzlement gave way to one only too familiar to Arthur and Helen, one of looming displeasure.

"In this race, you are losing? You do not win?"

"I'm afraid not," Arthur admitted.

"And this is the bed of my friend, the Lady of Gwent?"

"That's right."

"This I cannot allow. The Lady of Gwent is a great lady, if she wishes her bed to race then it must come first."

"Unfortunately. . ." Scowling, the General surveyed the Cockscombe team. They did not impress him. His arm shot out to point a finger first at the Vicar, then at Mr Crump. "You go, and you. You are weak and old. Too weak and old to push a little market cart along a road." The pointing finger moved to Mrs Merryweather. "You too are weak and old and also fat. It is good to be fat but not when carried. You go also."

"But. . ."

"Maiden in the guinea-fowl hat, you will be carried on this litter. Moja! Mbili! Together we push the litter of the Lady of Gwent to victory. When I, General Mkubwa, start a race I finish in the front!"

"We can't change pushers in the middle of the race," the Vicar objected. "That would be cheating."

"Cheating? You say I am cheating?" The General glowered. Storm clouds were gathering. Arthur hastily intervened.

"I don't remember anything in the rules about not bringing in replacements. For injured players, as in rugger."

"We aren't exactly injured", said the Vicar.

"You *are* injured!" the General thundered. "Come, go! Guinea-fowl hat, mount quickly. Arthur, Moja, Mbili, we push! We are ready. Go!"

With a mighty push, the General started the castors rolling and the bed shot away down the road. The displaced pushers watched it go with mixed feelings. "Not sportsmanlike I fear," said the Vicar. " Do I *really* look weak and old and fat?" enquired Mrs Merryweather. "I've been going to the Weight-watchers Club regularly except that on the last few occasions . . ."

"Weak and old or not, there's a lot to be said for the bar of The Gwent Arms," Basil Crump concluded.

Under its new management, the Cockscombe couch sped along the road like a hare, creaking in every joint and rocking drunkenly from side to side but still holding together. Soon other beds came into view ahead. The General and his auxiliaries struck up a rhythmic chant which imparted to the pushers the strength of ten and drowned in a wave of resonance all sensations of aching shoulders and blistered feet.

The first of the beds to be overtaken was that of the Ecologists, who had been delayed by the entanglement of their banners in overhanging boughs. A difference of opinion between Angus and Judy as to how they should be reinstated led to an erosion of the team spirit so essential to the generation of maximum push-power.

The Cockscombe team's rhythmic chant swelled in volume as their bed rolled on with ever-increasing momentum. Each passage of the chant ended with a sort of half roar, half grunt, followed by a thrust which almost lifted the bed off its castors. Arthur felt as if possessed by some primeval essence. As for Helen, rocking on her mattress and clutching its sides, this was perhaps the moment when the splendour of the General struck fully to her heart. Appearing like a spirit summoned in the hour of need, he was throwing all his strength and vigour into saving from defeat his honoured patron, the Lady of Gwent. A knight errant indeed, a man among men, a born leader. Only now did she realise to the full how privileged she had been to guard his person and enjoy his trust.

As they swung round a bend in the road, the spire of Shipton's church came into view. Three beds only now remained ahead. Snape's was in the lead, with Hartley's lying second and the Germans close behind. Short of some major obstacle ahead, the Snape bed looked like a certain winner. Emmeline's imagination was already dwelling on the glowing piece she would read in the *Star and Echo* and on the discomforture of her rivals, especially Mrs Rufford, swollen-headed as she was now that her campaign to prevent dogs from fouling pavements had culminated in the fixing of official warnings of a £5 penalty to almost every lamp-post in Shipton Wick. This would take her down a peg or two.

The war-chant of the General and his colleagues deepened and quickened as the distance narrowed between them and the Bad Schweinfaart pushers. The Germans were startled. Was a regiment or warriors with flashing spears and painted shields swooping through the peaceful English countryside? Looking back, they saw with alarm an object like a cross between a covered wagon and a pantechnicon advancing upon them at breakneck speed. Acting swiftly, the captain gave an order and the team pushed their bed on to the verge to let their rival by. Where the English law stood on such questions as runaway beds on the highway was uncertain, but it would do Bad Schwein-faart no good were its team to be accused, however wrongfully, of causing an accident in this foreign land.

On swept the Cockscombe bed. Ahead the Hartley's team were proceeding at a steady trot. The fit young men from the Blues and Royals, under the command of Lieutenant Denys Montagu-Bolingbroke-Stagge (known as Staggers) had main-tained an even, seemingly unhurried pace that had nevertheless kept them in or near the lead throughout the race. Miss Cheer, who weighed less than nine stone, was feeling seasick, but her plea to be put down was ignored by Lieutenant Staggers. The sturdy bed from Sandringham on its workmanlike castors had hitherto escaped injury or upset.

Lieutenant Staggers, unlike the German captain, had no intention of pulling to the verge to make way for the chanting pushers who were overtaking him. But, glancing back, he saw to his surprise that the near side rear pusher wore a military uniform of unfamiliar colour and design. The sky-blue tunic which the General had worn on his arrival had been exchanged for an active service dress consisting of a hunting green tunic frogged with gold braid, breeches to match and an impressive tartan forage cap trimmed with monkey's paws. On his shoulders, the Lieutenant noted, was the insignia of a Field-Marshal. With so many embassies, legations, High Commis-sions, military delegations and whatever from unfamiliar countries now around, a Field-Marshal, though acting in an unconventional manner, might well prove to be a distinguished visitor about to place an order for several hundred million pounds worth of jump-jet aircraft or ground-to-air missiles. While not actually drawing off the road, the Lieutenant thought it prudent to let the Field-Marshal's bed go by.

The straggle of bungalows and small, untidy houses that fringed the town began to appear. Ernest glanced over his shoulder to see the uncouth challenger gaining ground. His own monster castors were rolling as smoothly as oiled silk; the pushers' main problem was to keep up with their bed when it came to a decline. "Can't think how that grotty old contraption got as far as this," he said. "Falling to bits. Still, we'd better put a bit more distance between us. Come on, Syd."

The pace of both teams quickened as they reached the gentle slope that, after several bends, became the top end of the High Street. Strong as the Cockscombe bed was, built as it had been in the age of craftsmanship and of the finest materials with no expense spared, never could it have been subjected to such testing treatment at the court of Louis XVI. Helen was clinging desperately to one of the posts in which a nasty fission had appeared. Suddenly there was a deafening detonation, Helen was flung forward on to the mattress, the mattress was wrenched from its moorings, the rusty springs gave way and Helen found herself skidding painfully along the road.

"Halt!" cried the General, surveying a scene that had taken on the appearance of a battlefield. Bits of wood and metal ware strewn about and there was even a wounded body. The soldierly qualities that had won him high rank and honour came immediately into action. Although most of the bed had collapsed, all four legs with their castors were more or less intact. The bed was still battleworthy, in fact it would be lighter now that most of the superstructure had gone. The only problem was the passenger. The General picked up Helen's prostrate form and placed her on the surviving framework beside the soundest looking of the remaining posts.

"Now hug," he commanded. "Hug tightly. Now on. On to victory for the Lady of Gwent!" A tremendous push, accompanied by a stentorian war-cry, set the battered bed again in motion. Helen, her feet balanced on the wooden frame, embraced the bed post with all the desperation of a drowning sailor clinging to the wreckage of his craft.

The accident, Ernest reckoned, had given him game and match. His bed glided easily into the top end of the High Street.

Only a level stretch remained before the contestants were to swing left into the market square and then accross it to the Town Hall, where Colonel Martingale, the Mayor and other notables were assembled. Ernest felt already the warm glow of triumph, heard the cheers and acclamation of the crowd.

The folly of counting unhatched chickens has been stressed in many fables, parables, moral tales and warnings to the young. Human frailty being what it is, old as well as young keep on ignoring such warnings. Ernest Snape looked too long over his shoulder at the wreckage of his rival's hopes. While traffic in the High Street had been temporarily diverted, stationary vehicles had not been removed. A Long Vehicle loaded with concrete blocks stood by the side of the road. Too late, Ernest saw its rear end looming ahead. With an ear-splitting report, the hope of the Snapes crashed into the back of the stationary lorry. Two front castors, split and dented, rolled away into the gutter. Emmeline was hurled violently against a stack of blocks, screaming loudly as blood poured down her face. The disaster was total. Ernest lacked the spirit even to swear.

The General's team gave an unsporting whoop of delight. Swaying and creaking, their passenger still embracing the bedpost, they swept past the wreckage. But close behind, and gaining ground, came the German and the Hartley's teams. Again disaster struck, though not this time total. The castors of the German bed became entangled with the wreckage on the road and, as it swung round into the square, one of them gave way. The bed, limping along on three castors, fell behind.

Hartley's came on swiftly, drawing out to pass the General's team. The gods, and not for the first time, were on his side. A bull terrier, bored with inactivity and wishing to join in the fun, slipped its lead, dashed at the advancing objects and fell upon the ankle of one of the troopers in the Hartley's team. The young man tried to kick the dog away but its teeth only sank in deeper. With a cry of anguish, he abandoned his post. The bed lurched, swung around and came to rest against a lamp post with a mighty crash.

The war-chant of the General, Moja and Mbili, echoed insofar as he was able by Arthur, underwent a subtle change of beat.

The qualities of resolution, courage and relentless will pulsing through the chorus turned into a jubilant note of victory as the remains of Marie Antoinette's bed reached the steps of the Town Hall. Bad Schweinfaart limped in second and Hartley's followed, reduced to three pushers, the injured man having been removed to hospital.

The beaming General, or more correctly Field-Marshal, shook hands with Arthur, clapped Moja and Mbili on the back and lifted Helen, who was feeling more like a mangled bloater than a W.P.C., down from her perch.

"So! A battle, a *coup*, a race, all the same to Field-Marshal Mkubwa! He wins! The firstest! For the Lady of Gwent."

Colonel Martingale found himself embraced in a bear's hug while Arthur unashamedly sat down on the steps and panted. W.P.C. Wiggett endeavoured to remove some of the dirt from her face. The General – as he would always remain to his friends in Shipton Wick, no matter to what rank he attained – seized her handkerchief and did the job for her with his customary vigour.

"So! The maiden with the guinea-fowl hat! When I return to my country she shall be commander of my maidens' army! She shall have a big black Mercedes, many brindled heifers and white goats, and a numbered account in a Swiss bank! And when she has fed upon the food of my country, she will grow fat!"

The crowd cheered, cameras whirred and clicked, a BBC reporter asked "How do you feel about your triumph?", and Colonel Martingale, shaking hands all round, announced the names of the winning teams. "Thanks to their splendid efforts and to the generosity of the sponsors, I am glad to say that we have raised enough to plant six trees in the car park, *and* supply guards, and send the Comprehensive's steel band to West Berlin." Under his breath he added: "Poppycock."

Chapter Fourteen

THERE are some who spring from their beds, when the hour of rising comes, like salmon leaping up a waterfall; others who linger curled up in their warm nest until the last moment, and beyond, before reluctantly casting aside the bedclothes. Angus, in the normal course of events, belonged in the first category. He would even whistle or hum a tune on the way to the bathroom. But this was not, whatever happened – and a lot was about to happen – going to be a normal day. For a full five minutes Angus lay abed in the early morning darkness marshalling in his mind the plans, contingencies, precautions, hopes and fears surrounding the events to come.

By now Giuseppe and his men should be in the shed by the gate on the Dudgrove Turville road, thoughtfully equipped by Angus with several bales of straw for them to sit on during a longish wait. To replace the guns still at the bottom of the pond at Shuddering Park had been a simple matter. London was full of embassies whose cellars were well stocked with weapons of the newest type, kept topped up by the contents of diplomatic bags arriving from North Africa and the Levant. Angus' yellow van had a false bottom and the guns had travelled safely to the shed beside the gate into Lammas Wood. Angus had always believed that the simplest plan was best.

A simple plan. The fox was in the cupboard, the dart-gun primed, Giuseppe in the shed, a coal-black swift Mercedes in a nearby parking bay, a helicopter waiting at its appointed spot and, on the distant island of Phlogge, a party with supplies had recently landed from an Irish gunboat to prepare a comfortable reception centre for the kidnapee, if such a word existed. The distribution of a keg of Irish whiskey to each of the five inhabitants of Phlogge had eliminated any risk of interference by the natives.

First, the fox. After so much tagging, fitting with radio

devices, drugging, undrugging and generally being messed about, Sebastian's study foxes had become semi-tame, or at any rate resigned. Angus had experienced little difficulty in abstracting one called Rufus from his pen and shutting him in the broom-cupboard, comfortably settled on an old blanket, for the night. Now, with the dawn of D-Day, Rufus was popped into a sack. After a bowl of porridge, Angus once more checked the dart-gun and its syringe loaded with the correct dosage to immunise a hefty horse. Then he donned a mackintosh, pocketed a packet of biscuits and went forth into the darkness, now faintly lightening, gun in hand and bearing the sack over his shoulder. He locked the door with a tinge of sadness. Soon the cottage would know him no more. He had enjoyed his little interlude in Shipton Wick.

Rufus, resigned as he was to his role of study fox, was not resigned to being half-stifled in a sack and dragged over rough ground. There was nothing he could do about it except squirm and wriggle. "Never mind, old fellow," Angus told him. "No one's going to eat you. Just work up all the scent you can." Rufus' adrenalin must by now be flowing freely, causing him to stink. The more stink the better.

Angus dragged the sack through the wood, past a fallen tree-trunk he had selected as his place of concealment, through the gate beside the shed and to the yellow van which was drawn up on the verge. Rufus must bide his time inside the van until all was over. After a word or two with Guiseppe, Angus returned to the fallen tree-trunk. A grey dawn was gathering a little strength. Why did people write or speak of dawn breaking? An English dawn hadn't the strength to break the handle off a Dresden tea cup.

Others beside Angus were early astir. Judy Mustard, in fact, had scarcely stopped stirring for the last week. There was much to prepare not only for the demo, but for a ploy of her own.

Controversy about the demo among the Ecologists had been heated. Security would be tight. Security had done its best to have the venue of the meet changed, but the Prince hadn't wished to cause a break with one of Shipton Wick's oldest traditions. The hunt had been meeting at Cantilevre ever since the Lord of the Manor of the day, Sir Godfrey Wayne-fleete d'Aubergin du Bouillon, had summoned churls and freemen alike to a mighty stag-hunt in celebration of his safe return from the First Crusade. While Security had failed to shift the meet, it did succeed in forbidding access to the Cantilevre domain to all save members of the Hunt and those who could secure passes. All the demo would be able to do would be to assemble on the road outside the gates, where the police would certainly move them on or else change them without causing an obstruction.

So what was to be done? Forget about the Opening Meet, said some, and switch to the Boxing Day one. This was always held in the Market Square and attended by a large part of the population of Shipton and nearby villagers. A tip-off to the media would secure a good response and Stop the Hunt a lot of public sympathy.

Judy was not to be so easily deflected from her purpose. She had her supporters, especially among the younger, less compliant members of the group. A few arrests, a scuffle or two – nothing would do the cause more good by showing up police harassment and denial of the rights of free speech and assembly. This view was forcibly expressed by young Andy Stubbins, leader of the Militant Tendency at the Comprehensive, and by Owain ap Rhys-Jones, a graduate in pyrotechnology of the Aberstwyth branch of the University of Wales and the latest recruit to the Fire Brigade.

Put to the vote, Judy's side had been narrowly defeated. If only Angus had been there, she bitterly reflected, they would have won. Though Angus could be a bastard and she didn't trust him, she had to admit that when it came to oratory, he could talk a flock of sheep into dancing the rhumba. But, of course, she couldn't be sure that he *would* have been on her side. Now he'd gone off without a word on one of his dubious pursuits, just as matters were coming to a head. Just like Angus. Unreliable.

But now she had more important things to think about. If the demo could be kept from Cantilevre's lawn, there were other places where it could assemble. Better places in some ways. So long as the Prince was there. That was the crux. A demo without the Prince would be just another demo so far as the media were concerned. How to ensure his presence? This was the problem and she saw a solution. There was not much time to put her plan into effect but just enough, with a bit of luck. The first step was to obtain from the League Against Cruel Sports one of their excellent preparations designed to tease and mislead the sensitive noses of foxhounds. That step was taken.

Colonel Martingale was another early riser on this momentous day. Seasoned foxhunter that he was, every time the Opening Meet came round he got butterflies in the stomach. Of course there was no cause for worry. Cubbing had gone well, the new entry were coming along nicely, the horses were fit, hunt servants confident, no major setbacks had occurred. All the same, the Opening Meet put an end to rehearsals. Now came the real thing. And with the Prince among the field, a heavy responsibility rested upon the Master of the pack he had chosen to follow.

Loyal subject as he was, the Colonel could not but regard the Prince's presence among the field as a mixed blessing. Journalists and cameramen everywhere. Journalists. His lip curled. He well remembered how, when he had been a junior subaltern, some journalist or other had come nosing round the mess trying to unearth what he was pleased to call a scandal. (Something to do with the Colonel's lady.) He'd had the insolence to ask impertinent questions of his betters. He was deprived of his trousers and chucked into a horse-trough for his pains. That was the right way to treat journalists. Couldn't do that today, which just showed how the country had gone to blazes. Not even any horse-troughs to throw journalists into nowadays.

At the best of times, a Master's responsibilities were heavy. Uncooperative farmers, broken fences, lamed horses, injured or lost hounds, uncivil riders ignoring the Field Master's commands, and then the League Against Cruel Sports with its local cell run by that bitch Judy Mustard. He had grave misgivings about what devilry they might be up to at the Opening Meet. Whackers, it was true, had pretty well every shrub in Cantilevre's garden under observation and had combed Lammas

Wood from one end to the other the day before. Nothing suspicious.

An eye should be kept, he'd told Whackers, on that uncouth Scottish layabout who occupied the cottage on the edge of the wood. Whackers replied that an eye was being kept. His men had made a thorough search of the cottage, leaving behind a few bugs. Not much of a haul: several empty whisky bottles, correspondence about an inflatable whale, some dirty postcards, a letter from someone called Maggie – not from Number 10 but from an address in Ross and Cromarty – about sending flowers to Aunt Rosamund's grave. So far the bugs had picked up nothing but an indifferently rendered humming of the Mountains of Mourne. Irish. Suspicious, certainly, but hardly conclusive.

Colonel Martingale began rather earlier than was strictly necessary to don the various items of clothing required. More worries here. Had his breeches been properly cleaned? Boots impeccably shined? Coat conscientiously brushed? Waistcoat checked over? Buttons polished? Stock carefully ironed? More than ever was it important to be properly attired.

Once in the saddle, the Master's spirits rose. Saracen, his big grey, tossed his head and wrinkled his nose in acknowledgement of his master's pat on the neck. A better horse than Saracen would be hard to find. It was good to see the hounds surging round him, a sea of waving sterns. As a rule sport seemed better with a dog pack than when the bitches were out. Thanks, perhaps, to Challenger, who'd won the championship at the Puppy Show four years ago. Be scent never so weak, the mere ghost of a trace of a whiff, Challenger would pick it up, give tongue and lead the pack on and away through bramble and bracken, across plough and pasture, over bank and wall and hedge, through farmyard and barn and outhouse, wherever the scent might lead. No finer hound in the country than Challenger. And Caesar, his litter-mate, wouldn't be far behind.

On the stroke of ten forty-five the cavalcade – Master and hounds, huntsman and whippers-in – turned in through the gates of Cantilevre, trotted past the stables and into the orchard just beyond the lawn. Already the Hunt followers were assembled on their well-brushed, shiny-coated horses, eager for the fray. Most of the riders, he was glad to see, were properly turned out in well-cut coats, stocks and breeches spotlessly white, buttons polished, the top-hats of the red coated seated firmly on the head. Some of the women wore veils. Nothing more becoming to a woman than a veil, but he didn't like the midnight blue coats and habits some of them favoured these days. Nothing so smart as black.

No sign, as yet, of the Prince, but it was his custom to keep out of the way until the hounds moved off and then to join the field. No sign, either, thank God, of Stop the Hunt; Whackers and the local police between them had seen to that.

Stirrup cups were handed round. Nothing like a noggin of port on a cold day. The Master was kept busy touching his cap to some acquaintances and raising it to others, depending on their sex and status. He doffed it altogether to Sybil, who was on the lawn in her wheel-chair with other privileged spectators, and again to Mary Gwent.

At five past eleven precisely the hounds moved off amid a cracking of hunting crops and a tootle from the horn. Through the gate at the bottom of the orchard, past the farm buildings, along the track to Lammas cottage, round the headlands of a ploughed field and through the gate into the wood. Here the Prince joined the field.

Once in the wood, the hounds fanned out in search of that enticing foxy odour that would draw deep bell-like notes from their throats. Leaves were brushed aside by questing noses, clods overturned, brambles investigated. Almost immediately, Challenger gave tongue, Caesar joined in, others converged upon the spot and full-throated cries sounded through the wood. Away they went, heading diagonally through the copse toward the Dudgrove Turville road. A splendid start to the day.

Then came a check. The bell-like sounds changed to shorter, shriller and less confident cries. The hounds fanned out again, as if uncertain in which way their noses directed them to go. Quite normal, the Master noted, in fact standard behaviour; no fox would leave the shelter of a wood so long as he could avoid it by jinking about in the hope of throwing off his pursuers.

The music of the hounds changed key. Excitement was

rekindled, but excitement of a deeper, more frantic kind. The
Colonel, who knew his hounds so well, detected a note of
near-hysteria. This was no ordinary picking up of a line.
Something was up. Urging Saracen forward, he came up to the
hounds to find them milling about, raising their muzzles and
positively howling. They were distraught. If he hadn't been
living in the twentieth century he'd have said that they'd got on
to a wolf, a bear or some other beast of prey.

"Whip them off," he cried to the huntsman. As whips
cracked and horn blew, the pack suddenly decided which way to
go and, it seemed, what they were after. Their throats swelling
with the volume of sound, their tone one of passionate
exhilaration, they streamed off through the wood in an altogether different direction to that of the line they had been
following before. In the direction, unfortunately, not in the
open, huntable, rolling country towards Cuckold's Reach, but
of the outskirts of Shipton Wick and its bungalows and gardens
and hen-runs and irate householders with complaints about
woken-up babies, hens put off laying and frightened cats. One
elderly lady had even claimed a thousand pounds damages for
breaking a leg when trying to get her terrified cat down from
the top of a wardrobe.

There was no stopping the pack now as they streamed away
towards the town, giving tongue as the Master had never heard
hounds give tongue before. They were acting as if they'd gone
off their heads. Perhaps they *had* gone off their heads. As he
galloped after them, a thought came to him like a clap of
thunder. Crazy, mad, demented. Something had demented
them. He'd read about it – a diabolical chemical invented by
those unspeakable anti-hunt fiends, a synthesised essence of the
effluvium emitted by bitches on heat and a hundred times more
powerful. His hounds *were* mad – sex-mad. Poor devils. And he
knew the perpetrator of this infernal deed. That she-devil, that
hell-hag – one couldn't call her bitch, since bitches were clearly
so compellingly attractive – that offspring of a spitting cobra and
a plague-carrying rat. This time, law or no law, Judy Mustard
wouldn't escape retribution. No greater mistake had ever been
made than abolishing the burning of witches at the stake. Bring

back the stake, he cried through clenched teeth as he galloped on.

Angus also, concealed behind his log, heard the sudden change in the music of the pack. So far, all had gone like clockwork. The line had been laid, Giuseppe was in the shed, God in his heaven and all was right with the world. As the hounds moved off, confirmation came through on his CB radio that the object of the exercise was in the right place at the right time. "Gaffer to Mobile Three. Gammatox delivered. Strength as specified." So, the Prince was on his way. The dart-gun had a range of about a hundred yards and Angus entertained no doubts as to his marksmanship. Already the hounds were picking up the line of the bagged fox.

Then, commotion. A new note in the hounds' frenzied belling, abatement of the sound as they streamed away in the wrong direction, then nothing but a distant yelping, finally no sound at all. Catastrophe. Angus swore, tugged at his beard and spoke into the microphone. "Mobile Three to gaffer. Gammatox non-delivered." There was no reply.

A lesser man than Angus would have given way to despair. Plans so carefully laid, an organisation so skilful, difficulties so competently overcome; and then, at the last moment, all was undone. But his was a resilient nature. The milk was spilt, the plan aborted. So be it. There'd be another day.

The first priority was speed. He made his way quickly to the yellow van parked beyond the shed. No point in disturbing Giuseppe who would only, as Angus' old grannie used to say, throw a tantrum. He'd never really taken to Giuseppe. Too emotional.

The van smelt strongly of fox. "That's it, then, old fellow." Angus said as he undid the sack and shook Rufus out into the road. "Back to the dustbins of Bristol and good luck to you." As for him, it was up and away to the island of Phlogge – his very own island, he was thankful to say, having taken the precaution of putting it in his own name. Everything there should be pretty comfortable. The plotters had intended to maintain the Prince if not in quite the style to which he was accustomed, in a civilised way. Plenty of whisky and wine. He got into the van and drove off at speed. Silence enfolded Lammas Wood.

Silence did not enfold Shipton Wick. Never had hounds run so well. Through the Industrial Estate they went, skimming over spiked iron fences, around lorries and vans, lungs pumping, voices clamorous, noses to the ground, Challenger as ever in the lead. Human heads appeared at windows as startled workers looked out to see what was going on. Skirting the sewage works, the pack raced on through a housing estate and up the embankment of the old railway line. The rails had long ago been torn up and the embankment was overgrown and deserted. Along the former track raced the hounds until, surging over an iron fence like a mottled wave, they reached their journey's end in the old station yard.

Their journey's end, but not reward for their prowess, no assuaging of passion, no comely, nubile young bitches all agog to greet their ardent lovers. Suddenly the scent was there no longer. The hounds milled around, a maelstrom of waving tails and questing noses, baulked, baffled and betrayed. The Master's heart bled for them as he clattered into the yard at the head of the field. Only a hell-cat and she-devil could play such a foul trick on a pack of innocent and trusting animals. Now was their chance to tear her limb from limb. But theirs was too generous, too honourable a nature for that. They bore no grudge despite their scurvy treatment. And there was the hell-cat herself in the middle of the yard standing on a trailer bedecked with banners and placards, red in the face and surrounded by her sycophants. "Stop the Hunt and Save the Whale" was the message.

Secured by ropes to the trailer, there floated in the sky an enormous rubber whale, dipping and rolling in the wind. Clustered round the trailer were a score or so of persons instantly recognisable to the Master. If only there'd been a horse-trough handy not one would have escaped a ducking. He grasped at once the low cunning of the hell-cat. Journalists and cameramen could be, and had been, kept away from the meet but they couldn't be kept out of the old station yard. If they couldn't get at the Prince in the hunting field, the whole hunting field with the Prince included could be, and had been, brought to them.

Where was the centre-piece of this drama? With any luck, he'd have drawn the line at the Industrial Estate and gone home. Colonel Martingale should have known better. The Prince was made of sterner stuff. Where the hounds went there the true sportsman followed, whatever line they chose to take. The Prince was nearly always out in front and today was no exception. Close on the heels of the Master, the leaders of the field drew rein in the yard.

Now it was the turn of the ladies and gentlemen of press and television to surge round their quarry. Their quarry had been delivered to them on a plate, if a handsome horse could be so described. Journalists filled their notebooks in a frenzy, cameramen darted about in search of better angles for shots in which the Prince, some at least of the hounds, Stop the Hunt banners and the rubber whale could be tellingly combined. Questions pelted upon the cornered Heir as stones had rained upon St Stephen.

"How do you feel about whales?"

"How do you feel about women?"

"When are you going to get married?"

"Have you proposed to Lady Rebecca?"

"Is it true you had a date with Mrs Debenham-Freebody in a yacht off Stornaway?"

"Is there a nursery wing at Cantilevre?"

"How much did you pay for that horse?"

"How do you feel about abortion?"

"How do you feel abut Europe?"

"Do you think women should work on oil-rigs?"

"Are you going to marry Diana Dors?"

"How can British industry be made more competitive?"

"Are you in favour of legalised brothels?"

"Do you think Wales should be given independence?"

"Are you in love with Piggiewiggie Stickelburger?"

"How do you feel. . ."

The Prince shared the feelings of the hounds, though for a different reason. He felt baulked and betrayed. To be hunted by the media was no new experience but to be brought to bay in a

dismantled station yard, with an inflatable rubber whale overhead and surrounded by thwarted lovesick hounds, was carrying
royal approachability too far. Someone had blundered. He was
not to know that if it hadn't been for Judy Mustard, he might
now be trussed up in a van en route, by devious ways, to the
island of Phlogge, victim of what could safely have been
described as the kidnapping of the century.

Judy herself was equally unaware of the part she had played in
the shaping of the world's destiny. It was her moment of
triumph. National coverage was in the bag. This evening on
television news, tomorrow morning in every newspaper, the
message would be there for all to see and read – messages rather,
for leaflets galore had been circulated round the old station yard
relating to everything from badgers to nuclear power, from
battery hens to seal pups to tropical rain forests. The only fly in
her ointment was the absence of Angus. She had so much looked
forward to witnessing his discomforture. Still, wherever he'd
got to, he'd read all about it next day and realise that the Shipton
Wick and District Ecology Group could manage very well
without him and wouldn't welcome him back. If Angus had
escaped humiliation, Colonel Martingale had not. Action was
called for, almost any action, to get the Prince out of this mess.
Cracking his hunting crop at members of the media had
produced no effect, other than the zooming of several lenses in
his direction, gleaming at him like evil eyes. There was Judy
standing on the trailer, her hand on the cord by which the
rubber whale was tethered. Inspiration came. He drew from its
case attached to his saddle the humane killer with which Masters
of Fox-hounds are equipped, stood up in the saddle, and fired.
There was a pop, a whining sound like the moaning of an
anguished spirit, and the deflated whale collapsed in crumpled
folds about the heads of the Ecologists. A wolfish grin covered
the Master's lip as he cracked his whip. "This way, sir," he
called. "We'll kill our fox even if we can't pull down the
vixen." To the huntsman he added: "Tomtits' Bottom."

The huntsman sounded his horn and the hounds, forgiving
creatures that they were, eddied round him as he trotted out of
the yard bound for Tomtits' Bottom. Here, sure enough, they

found a fox who led them across Trollops' Spinney, past Sodom's Withies, round Spooney's Patch and back to Tomtits' Bottom. Away it went again past Panders' Folly, over Lechers' Lee, through Doxy's Coppice and back to Tomtits' Bottom, where it handed over to a brother who took the hunt past Muckheap Farm and Cowlease Common, across Stirks' Cut and so back to Tomtits' Bottom. Here a cousin took over and led the hounds through Winnowers' Grove, past Gibbet Corner, round via Cuckholds' Acre and so back to Tomtits' Bottom where it went to ground. So much for Judy Mustard and her fiendish tricks, thought the Master; in spite of everything, they'd had a good day.

So much, thought Reggie Whackers as he closed the door of Lammas cottage, for Angus MacBean. The fox had gone away and wouldn't been seen again in Shipton Wick or its environs. A pity. Matters had been nicely organised. Sebastian's report of the disappearance of one of his foxes, and of Angus' interest in the art of darting; guns located in the pond at Shuddering Park; delegates to an Ecumenical Conference in Cheltenham of which no ecclesiastical authority had heard; a visit by some kind of Arab, or near-Arab, to the Golden Fleece at Poggleton; Angus' excursions in his yellow van; these and other pieces fell into a pattern. The shed, the road, the wood, all were under observation by Reggie's men; vehicles in readiness, helicopters on standby, the SAS on full alert. A tidy little trap and then that Judy Mustard and her circus had to go and spring it. Reggie Whackers thrust his hands into the pockets of his mac, pulled his old felt hat down to keep off the drizzle, and walked away. A pity. But life was like that. There'd be another day.

Chapter Fifteen

BANQUETS in the Civic Centre were no new things in Shipton Wick, but this particular banquet had no precedent or, at least, none that anybody could remember. If you went back far enough no doubt Kings and Queens as well as Princes had enjoyed the town's hospitality. Councillor Mrs Hussey wondered whether former Mayors had faced similar difficulties when grappling with the invitation list. Around a core of "musts" lay a grey area in which dignatories such as the President of Round Table, Rotary, the Soroptimists, the Civic Trust, the Chamber of Commerce and the District Council, the Chairman of the Bench, the Rural Dean and many others competed for a place.

Then came the problems of seating, every bit as knotty. The Prince must be seated on the Mayor's right hand. Who was to be his other neighbour? Protocol pointed to Mrs Rufford, as wife of the deputy Mayor and president of the Lions. But Muriel Rufford was, by general admission, terribly dull. Questions of dogs fouling pavements, and a ramp for wheelchairs in the Market Place toilets, were ever uppermost in her mind. Councillor Mrs Hussey doubted whether the Prince would find such matters of compelling interest. If not Mrs Rufford, then who? It seemed impossible to bestow the honour upon one lady without giving offence to at least a dozen others, and their husbands as well.

And then, all these ladies who came under review were middle-aged or worse, besides being married. Wouldn't the Prince prefer to have one of his own generation at his side? Lady Pandora perhaps? His name had been linked with hers in the press, which of course meant nothing; it had been linked to practically every presentable young woman in the kingdom, and indeed others not so young – hadn't there been something about Diana Dors? – or even not in the kingdom. Lady Pandora might do but you could never be sure what Lady Pandora would *do*. The Palace and the Foreign Office between them had barely succeeded in convincing the General that she really hadn't employed her familiars Mustard and Cress to cast over him an evil spell, when the gossip columns made a meal of her impersonation of Princess Margaret and subsequent election as Rector of the University of St Neot's. No, on the whole, *not* Lady P.

While still pondering this dilemma, Councillor Mrs Hussey encountered Sybil shopping in the High Street in her Mini Metro. Time was when a toot on the horn summoned from the shops assistants eager to receive her order and place it in her car. Nowadays Miss Cheer grumpily accompanied her and vanished into the supermarket while Sybil's car, with Sybil in it, remained on an awkward corner or double-parked, further snarling up the traffic.

Sybil beckoned the Mayor to her side. No time was lost in plunging into the topic uppermost in both ladies' minds.

"You must, of course, see that the Prince has someone *convenable* next to him on one side at least. I suppose on the other it will have to be someone from the Town Council."

"It will."

"Now who would be most suitable?" Sybil pondered. How infuriating of Jo to have vanished into the jungles of Bootle at a time like this!

"I have been wondering too," the Mayor admitted.

"I know! Get hold of Arthur. We *all* know who the Prince would like to have by his side."

"Do we?"

"But of course. Arthur will arrange it. The Prince will bring down *you know who*."

"Oh."

"Yes, that will be much the best plan. We couldn't have the poor young man totally swallowed up by Town Councillors' wives."

Councillor Mrs Hussey forebore from remarking that Sybil was one too.

"I shall be next to Henry Gwent, of course. Mary Gwent

between Arthur and Peter. I daresay she ought to have Sir Hubert, but he's such a bore about those sea slugs of his. That woman who keeps the Health Food shop is on the Town Council, isn't she? Mavis Pellett. I daresay she'd do for Sir Hubert. I expect she takes an interest in sea slugs.''

Miss Cheer emerged from the supermarket. ''Check-point tailback as usual. Some of those women must be stocking up hotels.''

Councillor Mrs Hussey decided to swallow her pride. ''I will send out an invitation. To You Know Who.''

''Arthur will arrange it.'' Sybil waved and departed, weaving a skilful way between a double-barrelled articulated lorry and a huge delivery van.

Arthur, contacted on the telephone, was offhand.

''You Know Who? Who's that?''

''I'm asking you.''

''It all depends on which paper you read. I should think he could manage with the wives of local worthies for the evening. He can't have roses all the way.''

''Possibly we're not a very glamorous lot. . .''

''You can tart yourselves up. Oh, and there's the General. Field-Marshal I should say. He's to be in attendance and he wants to sit next to the girl he insists on calling the maiden with the guinea-fowl hat.''

''W.P.C. Wiggett. I'm afraid we really can't . . . We haven't even asked the Chief Constable.''

''Don't say you haven't been warned.''

That's her problem, Arthur thought. For the first time in his life, he found himself looking forward to a municipal dinner. Or, at least, not to the actual dinner, but he'd made up his mind and intended to communicate his decision without delay. One didn't rashly embark, anyway he didn't, on a second time round, but he'd had enough of fried eggs in the kitchenette, no one to brush his suits and evenings either solitary or peripatetic. Better, he seemed to recall a quotation, the tranquillity of the marriage bed than the turbulence of the chaise-longue. They'd have the flat off Knightsbridge, he'd keep his horse at Shipton and come down to hunt whenever duty permitted. Time to settle down.

Really, thought the Mayor, Arthur wasn't at all helpful. You Know Who must be eliminated. Perhaps it had better be Muriel Rufford after all. She was pondering the question when her telephone rang. Councillor Ernest Snape was on the line.

"About the seating at the banquet," he began, sounding very Snape-ish.

"Oh yes?"

"Naturally you will take advantage of your position and place yourself next to the royal guest. That can't be helped. But on the Prince's other side?"

"The wife of the deputy Mayor, of course."

"I wouldn't go too much for that 'of course.' "

"What do you mean?" There was a pause.

"I seem to remember a spot of bother about planning permission for a double lock-up garage next to Bob Rufford's home. Which was refused when the vendor of the plot applied."

"I don't know what you mean. Bob got planning permission."

"Yes, after he'd bought the plot without it for a knock-down price. Then he applied for the permission and got it. The vendor wasn't very pleased."

"I daresay not, but what on earth has all this got to do with the seating arrangements at the banquet?"

"I don't think the wife of a councillor who's been hanky-pankying with planning laws ought to have a place of honour."

"Really, Ernest Snape!"

"The *Star and Echo* would be interested. Scandal in the Town Hall. The previous owner of the plot says he can prove his point."

"What point? Are you suggesting bribery and corruption?"

"I think an enquiry as to how a junior planning officer with several children *and* a mortgage could afford to take his wife on a luxury cruise round the Greek Islands on one of Bob Rufford's tours would lead to interesting revelations."

"Blackmail!"

"I shouldn't waste time if I were you fiddling about with words. Mud sticks."

"You're talking utter nonsense. Of course Bob Rufford has

done no such thing . . . What are you suggesting?''

The Mayor's heart had sunk. She knew quite well what was coming.

''That Mrs Rufford should find a less prominent seat at the dinner table. Mrs Snape would be willing to take her place.''

''But Mrs Snape. . .''

''Mrs Snape what?''

''For one thing,'' Councillor Mrs Hussey answered, clutching at a straw, ''for one thing, I'm afraid she suffered badly in that unfortunate accident. Disfigured in fact. A disfigured neighbour at a dinner. . .''

It was the wrong gambit. Lemons were not as sour as Ernest Snape's voice. ''Mrs Snape has entirely recovered. She will sit next to the Prince at the banquet.'' He rang off.

Gloomily, the Mayor drew towards her the sheet of paper bearing the latest seating plan.

When Sybil turned into the drive at Hartley's, she saw a familiar, small and dented car by the front door. Jo and Simon where in the kitchen ravenously tucking into the contents of the fridge, the bread-bin and a cupboard of preserves. Except for Jo's hair, which while rusty and matted could still be seen to be basically golden, and for Simon's beard, no less rusty and matted, it would have been difficult to tell them apart. Both looked lean and hungry. They couldn't be hungry for much longer at the rate they were getting through the food.

''So you've left Bootle,'' Sybil said. Jo waved a ham-bone at her mother. ''Only to borrow a helicopter. Simon's going to display his montage of The Uncreation from the air. Breaking new frontiers in communication.''

Simon nodded and, so far as he could be heard through a mouthful of cheese and chutney, added: ''Four-dimensional art. Extending the threshold of perception.''

''You both need a bath,'' Sybil said.

''A monumental understatement,'' Miss Cheer confirmed, surveying with fury the state of her kitchen.

''I daresay it will take you a little time to borrow a helicopter. Meanwhile you had better stay here. Miss Cheer will find you some clean clothes.''

A plan was beginning to take shape in her mind. Wheeling herself rapidly into her writing-room, she consulted her book of ex-directory numbers, drumming her fingers on the table lightly as the shape slowly formed. First, the facts. She dialled the Mayor.

"About the seating plan."

"It's all arranged," Councillor Mrs Hussey replied. "You are next, as you requested, to the Marquess of Gwent."

"And on the Prince's right hand?"

"Mrs Emmeline Snape."

"Mrs *Snape*?"

"You Know Who was not available, I'm afraid. Ernest Snape is one of our oldest and most valued Councillors."

"Mrs Snape. . ." Sybil's voice was dreamy. "Mrs Snape. Has she ever been abroad?"

"I really don't know." The Mayor sounded startled. "I think she's been to stay once or twice with a sister on the Isle of Wight. Why?"

"Nowhere further than that?"

"If you'll forgive me, Mrs Paxton, I don't think this is any affair of yours or of mine either if it comes to that. Now you mention it, I think they did go once on a coach tour in North Africa. Bob Rufford had some empty seats offering at cut rates. Why do you ask?"

"Idle curiosity," Sybil said, and rung off. North Africa. Just right. Libya of course. Thoughtfully, she reached again for her book, turned to one of the pages, and dialled a number. "MI5? Give me Mr Winckles, please."

The Mayor cluck-clucked as she replaced the receiver, murmuring (not for the first time) who does she think she is? She drew the seating list towards her, struck out the name of the Marquess of Gwent and substituted that of Field-Marshal Mkubwa. That would teach her.

It was not to be. The BBC's one o'clock bulletin brought news of events in the distant Republic of Hapana that were to have their impact on the seating plan. There had been a *coup*. Elements of the army, rising in revolt against the Good Shepherd

Dr Dudu, had seized the radio station, the airport and, it seemed, Dr Dudu himself, and claimed to have liberated the suffering people of Hapana from a ruthless and bloodstained dictatorship sustained by American imperialism working through the CIA. The six o'clock bulletin reported that the outcome of the *coup* hung in the balance; the rebels still held the airport but a government spokesman, having either re-taken the radio station or found another, claimed that dissident elements in the army, aided by Cuban mercenaries in the pay of the ruthless and bloodstained Trotskyite World Revolutionary Council, had been overcome. They were now held by the benign and democratically elected government of Dr Dudu in the old Anglican cathedral pending their execution.

Later bulletins corrected earlier statements. It appeared that the blood-stained and ruthless Trotskyist dictatorship of Dr Dudu, sustained by Libyans and Angolans with the help of the World Congress of Churches, had surrendered to liberators trained and organised by the benign and enlightened CIA. Either way, it was clear that the government of Dr Dudu was in trouble and that the place of his highest-ranking officer was at Dr Dudu's side.

His highest-ranking officer, however, seemed to have disappeared. Arthur made enquiries. H.M. Government, a Foreign Office spokesman told him, was backing Dr Dudu. The Foreign Secretary was about to make a statement in the House condemning unequivocally this latest example of banditry and the flouting of international law. Rebels capturing airports and radio stations, innocent lives put at risk, seizure of democratically elected heads of state, mass executions, these things were not to be tolerated.

"So what is HMG going to do about it?" Arthur enquired.

"Nothing, of course."

"Is Dr Dudu a bloodstained ruthless Trotskyite dictator or an agent of American imperialism acting through the CIA?"

"No idea."

"Then why is HMG backing Dr Dudu?"

"He's the sitting tenant, as it were – the probable winner. Of course if he's chopped, then we shall welcome the liberating forces of the people who have overthrown the bloodstained ruthless tyranny of Dr Dudu.''

"So where does that leave General Mkubwa?''

"At RAF Lyneham, ready to take off at any moment.''

"To go to the aid of Dr Dudu?''

"To fly to Switzerland if things go the wrong way.''

In that case he won't be coming to the dinner, Arthur thought. Just as well. The draft of the Prince's speech had just arrived. Arthur set himself to amend it so that the author, with luck, wouldn't notice. The Prince had got the grammar of the first paragraph so snarled up that the Mayor might easily be confused with Shipton's emblem, that short-legged extinct bird. And, touching on the town's long history, he'd mixed up the battle of Ethandum with the battle of Ecgbrythestan. And he really mustn't promise to protect the badgers when Ministry vets were moving in next month to gas the lot.

Meanwhile, Arthur has his own fish to fry. Charlotte, busy helping out at The Red Lion, had invited him to a quick lunch at The Old Coach House before both returned to their labours. "Come and look at Seven Up,'' she said before they sat down to the repast. "He's got a tender fetlock I'm afraid.'' They strolled down to the stables. Beyond lay a slope to the river where an old mill, now demolished, used to stand. The stream was fringed with trees whose damp, bronzy leaves still clung to twigs and boughs. Arthur breathed in deeply: a good, rich, satisfying, autumny smell suggesting to his mind repletion, the summer's labours over, harvests gathered into barns, fruit into store, the seed of next years' husbandry already lying in the damp earth. And the start of the hunting season.

"I should think a poultice,'' he said.

"Me too. I'm sorry you'll be going soon.''

"Me too. But I'll be back now and then I expect.'' There was a pause. Arthur added: "In fact I'm thinking of keeping my horse down here and coming down to hunt at weekends when I can.''

"What a super plan. Why not stay at The Old Coach House? I know mummy'd love to put you up.''

"I'd love that. I've got what *I* think is an even more super plan. The question is, do you.''

He expounded. "Oh Arthur. . .'' They were late for lunch. "It doesn't matter,'' Marjorie Evers said. "It's all cold.''

"Good news,'' said Charlotte. There's only one word, her mother thought, to describe her: glowing, with a sparkle in her eyes and her dark hair blown about her head in becoming ruffled waves. Arthur looked possessive. Marjorie embraced her daughter. "I'm so very, very glad. I've seen it coming but one never knows. . . How delightfully *conventional* this is.'' It hadn't been at all the same with that Italian with a chain of fish-and-chip shops. All forgotten now.

"I'm rather a conventional chap,'' Arthur stated.

Chapter Sixteen

SHEEP-DOGS, Sybil thought. She had watched them on television. There were the sheep, watchful, nervous, confused, anxious only to bolt over the hill and away from pens and humans. There was the dog, watchful, stealthy, subtle, edging a few inches this way and a few inches that, ready to dart like an arrow to cut off every attempt on the sheeps' part to escape. Jo, like the sheep, was watchful, shy, possibly confused and certainly ready to make a dash at any moment over the hills to Bootle. How to edge, inveigle, entice her into the pen of the civic banquet? Peter only made matters worse.

"You'll get a good meal," he suggested.

"I've had one, thanks."

"Interesting people."

Jo looked her contempt.

"It would please your mother."

Silence.

"Anyway," he said to Sybil, "I don't think you can possibly get her in. The seating's all arranged. There's no place for her."

"Thank God," said Jo.

"I think one will be found," Sybil replied. Now that Jo had had a bath, however reluctantly, washed her hair and put on clean clothes, she really did look stunning, thought her mother. That hair, like ripe wheat, that radiant complexion. Perhaps it was the goats' milk cheese, which seemed to have replaced the pot. No one to hold a candle to her, Peter thought. Fit for a Prince. . .

"That helicopter," Sybil said in thoughtful tones.

"What about it?" Jo asked.

"Helicopters don't grow on bramble bushes. But I know where one might be found. That is, borrowed."

"They can be hired," Simon observed.

"Only with money."

"Well, where's this helicopter that's going for free?"

"Of course I can't promise anything. But there are several helicopters in the Queen's Flight."

"What makes you think the Queen would lend us one?"

"I don't suppose the Queen would. But her eldest son. . ."

There was a pause, broken by Jo. "You want me to get my hooks into your precious Prince at this ghastly dinner and, if they sink in deep enough, he'll come up with a chopper."

"A possibility," said Sybil. "No more."

"Prostitution," said her daughter. "And you the madam."

Sybil thought hard about sheep-dogs. That slow, stealthy movement. "Of course it might come to nothing. Worth just, perhaps, a try. A little experiment."

"Well, it's not on."

Simon intervened. "All the same, it might be an idea. Just might."

Sybil, surprised, looked with fresh interest at the young man. From what could be seen through all the hair, he might be quite good-looking.

"You mean," Jo said fiercely, "I prostitute myself at this ghastly bunfight with a royal, if I can con him, for the sake of a grotty old chopper?"

"A new one, probably," Simon said. "Anyway newish. A dinner at the Civic Centre wouldn't kill you, after all. You could skip the meat. Just an off chance."

"Very long odds," said Peter. Sybil had an inspiration. "How about a bet?"

"What sort of bet?"

"Ten to one he doesn't offer to lend you a helicopter." Even a hint of an offer, she thought, would do. She had taken the precaution of getting the private number of the Captain of the Queen's Flight.

"Not good enough," Jo said.

"Fifteen to one."

"Twenty. In fivers."

"All right," Jo said. "All bloody silly but I suppose if Simon wants me to be a sacrificial lamb. . ."

Good for Simon, Sybil thought. "Now, what can you wear?"

This was the question that had been preoccupying the chosen ladies of Shipton Wick for weeks. The town's three boutiques had done excellent business, although the more adventurous of the ladies had shopped around in Bath or Cheltenham in search of something that other Shipton ladies hadn't inspected and rejected. Emmeline Snape was one of the adventurers. Ernest had been uncharacteristically generous in setting a price limit and Emmeline resolved to make the most of it. She came back with an emerald green number adorned with silver sequins which displayed to the best advantage, she considered, the graceful curves of her figure. If the Prince thought he was in for a dreary evening with a lot of small-town frumps, he'd have a pleasant surprise.

Alas! for human hopes. For a second time, the counting of unhatched chickens proved the undoing of the Snapes. At the last moment, when Emmeline was in her pink négligee painting her toenails before donning the dress, the doorbell rang. Muttering angrily, Ernest opened the door to see two strangers – a man and a woman, both respectably dressed – standing on the step.

"Go away," he said, starting to slam the door.

"One moment, sir, if you please." The male stranger held out a hand to display an official looking docket, a pass or warrant of some kind. Ernest hesitated. "Special Branch," said the man. "We wish to interview Mrs Snape. Mrs Emmeline Snape. Acting on information received. With regrets for any inconvenience this may cause."

Inconvenience! That derisory word was to remain stamped upon Ernest's mind for years to come. The next two hours were the worst he was to experience in the course of a long life with its share of troubles. The respectably dressed visitors were quiet, polite, even at times apologetic, but as deaf to reason as the most monolithic of pillars. Ernest raged: intolerable insult, invasion of privacy, methods of the police state. He invoked the editor of *The Times*, the Director-General of the BBC, the local Member of Parliament, the Home Secretary, the Attorney-General, the House of Lords, the Queen. In vain. Emmeline, swathed in her pink négligee, protested, screamed, threw a pot of face-cream at the invaders and went into hysterics. The questioning went relentlessly on.

"In 1979, you visited Libya. What was the purpose of that visit?"

"You spent a day in El Aghaila. Whom did you meet there?"

"I must ask you to search your memory. With whom was your assignation in Shabbat?"

"What was the message you delivered to a blind man with one leg in the Kasbah in Tripoli?"

Time passed. Six thirty, six forty-five, seven o'clock. "Can't you understand?" Ernest cried. "An appointment. An appointment of the utmost importance. A dinner, *the* dinner, and Mrs Snape is to sit next to the Prince! On his right-hand side!"

"You say Mrs Snape is to sit next to the Prince? On his right-hand side?" Both interrogators looked extremely grave.

"You imbeciles! It's seven o'clock! We must leave in twenty minutes at the outside. Twenty minutes. Can't you understand?"

The interrogators exchanged glances, looking graver than ever. "I'm afraid, sir, your wife's replies are most unsatisfactory. We must detain her for further questioning. With regrets for any inconvenience this may cause."

"Inconvenience!" It was a wail of despair. Ernest fled to the telephone. The Mayor was in her hall adjusting her chain of office when the bell rang. She had half a mind not to answer, but there was a little time in hand. She lifted the receiver.

It was difficult, at first, to grasp what Ernest Snape was saying, but as he made his meaning clear a look of horror spread across her face. A vision of an empty chair filled her mind. The reception, the introductions, the smiles, the sherry, the bright dresses and brushed dinner jackets, the citizens of Shipton at their best, and then – the gleaming dinner table, the polished silver, the sparkling glasses, the tastefully arranged flowers, an *empty chair* on the Prince's right hand. Empty. Too late now to re-arrange the table. An insult to the Prince. Television coverage, front-page news. Shipton Wick Council Insults Prince. Prince Slighted in his Home Town. The Empty Chair.

Ernest had rung off. One hand on the hall table to steady herself, with the other she re-adjusted the mayoral chain which had slipped awry, and no wonder. No time for deliberation, for pondering how to pull this chestnut out of the fire. She must face the music. Perhaps a quick word in Mrs Rufford's ear. . . But Muriel Rufford wasn't a quick thinker, able to adapt to sudden changes of plan. Chaos lay that way. The telephone rang again and automatically she responded. This time the voice was cool, calm and collected.

"I hear there has been a *contretemps* about the seating arrangements."

Contretemps. You could call it that, the Mayor supposed. She was too shattered to wonder how the news had reached Sybil's ear.

"Naturally you don't want to have an empty chair on the Prince's right hand."

"No."

"Filled by a young, attractive and intelligent girl, the Prince might find the change of partner *convenable*."

"*Convenable.* Yes."

"Fortunately, Jo has unexpectedly returned from a visit to the North and is prepared to fill the gap. She and the Prince have a lot in common and I think she'll entertain him very satisfactorily."

"Well. . ."

"You have only to say the word. It's now seven fifteen."

The Mayor swallowed hard, took a deep breath and replied: "All right. Send her along."

God knows, she thought with desperation, what we're in for. Jo and the commune out towards Charlton Mansell. The Munshi. Nuts and dates, pot or worse, goats' milk cheese and what used to be called Free Love. Dirty clothing and dirty words and ugly rumours about a poisoned child. Next to the Prince. Shipton's welcome. Too late now. Clasping her chain as if clinging to a raft in a stormy sea, the Mayor stepped forth and climbed into her car.

Outwardly, the scene at the Civic Centre was all that she had hoped it would be. The rank and fashion of Shipton Wick and its environs were assembling looking clean, tidy and full of loyal goodwill. The labours of Astrid and her fellow stylists at the salon Marie-Louise had been well rewarded by immaculate coiffures. The Mayor and Mayoress of Poggleton were there, come to share in Shipton's great occasion. The Burgomeister of Bad Schweinfaart and his consort were not; they had received an invitation but had declined, nervous perhaps about another English joke. The Gwents, Sir Alciabiades, the Evers, Colonel Martingale, Arthur Longshott, the Chairman of the Bench, several of the leading local farmers and a host of lesser fry, pillars of Shipton's commercial world, were present and correct. But no Councillor Ernest Snape and his consort.

And there was Jo, conspicuous with her long golden hair. The Mayor almost gasped. Here was no slouching teenager in patched jeans, a dirty old anorak and disintegrating sandals, or no shoes at all. Here was an attractive, one could indeed say beautiful, young woman, draped in a full-skirted, patterned dress falling in folds about her ankles with a striped linen bodice of many hues.

"What a super dress! May I ask where you got it?" several of her fellow guests enquired. Jo was elusive. In fact, she owed it to Miss Cheer. "There's all those nice tablecloths at the back of the airing cupboard," she had said. "Never used nowadays. No proper teas like there used to be with silver and sandwiches, now its all mugs and plastic trays. Dainty sort of tablecloths some of them, hand-embroidered in Italy, or patterned stuff from Spain. Garish in my opinion but they wouldn't need much messing about with. Drape them, that's all."

Miss Cheer had a Singer and an unexpected dressmaking flair. It hadn't taken long to convert two or three tablecloths into a stylish little number which Jo wore with an air. Sybil, threading her way about the room with her usual speed and skill, felt well satisfied. Jo mightn't get a helicopter – Sybil devoutly hoped not – but she couldn't fail to win royal approval. And from that, who could say what might flow?

The Prince, attended only by Arthur, arrived quite unobtrusively. He greeted the Mayor like an old friend and, when his other dinner partner was presented, gave her a warm and charming smile. The Mayor felt that a weight had been lifted from her shoulders. It was going to be all right.

The Mayor of Poggleton sat on her left hand. A rather brash young man, she privately considered, one of the pushing, go-ahead business man types, given to announcing that he was taking Poggleton into the 1980s. A dig, of course, at Shipton with its old traditions. Ethelbald the Elder had never slept at Poggleton because in his day Poggleton wasn't there. And from what she had seen so far of the 1980s, the proposal to take Poggleton or anywhere else into it seemed ill-advised. Still, this was Shipton's finest hour and Shipton could afford to be generous. "I hear glowing reports of your new Sports Centre," she remarked.

"We're fortunate in Poggleton in the generosity of our community. A lot was donated."

"We, too, have some very generous donors. It's a question of priorities. At the moment the bowling green needs a new pavilion. And in the long term of course the sewage works. . ."

The Prince was getting on like a house on fire with Jo. She seemed to be doing most of the talking. Words and phrases such as Khama and Kiriya, Tree of Life, Dhammapada, Vishnu, Siva, Ocean of Love, transcendental meditation and four-dimensional art floated to the Mayor's ear. She wondered whether Jo wouldn't be more tactful to direct the conversation towards polo, fox-hunting, racing and other manly sports, or even foreign affairs or youth opportunities. But the Prince must be accustomed, conversation-wise, to taking what came. She thought she caught the word helicopter. The Prince laughed.

Then it was her turn. The question of conversational gambits had caused her several disturbed nights. The municipal affairs of Shipton Wick – no. Enquiries as to the health, activities, matrimonial status and breeding successes of his family, a great standby with ordinary folk, would be both impertinent and superfluous, since everyone knew the answers already. "Have you read any good books lately?" seemed a trifle bleak. Sport? the Hunt might lead somewhere, although it had led earlier in the day to complaints about the hounds running amok in the Industrial Estate and frightening children. Shipton's history: she might do something with that. Ethelbald the Elder was, after all, a forerunner, if not an actual ancestor, of the present monarch. The topic on which she'd really like to engage him, the identity of You Know Who, must unfortunately be ruled out.

It was, after all, the duty as well as the privilege of the royal guest to set the ball rolling and this duty he gracefully performed, complimenting the Mayor on the food and company provided at the banquet and on the beauty, interest, and amenities of the town. Shipton Wick, it seemed, met with his unqualified approval. The Mayor's spirits soared. Soon they were discussing the probable identity of the town's emblematic bird. Probably flightless, as it looked so top-heavy; an interesting supposition, since flightless birds had died out, if they had ever existed, in Europe, which suggested that the emblem was of great antiquity, as indeed everyone had always supposed. The Prince thought it looked something like a gallinule.

Next were to come the speeches and then light relief (merry pasteroles and rondos) from the Shipton Singers. But an interruption occurred. A commotion could be heard outside. The sound of a booming voice, in fact a bellow, came to their ears. The Prince's personal detective eased his gun in its holster. Conversation stopped abruptly, except for Jo affirming her dedication to transcendental four-dimensional art. Then her voice, too, fell silent. There was an even louder bellow, the door flew open and a familiar figure strode in.

"The Prince! Where is the Prince?" The General stood still, feet apart, for an instant, and then spotted his quarry. "Ah, the Prince. I have come to bid the Prince farewell. Goodbye, farewell, kwaheri. No longer can I stand at your side prepared at your command to slay your enemies. My heart is sore. But I have been recalled to lead my country's army and crush my country's foes. I shall crush them as grain is pounded in the mortar. The wind will sweep the ashes of his enemies to be scattered in the mountains. So, I go."

The General had resumed his medals – rather more, it appeared, than before – his sky-blue uniform and his gun. Arthur broke the startled silence. He expressed regret at the

General's impending departure and hopes for his military success.

"Dr Dudu, then, has re-established his authority? The *coup* has failed?"

An expression of depthless contempt convulsed the General's face. "Dudu, that unclean hyena, that dog's vomit, that baboon's abortion, that blood-sucking bat, that eater of babies, that traitor to my suffering people! Dudu has been overthrown, cast forth, trampled under by the forces of freedom, progress and peace! Our glorious leader, liberator of our people, champion of human rights, democracy and peaceful co-existence, our mighty and victorious leader Socrates Simoni – he is now President of our Republic! To his side I go."

"So the Good Shepherd has turned into an unclean hyena," Arthur commented.

"So now," the General thundered. "I go, and with me goes the maiden with the guinea-fowl hat. On her I have bestowed the command of my maidens' army, an ever-victorious and resourceful army. There is a division of canoeists, a division of trackers, a division of cooks, a division of combat warriors armed with Armalite rifles and a division of strumpets. She shall command them all. She comes with me now. The aeroplane is ready. I go. She goes."

"Well, I'm rather afraid," Arthur said, "she's actually a member of our constabulary. Signed on, under contract and so on. I rather doubt. . ."

The General's face clouded over. "She comes. Our great leader, our Generalssimo Simoni, commands it. I command it. She comes."

"I hardly think that tonight. . ." For once, Arthur was at a loss. An explosion threatened. The Prince, calling on his diplomatic skill and remembering his homework, stepped in. Hapana, though non-aligned, was believed to incline towards the West, if only very slightly, and provided that an already copious flow of interest-free loans, grants, subsidies, technicians, capital investment and other forms of aid were not only maintained but substantially increased. And then, there was the molybdenum. Also a pleasant game park with several lodges where the food was said to be passable, popular with politicians and senior officials of nationalised industries seeking relaxation in the sun. Perhaps some measure of intervention from the Palace, the Prince hinted, might facilitate matters, always providing, of course, that the lady was willing. The General beamed.

"She is willing. When Field-Marshal Mkubwa summons, maidens come."

"I don't know whether she's on duty at the moment," Arthur said.

"She is in my car. With Moja and Mbili who have brought her from the house of her aunt. Her aunt comes too."

"Good heavens," was all that Arthur could manage to say. Abduction? Kidnapping? The white slave trade? Would W.P.C. Wiggett's aunt be drafted into the division of strumpets?

"Also," the General added, "fifteen birds. Small birds of many colours who squeak. In my country we have many birds with colours but they do not squeak. So the aunt of the new Commandant-General of my Maidens' Army takes with her these birds."

"In that case perhaps. . ."

"Tomorrow I place myself at the head of the army of the Lion of Hapana, our great Generalssimo Simoni, to crush Dudu and his traitors as the lion's jaws crush the bones of the gazelle. Also I will send a present to your mother the Queen."

The Prince said that that would be very kind.

"There are many animals in my country. The Queen likes animals. She shall have animals."

"Her tastes run mainly to horses and corgis", said Arthur.

"Those we do not have. Okapis and bongos. Very rare. She shall have okapis and bongos."

"I'm sure she will appreciate those. . ."

"So now I go. You will hear of my victories on your radio, read of them in your newspapers, see them on your BBC. Many victories. There is a television crew on the way. Farewell!"

The General beamed again, waved to the company, saluted the Prince with a hand that quivered like the strings of a giant cello, about turned and strode masterfully from the room.

The revival of conversation was like mice emerging from their holes to twitter. The sound gathered force until it rivalled in decibels a shed full of agitated broiler chickens. The speeches were commendably short and the Shipton Singers with their sprightly melodies restored the equilibrium of the guests. The General will be missed, Arthur thought, but without him Shipton will more confidently pursue the even tenor of its way.

The Prince looked at his watch. Although no hint of impatience had escaped him, he was eager to be back at Cantilevre. He was expecting a guest, a very special guest, young, beautiful and altogether *convenable*. You Know Who.

"You look like the cat that swallowed the canary," Jo's mother said. "Did you get your helicopter?"

"Something better. Simon's going to be commissioned to paint a mural in Cantilevre's dining room. It's a big room, two turned into one. Any subject he likes. Of course it will be The Uncreation. Isn't it terrific?"

"I hope Simon thinks so." On reflection, Sybil thought he would. He needed a lot of cleaning up but, underneath all that dirt and hair, Sybil had detected the lineaments of a young man of dawning common sense.

Not every citizen of Shipton Wick had been concerned in preparing, serving and eating the banquet for the Prince. The moon was almost full, the skies had cleared, it wasn't raining, and Daryll and Astrid had decided to go badger-watching in Lammas Wood.

"This is the last time," Daryll said gloomily.

"You mean the gassing."

"Nothing can stop it now. Those pig-headed farmers with their miserable cows."

"Surely there's *something* we can do!"

"I think we've done all we can."

The night, the moon, the motions of the stars were on their side. They saw the badgers. Astrid hadn't seen them before. There they were, two of them, scarcely to be discerned in the wood's dark depths but emerging in an open patch where moonlight shone upon the white streak down each cheek and the white on chin and ear-tips. Like bulls-eyes, Astrid had said. They snuffled busily in the leaf-mould, questing, unsuspecting, inexplicably endearing. They crowned the night. And they were doomed.

The human pair walked back in a melancholy mood. "They *can't* be murdered," Astrid said, almost in tears. "We've got to save them somehow."

"Demos, petitions, all that Judy stuff is useless. Kicking at a brick wall. But. . ." Daryll's words came hesitatingly as an idea took shape in his mind. "Suppose . . . translocation."

"Trans. . . . .?"

"Sebastian's dart-gun. They do it in Africa and places like that. People dart the animals, take them to a game-park or some other place where killing's not allowed and then release them. Translocation, that's what it's called."

"But where would we take them?"

"That's the difficulty. That's . . . wait." The idea was growing. "I've got it! Shuddering Park."

"Oh, Daryll, what a marvellous idea!"

"Whoever bought it doesn't seem to go there, let alone move in. It's still deserted. Woods, undergrowth, privacy. Just right, I should say."

They walked more quickly, excited by the idea. Sebastian would have to be enlisted. They were sure Sebastian would play.

Lammas Cottage loomed ahead, dark and deserted. "Good riddance," Daryll said, thinking of Angus.

"I suppose so. . ."

"Surely to goodness you can't see anything in that. . ." He was at a loss for the word. You couldn't call Angus a twerp. Show-off. Twister. Well, forget him. Daryll had something more important, more important even than the badger rescue operation on his mind. "Look, Astrid, I've had, well, a sort of idea. Wild as horses, off the map, a non-starter I expect. It's just that. . ."

Words failed. The night was getting chilly but he felt sweat on the palms of his hands. His breath was coming faster. Lammas Wood looked like some big black animal crouching in the dark.

"That what?"

"This cottage. It's empty now."

"I know."

"I spoke to Tony Borrowdale. It isn't wanted for the farm. I think I might get it for a pretty low rent. Just might."

"That would be marvellous, Daryll."

"Yes. But only if. . ."

Astrid didn't answer. Her breath, too, was coming faster and a kind of tingle ran down her spine. Her heart was thumping and her hands felt cold.

"I wondered . . . suppose you . . . suppose we. . . Not much there of course. A Rayburn. Electricity. Open fire. There's worse places for a start. . ." A bright vision came into his mind: a log fire, curtains drawn, something tasty simmering on top of the Rayburn, Astrid's hair a tawny halo with a reading lamp beyond. . .

Astrid turned her head to see the moonlight shining faintly on his thin face, his eyes dark like sockets, his narrow shoulders, the fringe of indecisive beard. A stab of pity awakened in her heart, an instinct to protect, as towards a fledgling or a puppy. She stumbled on a fallen branch. Daryll stretched out an arm in support. Then the arm, both arms, enfolded her.

"Oh, Daryll!"

Unbelievable. The vision was going to come true.

Typeset by T H Brickell & Son Ltd
Shaftesbury, Dorset

Printed by Redwood Burn Ltd
Trowbridge, Wiltshire